Chain
of
Evidence

by
D.B. Corey

ISBN: 978-0-9893696-0-2

Published by:
Intrigue Publishing
11505 Cherry Tree Crossing Rd #148
Cheltenham, MD 20623-9998

Cover Design by Iconix
Author website: www.dbcorey.com

Printed in the United States of America
Printed on Recycled Paper

Chain
of
Evidence

For Maggie—my muse and my encouragement

D.B. Corey

CHAPTER 1

Someone called her Stacy. A fitting name for one so alluring. Wanton desire in a tight red dress. A sure thing for the right man, but not for me. I didn't have a shot in hell.

I eased in beside her at the bar and she turned toward me. The music was loud, and I had to yell to say hello. She turned away without a word, sparing herself the pretense of a make-believe courtesy. With little more than a glimpse she deemed me unworthy, and that simple gesture allowed me to chart the evening's course.

Time slowed, and I waited. The perfect moment can present itself without warning and I may not get a second chance. The more minutes that passed, the more invisible I became, and soon Stacy and her gaggle of friends were in a world where I was not invited. They laughed and caroused and teased one another, and one or two of them went off to dance with men. Stacy drank white wine, and that was perfect for me. So I waited.

Then the moment was upon me. Stacy's wine sat unattended, unnoticed by anyone, except me. I reached for a napkin and passed over her glass. No one saw the cyanide drop. No one saw it dissolve in an instant, and as I turned from the bar they continued their boisterous antics…as if I hadn't been there at all.

I made my way to the exit and listened for the sounds that I expected to hear. Frantic cries for help among a cacophony of confusion. And when I heard them, I turned to look as anyone might. I watched the bouncers push through the crowd, saw them knock people aside as they rushed to her. And among the music and the screaming, the dancing and the panic, I knew what the bouncers did not. I knew she was dead before she hit the floor.

Now I wait for her on a concrete sidewalk as a crescent moon arcs over the city—the Cheshire's grin, pasted on the night. My watch reads 3:36 and a thin layer forms on my skin. Humidity? Or sweat. Does it really matter? Baltimore is always humid in August, but more so tonight, and breathing is like sucking air through a wet sponge.

The sound of an approaching engine heralds her arrival. Headlamps bounce off the black surface of Pratt Street and a body transport turns the corner. Launching my cigarette into the night, I track its fiery path before turning toward the medical examiner's building. Stacy's image fills my thoughts as I pause beside a glass door that reflects my image.

My eyes sweep my length. I want to be presentable before stepping inside. Removing my glasses, I clean them with a section of my lab coat. Their circular rims portray me in a scholarly light and I like them, so I take extra care. Pressing my badge against the reader, I smile at the click of the electric lock.

Yes. She *is* desirable. Especially now, that she lacks a pulse.

I stroll past the main lobby information kiosk and nod to Officer Bowers. He is the night guard; a college kid in his third year working his way through. I point my travel toward the autopsy lab forty feet down and on the left. I hear the Latino janitorial crew jabbering in the Spanish I never learned in school. I doubt they're legal, but it doesn't matter. I don't really give a shit one way or the other.

The metal double doors of the lab hiss closed behind me and it's too cold in here again. We keep it that way by design. It's better for the dead. The lab's construction is cinderblock, painted a flat sea-green; a horrid color to say the least. Too bad they didn't consult me before painting. I'd have suggested a color that didn't remind everyone of bile.

They made a good choice with the suspended ceiling, however. The ample lighting serves the space well, as does the classic L design of the room. All they omitted was music. I mean, how hard could it have been to pipe in a bit of opera? But since they didn't, it falls to me to bring a little culture to an otherwise provincialist environment.

I glance at the clock on the wall. The transport should be at the dock. I pick up my pace down a center aisle that runs the length of the lab, jogging between gatherings of gray metal desks, to another set of metal double doors.

On the right, just before the dock, is the staging area; a secondary 20 x 20 room separated into its own quarter. That's where we do the city's work. It has all the pathological amenities: stainless cabinets and counters bolted to the bile-colored walls, gurneys with equipment trays parked side by side, tools and safety apparel stacked and organized in the cabinets, all there in support of three autopsy stations with their centerpiece stainless-steel tables; units tricked out with electricity, plumbing, and powerful parabolic lamps, fixtures I always thought resembled space weapons straight from a science-fiction movie.

I hear the telltale beeping of the van, backing into the loading area as the rollup door creaks its way skyward; triggered by Security in the central control room. A driver I've never seen before makes his way to the back of the van; an odd little man in an Orioles cap and coveralls. I walk over and offer my hand.

"I'm Doctor Harvey Morral, third-shift medical examiner."

"Hi, Doc. Andy Bikke's the name."

"Nice to meet you," I say. "So where's Alfred? The regular driver."

"Personal time off. Somethin' with his family's all I know. I'm just fillin' in till he gets back. So listen, Doc, I'd love to chew the fat, but I got another pickup. Can we get me unloaded?"

"Of course," I say, not wanting to take any longer with this bumpkin than I have to.

Andy disengages the safety latch and slides the gurney from the van. The wheels drop and lock as they clear the vehicle, and I lead him to the staging area to shift the body to an in-house gurney. Andy hands me a clipboard.

"So where'd you get this one?" I ask, signing the chain of custody.

"Picked her up at a club off Shawan Road. Wurlitzer's. Ever been there?"

I smile with the recent memory. "Can't say that I have."

"This one just dropped dead, from what they say. The Homicide boys were talkin' like it's that cyanide killer that's been causin' all the trouble. Thinks she was murdered."

My eyes cut to his but I say nothing. I find it pleasing that those idiots in Homicide have already taken to making calls at the scene, pinning sudden unexplained deaths on the Cyanide Killer without the benefit of forensics; especially since I would be supporting their theory when I send Tox specimens that belong to one of CK's victims.

I hand Andy his clipboard with his copy of the documentation, keeping one for the Office of the Chief Medical Examiner, and one for me.

Andy says his goodbyes and goes out the way he came in. Activated once again by Security, the overhead rattles its way down as the van pulls away. When it closes fully, I lock the interior dock doors and walk back to my desk.

In the lower drawer I keep my iPod speaker system, a compact little unit that packs a wallop. Aiming it toward the autopsy bay, I dial up my favorite piece. *Rigoletto*. After all, the Duke is much like me. As I return to the gurney, the peppy *Questa o quella*—this girl or that girl— saturates the lab.

Pulling back the forensic sheet, her beauty gives me pause. I gaze at her five-five corpse, her dark-brown hair splayed against the snowy white of the gurney's sheet, her translucent blue eyes still clear, fixed open, and even in death she maintains her allure.

"So, we meet again," I say, but then I remember. "Well, not 'again', per se. We never actually met to begin with, did we, Stacy?"

I brush her face with a feather-like touch, lambent wanderings across un-mottled skin. Removing her dress, I take my time. Red has always been my favorite color. Working my fingers through her long dark hair, my breathing changes and takes a rhythmic metre. My hands linger about her chest before moving on to their ultimate goal, and I register every inch as territory conquered. I want to slow down, bask in this the rarest of moments, but cupidity tightens its grip and I cannot stop myself. I shoot an uncertain glance at the double doors, but I know I engaged the bolt. I check the wall clock. There is plenty of time.

"I saw you several hours ago," I say to her. "At Wurlitzer's. You remember me. I am the reason you are here. I am pleased you did not keep me waiting."

I brush my face against hers and relish in the cool of her skin. Moving my lips to hers, I steal an empty kiss—hollow and unresponsive. The lust within me rises.

"You like this, don't you?" I whisper. And when the moment passes and she does not answer, I move to the foot of the gurney. Untying my scrubs I allow them to drop, and as the Duke sings of the flighty woman, I part her legs.

CHAPTER 2

The big-faced clock on the wall read 5:15 in the morning, and Detective-Sergeant Moby Truax stood in a small kitchenette, tucked in a corner of the squad room.

With the aroma of brewing coffee in the air, he regarded the liquid in his mug—the remnants from the preceding pot—with trepidation. He folded in three packs of real sugar with a plastic spoon as an ancient memory found its way to him.

He recalled sitting in his 4th period English class when Mister Bater called on him. The memory of the crusty old educator pushed a smile onto Truax's face.

"Master Bater," he said, uttering the name the students used behind his back. "How did that guy ever make it through puberty?"

"Mister Tru-ax," Bater said, pronouncing his name as if it included a hyphen, "Please recite the next line to the class."

A single line of prose appeared in his mind. Standing in the middle of the kitchenette, Truax spoke the words aloud, stumbling over their order, but the words finally came.

"You can't eat the orange and throw the peel away. A man is not a piece of fruit."

It was a line from Act II of *Death of a Salesman,* the story of Willie Loman; a man who, late in life, realized himself a failure. Truax found it strange that he dredged up that particular memory. Maybe it came to him because he thought himself like Loman, and now, some forty years later, knew just how worthless Willie Loman must have felt. He tossed the plastic spoon in the trash and stared at the hours-old coffee in his cup.

A piece of fruit. Damn terrible way to regard a man's life.

The coffee brewing in the pot still had a ways to go, so he ambled back to his desk in the rear of the squad room.

"Your phone was ringing," Danny Collins said from two desks over.

Collins was one of the few senior detectives left in Maryland State's Special Investigations Unit who hadn't retired, although it was no secret that he'd be making his move before long.

"I heard it," Truax said.

Collins shrugged and went back to what he was doing.

Truax dropped into his chair and scooted forward, pulling himself more than anything else, and logged a mental note. He should try to get back to the gym. "Try" being the operative word. He slid on his glasses and cursed as the broken left temple dug into his skin. He *knew* it was broken, and chastised himself for letting it slip his mind yet again. He wiped a fingertip across the scratch. There was little blood, so he sealed the wound with a dab of spit.

Returning to his task, he rolled the mouse. The Starfield screensaver disappeared and his report on the night's homicide filled the monitor. A white female. The latest in a string of five dead women.

Stacy Culver: Thirty-one years old, five-foot five-inches tall, one-hundred-eighteen pounds. Dark brown hair. Blue eyes. Preliminary COD: Poisoning.

He elected not to add his personal observation of 'gorgeous' to the report, despite it being a fact. Saying so, *officially*, would not be wise, especially considering the climate of the division lately.

She smelled of almonds, Truax thought. *Same as the others*. He noticed it while crouching over her body next to the semi-circular bar where she dropped. He questioned the bouncers at Wurlitzer's and each gave similar versions: Rushing to her when they heard screams, afraid to touch her for the pink foam around her mouth, and when an off-duty EMT finally reached her, she found no pulse.

Truax held that thought as he double-clicked on the icon of the homicide he investigated prior to this, the one that occurred two weeks earlier.

Rosa Neunyo. Female. Age seventy-one. Five-nine, one-hundred-ninety-three pounds.

Unmarried. Lived alone in a rundown two-bedroom house in Middle River.

Preliminary COD: Poisoning.

Poisoning, Truax thought. As were the three that came before her: Dorothy French and Harriett Brennermann, women in their late sixties. But then there was Emma Baumgartner—a woman in her early thirties. She didn't fit the profile. She was too young. And now there was Stacy Culver. She was too young as well.

The killer left nothing, and killers always leave something. Some physical evidence: hair, fibers, DNA if he was lucky—the Holy Grail of investigative work. But all the Cyanide Killer left was the weapon and the bodies. The victims weren't robbed or molested, assaulted or raped. They were just dead.

He saw just two commonalities: cyanide was the weapon, and all the victims were women; three in their sixties, the other two, half that age. Young Stacy Culver paired better with Emma Baumgartner, young women poisoned, found dead in or near a bar. He'd have to wait for the forensics and autopsy reports on Culver to confirm his suspicions of poisoning, but as far as he was concerned, he was dealing with two killers.

But that was only as far as *he* was concerned. His new captain had a different theory entirely.

Closing the files, Truax leaned his head back and peeled off his glasses. He rubbed his eyes hard and enjoyed the pressure. It felt good, but his mother always said it would make him go cross-eyed.

A lie parents tell their kids, he thought. *Ranks right up there with "jerking off makes you go blind."*

Dropping his head, he closed his eyes and placed his index fingers on his temples. He began moving them in a circular motion. It would stimulate blood flow, or maybe even wind up his brain. He didn't care which. This he performed daily and then tested his memory to see if any of it had miraculously returned when he wasn't looking. After all, that's when it disappeared.

He struggled to recall details from the first victim, Dorothy French. Details he just read. He remembered some, not all, and of late he caught himself referring to notes and reports and forensic documents to recall the minuscule leads he *did* have: the so-called eyewitness reports collected at the murder scenes, heavy on imagination but light on fact. Now here he was, four months later at a dead end. There were no new developments on the Cyanide Killer—CK, the papers dubbed him, a tacky tabloid name created to sell newspapers in an age of internet news.

He replaced his glasses, taking care not to scratch himself as before, and congratulated himself for remembering. He rolled the mouse pointer over the case file icon of the French woman, but before he could open it, a fresh-faced Detective Nichols arrived at his desk. The expression he wore could only be interpreted as bemusement.

D.B. Corey

Truax skimmed his scalp with his fingertips, enjoying the feel of day-old nubs; a new habit acquired after abandoning the barber shop and its fifteen dollar haircuts. They were a waste of money; money he didn't have. So he began shaving his head. Oddly, the sandpaper-like stubble reminded him that he should mow his lawn.

He peered over the top of his glasses at Nichols, a lanky high-school-looking kid in his early thirties, with a full head of wiry red hair.

"Whadda ya want, Rookie?" Truax bristled.

"Whatcha doin', Pops?" Nichols returned, a snarky grin stretched across his face. "Still working the cyanide case?"

Truax didn't answer. Instead, he waited for the next volley. It would come, he knew. Captain Atkins had handpicked Nichols from Vice, and because of his golden boy status, he never missed a chance to screw with the old man of the squad.

"So it's been what?" Nichols continued. "Six months? Seven?"

Truax suppressed the thought of reaching for his service weapon and putting a round between Nichols's eyes. "Ya know, Nichols, I'da thought they'd have taught you to add in college. Four. Four months. What of it?"

"Ah! So you *do* remember! A couple of us had a pool going as to what you'd say. I was waaaay off. I guessed you'd say nine. I think Bradley won. He said four-and-a-half. His guess was closest."

"I'm busy. Whadda ya want?"

"Oh…nothing. Thought I'd come over and let you know that the coffee you made is ready. Figured you forgot."

Truax felt the heat in his face. "Yeah. Thanks. Now if you don't mind, run along and join your little playmates. You don't want to miss milk and cookies."

Nichols grinned and plopped down on the corner of Truax's desk. "Not a bad comeback, Moby. Hey! Moby!

11

That's a nickname, right? How'd you get it anyway? Moby...What's it mean?"

Truax stared at Nichols and removed his glasses yet again. Without them on his face, he was less vulnerable. Less weak. "Do you know how to read?"

"Yeah. Of course I can read. Why?"

"Because, if you can, you might find the answer in a book by Melville. Maybe try something new and different for you. Approach it like it's an investigation. Go to the library. Figure it out. But before you do that, get your ass off my desk!"

"Look, Truax," Nichols said, climbing back to his feet, all mirth draining from his voice. "Don't take it out on me. It's not my fault you can't catch this guy. Besides, maybe you're losing your touch. You're almost sixty, after all. You're getting too old for this sort of thing. So why don't you just retire and stop taking up space. Go to Florida. Or wherever it is people go when they get old."

The comment launched Truax from his chair.

"And why don't you go *FU*—"

With his blood pressure banging in his ears, Truax pulled up short. He let Nichols get to him—the last thing he wanted. He eased himself back into his chair, averting his eyes as a recurring comfort tugged at him. Digging into the empty pocket of his shirt, he said, "Thanks for lettin' me know about the coffee, Nichols. 'Preciate it."

"Still pretty spry, I see," Nichols said. "Caught me by surprise, you did. That'll never happen again." He turned toward his desk. "Oh...and by the way," he said over his shoulder, "Captain Atkins said he don't want you working all night. Wants you to go home. Says you need your rest."

Truax checked his watch. 5:53. The sun would be up in another hour.

"What? What the hell are you talking about?"

"Said you weren't answering your phone. Said he wants to see you in his office later today."

"Today's Saturday."

"Captain says to be there at 8am."

Truax began rummaging through his desk drawers. He spotted a brittle stick of gum in a yellow wrapper. "What's he want?"

"Didn't say," Nichols replied. "Just said to tell you."

Truax glanced at the Culver file on his monitor and back to his watch again. 5:56. Stacy Culver would have to wait.

CHAPTER 3

The gurney bumped against the wall with practiced urgency, its wheels squeaking like old bedsprings. Sweat burned Harvey's eyes and all around him disappeared: the bright light, the cold room, the smell of death. Everything vanished as he locked his hips to hers. Speed and power merged in a primal frenzy, and he cried out as he delivered his seed. A bone-rattling orgasm racked him to the core, and he collapsed across the body of the dead woman beneath him.

Harvey lay upon her and his breathing slowed. The cold of the room settled on him and lowered his temperature. His spasms eased and he summoned his strength, pushing himself from Stacy's body before withdrawing from her.

He checked his reflection in the stainless-steel cabinet. His hair was mussed, but he kept it short, and it was easy to correct. Patting it down, he returned to Stacy's body, and transferred her to the autopsy table, where he rinsed his deposit from her.

After taking photos and performing other preliminary tasks, he placed his scalpel for the Y incision—upper right to center, upper left to center, center to pubic bone.

But as she lay naked on the cold steel, he hesitated before setting his blade, marveling at her similarity to the first woman he had there; his first act with the dead.

D.B. Corey

He remembered her; the woman with the dark brunette hair. She lay naked and unashamed, unaffected by the cold stainless of the autopsy table—the beautiful brunette who stood tall and loose beside the bar where he first saw her.

He met her in a Baltimore nightspot, 'met' being an exaggeration. Stood *beside* would be more accurate. He leaned in and asked her name. She offered a sardonic smile, and replied with an explicit, "Fuck off!"

It's not as if he had never been rejected before, he was accustomed to rejection, and anyone who knew him would attest to that. But *rude* rejection, delivered for the purpose of causing humiliation, was something he couldn't abide. He wasn't exactly easy on the eyes, as they say, and he'd be the first to say so. As his old high school gym teacher used to say, "There's some that gots, and some that don't gots." Harvey was a don't gots.

His appearance was pedestrian at best, and he harbored no illusion that he was anything more, but her rejection cut deeper than most. She seemed to derive some twisted satisfaction from belittling him before total strangers, all because he dared speak to her.

Suffering her ridicule, he left the club and went to work early. At precisely 2:32 a.m., he logged in the first body of his shift. The paperwork listed her as an alleged homicide victim: Ms. Dorothy French—a portly, sixty-nine-year old African American woman with brown eyes and salt & pepper hair.

The boys in Homicide suspected murder; poisoning to be exact. But then they always suspect the worst. It was in their nature, he supposed. But criticizing the cops wasn't his job. Performing autopsies and acquiring specimens for the crime lab, was.

He scarcely had Ms. French on the table and prepped, before the EMTs showed up with another body, a young woman from a late night restaurant on the outskirts of the

15

city. She had the light-blue coloring of asphyxia and a large chunk of something lodged in her trachea. Apparently, no one in close proximity knew the Heimlich. Such a pity. She was quite lovely—and, she looked familiar.

It took a minute, but he soon recognized her as the brunette from the bar, the woman who demeaned him scant hours before. Women with looks such as hers were uncommon in this place. Most who made it here were victims of physical trauma: accidents or assaults or overdoses; diseased whores beaten to death by their pimps, or drug addicts found days after death.

But this one—

Fantasies hatched in his mind as he fixated on the nightclub moment that excised his manhood. He conjured up methods of revenge as he drank her in, lying there in death, and his imagination reveled in possibilities both sadistic and salacious.

He abandoned procedure and started on her clothing, not cutting it from her body as called for, but peeling it off an item at a time, savoring her perfume and the stimulation of one-sided foreplay. With each second that ticked by, he moved farther from ethics and oath.

He knew it was wrong, knew that he was fulfilling some personal vendetta, and even stalled his pursuit once or twice, thinking his actions rape of some kind. But is it rape if they no longer live?

As she lay naked on the gurney, her beauty and the near perfect condition of her body overcame him. How long had it been since he enjoyed a truly beautiful woman? And how could he, in all good conscience, let her go to waste?

As a boy, he discovered the thrill of masturbation quite by accident, but that night, as a man, he stumbled upon something infinitely more gratifying, albeit cloaked in a shroud of social stigma. Until that moment he had counted his conquests on one hand, but that first encounter in the lab changed that, although for a time, women came to him as the brunette had—inanimate, and in the middle of the night.

But the women he coveted were a rare few; an undamaged few, and as the days passed he conceded that the physically mutilated, or the sexually diseased, or the heroin addicted, were more the norm for this place. They were women in name only, and when the supply of pristine flesh trickled to a stop, he knew he could no longer rely on random Chance. He had to find another source.

Then Fate stepped in. The Cyanide Killer had come to town.

Harvey shook loose the memory and began with the Y incision on Stacy. Sated, he no longer spoke to her and allowed the work to occupy him.

He removed and weighed her organs, and then sliced off the required samples. Had he not killed her, he would have drawn her bodily fluids—blood, urine, bile, vitreous humor—and stored them in color-coded vials for the microbiology techs. They, in turn, would test for drugs, medication...and poison; poison they would find if they were worth a shit.

But tonight, with Stacy, he'd substitute her fluids with those he previously drew from a legitimate CK victim. Fluids he stored in a small refrigerator at home, fluids that contained the exact concentration of cyanide that CK used in all his killings. He'd send the specimens to the microbiology lab, and pass them off as belonging to Stacy. They would analyze the blood, determine the blood type, and discover cyanide in the exact proportions that CK used. But that wasn't enough.

Moving to her abdomen, he opened her stomach looking for solid contents. He found a partially chewed, partially digested chunk of pizza crust, and dropped it into a small beaker of the bile he had stolen. The poison was in Stacy's body, but not in the food she ate. If he were to maintain the façade, he had to mimic the Cyanide Killer's work, and because the lab techs should discover the cyanide in the blood, the food she ate must match that same poison in the same concentration. After that, there could be only one conclusion: that the Cyanide Killer had murdered her, just as he had all the others.

Secure in his methods, he continued his work, stitching her up as the sounds of the arriving day shift trickled into the lab. Hearing the hiss of the doors, he turned. His boss, Doctor Joe McGovern, ambled toward him.

Harvey thought McGovern small as men go. Just under five-eight and slim. Most men his age carried a paunch, but not Joe. McGovern approached with his half-moon reading glasses resting on the top of his head, right at the spot where his receding hairline began, and in his hand he carried a black coffee mug that read "The World's Best Dad."

The coffee was still hot, and as McGovern coasted to a stop at the autopsy table, he blew short puffs of air across the surface, agitating the steam in several directions while his eyes painted every square inch of young Stacy Culver. Judging from his expression and the involuntary guttural sound that slipped out, Harvey figured McGovern wasn't seeing her in a strict clinical light.

"Morning, Harv," McGovern managed, his eyes exploring Stacy's bare chest, unfettered by the baseball-type stitches holding her together. "Easy night?"

"Yeah, Joe. Not too bad. Just this one, and one earlier."

"That's good. About time somebody closed the damn floodgates for a night or two. So what's her story?"

"Not sure. Word is she dropped dead in a club. I didn't see anything obvious. She's young, healthy...very pretty. In good shape. Her muscle tone suggests she worked out regularly. Could be drugs, could be allergies...could be a lot of things."

McGovern puffed on his coffee again and took a tentative sip. "Could she have been poisoned?"

"That's what Homicide said."

"Really? And how'd you know that?"

"The body transport driver. Said he overheard them talking when he picked her up."

"Huh. No shit. Well I guess we'll have to see what the lab turns up before we can be certain, and that'll take a week at least. Maybe longer. Damn cutbacks. Well, finish up and get out of here. I have to go read all those interesting reports. Just drop yours on the way out."

Harvey nodded and continued with Stacy as the day shift activity increased. He bathed her with care as three of Saturday's day-shift trickled in. He listened as they stood around his table, drinking their morning coffee; eating their morning doughnuts.

"Sweet Jesus," one said, his mouth full of pastry. "Look at the rack on this one. Now here's a gal I'd love to meet while still alive."

"Do you mean *you* still alive?" someone said. "Or *her* still alive."

As his associates broke into giggles and continued to poke fun, Harvey mustered a benign smile. He thought them buffoons, none of whom had the sand to take her alive *or* dead.

CHAPTER 4

Truax drummed his fingers on the armrest as he waited for his new commander. Chewing a spent stick of gum kept his attention focused on the wall clock as he tried to will the big hand to move. It was useless, he knew. Telekinesis wasn't his super power. Recall, was. At least, it used to be.

The minute hand settled on the 51st position after seven. He balled a fist and thumped the arm of the chair. *More time wasted.* Had he had more warning, he could have made it to the store for a pack of cigarettes, but as it was, all he rummaged up was a rigid stick of gum that chewed like a piece of cowhide.

He shifted back and forth in the chair, but it did little to hurry things along. Climbing to his feet he paced left, and then right, and then began to ponder his thirty years of detective work, and how it compelled him to wonder about things. And right now, he wondered what this little get-together was all about.

He suspected it had to do with the cyanide case. He'd been on it from the outset—the full four months—with the only results being dead ends.

Or maybe he was here because of his other four cases, the homicides not related to the cyanide killings. He didn't know. What he *did* know, was lately, his production was in the shitter.

He unconsciously skimmed the palm of his hand across the top of his head and allowed the unshaven bristle to distract him. He let his attention drift to the detective novels he read in his youth: Sam Spade and Philip Marlowe, Nero Wolfe and Mike Hammer; all childhood heroes and all partly responsible for his path in life. He managed a smile and toyed with the thought of buying a fedora. He grinned broadly, knowing it could only help his wardrobe.

Idle daydreaming gave way to yet another technique to pass time—cataloguing his environment. He liked to exercise his powers of perception when he had nothing better to do. Like now. So he took in the room.

The potted plants sprinkled here and there had to be the work of the receptionist, simply because they were green and still alive. Her desk sat at one end of the rectangular room, and a model of a 1800s sloop sat atop an oak credenza that presumably contained office supplies. The wall clock he had directed his willpower toward, mimicked the design of a spoked ship's wheel, and overlooked the space as would the helm of an actual vessel; its minute hand now resting on the 58th position after seven.

The out-of-character nautical decor was ostensibly the work of his new captain, one Donald Atkins, Special Investigations Unit Commander; the department's idea of new blood.

He'd heard the scuttlebutt from a few of the older detectives concerning the subject matter of their private sit-downs with Atkins. Danny Collins had nearly as much time with the department as Truax.

"All Atkins discussed was retirement," Collins had said. "I figure maybe it's time. Better to go out when I want to, not when they tell me to."

That's all fine and good for Collins, Truax thought. He'd been supplementing his pension with a 401K comprised of every dollar he ever made moonlighting.

But one thing was certain. Atkins wanted to run things his way. He marked his territory like a dog pissing against a hydrant—revamping procedures, personnel assignments, and performance evaluations—any management tool that allowed him to sweep aside ossified relics like Truax; obsolete cops to be retired or otherwise disposed of like a worn-out pair of shoes.

Deep in self-absorption, Truax neither heard nor saw her coming until her voice startled him from his stupor. It was familiar, and possessed a fondness born of an old friendship.

"Moby Truax!" the woman exclaimed. "As I live and breathe."

The voice belonged to Carol Saunders, and the smile playing across her face made him forget for a moment, why he was there. She strolled in with the fragrance of Channel No. 5 trailing a step or so behind and with the delight of a child waking to Christmas morning, she embraced him.

A warmth washed over Truax, one he hadn't felt in ages.

"Hi-ya, Carol. Long time no see."

He took her in from top to bottom and realized just how long, a "long time" had been. She had gained a little weight, but she wore it well, and he could see the years had been kind to her. She was maybe ten years younger than him and he thought that she should be at least a little gray, but brown hair dye works wonders and easily knocked five years off her undisclosed age of...well, her undisclosed age. He smiled. Even carrying a few extra pounds, Carol was still a damn attractive woman.

"You're lookin' good," Truax continued. "How ya been?"

Carol dropped her purse on her desk and leaned over to power up her computer. Truax's eyes followed her top as it fell open.

"Oh, you know...the same," she said, straightening up.

Truax's eyes snapped back.

Standing pin straight, she gave him the once-over. "You're looking pretty good yourself, I see...other than looking like you slept in your clothes."

The corners of her mouth started an involuntary, unstoppable climb upward. "I like the crumpled shirt-and-tie look on you. I hear it's all the rage with the kids. I especially like the way it goes with your jacket, not that there's anything wrong with tweed in August."

Truax's grin threatened to overcome his face.

"I don't see much reason in wearing $300 suits to pillage dumpsters," he said, "and it's nice to see nothing's changed between us."

Carol's smile leaned toward the seductive.

"Why change a perfect relationship, Moby? Besides, its husbands I seem to have problems with."

Truax grinned. "Me too. Wives, I mean."

Carol pulled out her chair and sat. "You never re-married?" She gestured toward the chair. "Sit. Relax."

"Not much point in it," he said, re-claiming his chair. "Takes a special kind of woman to deal with the shit my job brings. How about you? Still driving the boys wild?"

"HA! I wished. Then again, maybe I don't. Not having to pick up after a man has distinct advantages. Plus, the toilet seat's always down at my house."

Carol paused and studied his face.

"You know? Something just occurred to me. The last time I saw you was at the gym. That was a while back, and you still look in great shape."

"I try, Truax sighed, "but it ain't so easy anymore."

Carol nodded. "Tell me about it. I run every morning. Gets harder every year." Her eyes lifted, surveying the area above his eyes.

"So when did you start shaving your head?"

Truax sanded his fingertips against the stubble, as if to acknowledge her question.

"About nine months ago. When I turned fifty-eight. Wanted to do something different."

Carol feigned shock.

"*Fifty-eight*? Get out! You don't look no fifty-eight. Forty—forty-five, maybe."

"You know what they say about flattery, Carol."

"Yeah, but I mean it. Fifty-*eight*? Damn, Moby! Well, I was gonna ask you out for a drink, but not now. You're just too damn old."

Truax rocked his head back and burst into hysterics, and Carol joined in. The pair chortled in unison for several seconds before laughing themselves out. Truax shifted in his chair as his chuckling waned, but he retained his famous crooked grin. "So, what brings you in on a Saturday?" he asked.

"I work a lot of Saturdays, ever since they laid off most of the admin staff. It's cheaper to pay me a little overtime than to carry those extra employees. Guess I'm lucky I still have a job, you know?"

"Yeah, I know. So Carol, why am *I* here?"

"Wish I could tell you. I didn't know you'd *be* here. Seeing you was a big surprise. A pleasant one, though."

"C'mon, Carol, you musta heard something. What gives?"

"No, really. You know—" She lowered her voice. "You know Captain Atkins is of the new breed. Young hotshot out to make a name. Word is he wants to run for Commissioner in ten years."

Moby raised an eyebrow. "Ten years? That's aggressive."

"He's an ass-kicker for sure, pardon my French. But working for a thirty-something wonder boy takes a little getting used to."

Truax nodded in agreement. "Don't I know it."

"He doesn't tell me shit unless he *wants* me to know," she continued. "Are you still on the cyanide case?"

Truax nodded.

Her voice became hushed, just above a whisper. "Then I'd guess that's why he wants to talk to you. He's been getting a lot of heat from the top brass lately, and when I put their calls through, he closes his door. Even so, I hear things. He's getting his ass chewed ou—"

"Morning Carol," Atkins said strolling through the door without a sound. The stealthy arrival launched Carol from her chair.

"CAPTAIN!" Carol blurted, clutching her chest. "PLEASE DON'T DO THAT!"

"Sorry," he said. "Didn't mean to startle you." Atkins stuffed his newspaper under one arm and gave no indication of overhearing. "Hope I'm not intruding," he said. "Seems you two are catching up. Been a while, has it?"

"Carol diverted her eyes, seeking refuge in the nearest piece of paperwork. "Detective Truax and I are old acquaintances, Captain."

Truax stayed mute and wondered if his hearing was the next mark on Aging's hit list. For the second time that morning, he'd been caught off guard.

"Be with you in a minute Detective," he said without looking. "Carol...Coffee?"

Carol waited until Atkins passed by on the way to his office before looking up. "I was just about to make a fresh pot," she said, shrugging toward Truax.

"Great," Atkins replied. "I didn't have time to stop on the way in." Atkins disappeared into his office. "Need any help?" he called.

Carol's eyebrows went up accompanied by a puzzled look. "For coffee? No… No, I can manage."

"Just asking. Detective? You ready?"

"Yes Sir," he said, thinking a cigarette would be a good thing about now.

"Good," Atkins said. "Come on in."

Atkins removed his suit jacket and hung it on a wall hook, its lightweight medium-brown fabric blending with the color of the room. "Have a seat, Detective," Atkins said, pointing to a chair as Truax stepped in. Carol eased in behind him carrying a pot of coffee and two mugs. Setting them on a small table, she poured a single cup, and handed it to Atkins.

"Coffee, Detective?" Atkins asked.

Truax regarded his new boss with a mixture of apprehension and pessimism. Pleasantries coming from suspects heightened his awareness. Pleasantries coming from superiors heightened his suspicion...unless born from genuine fondness, which in this case, they weren't.

A mere two months in command was insufficient for Atkins to become chummy with the help, and as far as Truax was concerned, he hadn't time enough to get his feet wet, unlike the area behind his ears.

"Thanks Captain," Truax said, settling into one of the oxblood leather chairs facing Atkins's center of power, "but I'll pass. Makes me have to go."

Atkins nodded for Carol to leave them. "Ah, yes," he said, dropping with bravado into a larger leather chair behind an oak desk that consumed a quarter of the room. "I have a similar problem."

"I doubt that, sir, unless you're over fifty."

Truax considered Atkins thin. *Rail* thin. And that was *too* thin. He quipped that if Atkins turned sideways, he'd disappear. Atkins wore his short blonde hair plastered to his head with some kind of goo, and seeing him in his oversized chair reminded Truax of five-year-old Edith Ann, Lily Tomlin's character on *Laugh-In*; the rude little girl who sat in a giant rocking chair, and informed anyone who would listen of her views on the world and her baby brother.

"Fifty you say," Atkins returned. "No, I'm not fifty. I have some time before that happens."

"I'd guess about fifteen years, Captain." Truax said, a hint of condescension in his voice.

"Very astute, Detective," Atkins returned, "And please…call me Don."

"Ah...no Sir. I'd rather not."

Atkins flashed a look of displeasure, and as soon as it had appeared, it vanished. "Very well, Detective," he said with a mannequin-like smile. "Suit yourself. I get it that you want to get a feel for me and my command style. No problem. Whatever makes you comfortable."

Atkins picked up a mug emblazoned with the yellow and black Maryland State Coat-of-Arms and blew away the steam rising from the coffee within. Taking a cautious sip, he flinched. "Damn! Hot!"

Steam was the clue, Truax thought.

Atkins blew again, this time sending a long steady stream of air across the top of the mug. "I guess you're wondering why I called you in." He took another careful sip, his eyes never leaving his guest.

Truax sat forward and knitted his fingers together. "As a matter of fact, Sir."

"Okay. I won't keep you in suspense any longer. Just as you want to get a feel for me, I also want to get to know my detectives...outside of what their service records tell me. Yours, I saw, was exemplary, if you discount the three insubordination incidents from earlier in your career, the last, I noted, occurring not all that long ago. But forget about that for the time being. I'm interested in your likes, your dislikes, how you spend your off-duty time, what hobbies you enjoy, is there a special woman in your life...your plans for retirement."

And there it is, Truax thought.

Atkins's words hung in the air like a challenge from a drunk in a bar. Truax's eyes narrowed. Should he respond in kind? His gut said no. *Wait to see what develops,* it told him. *Be on your toes, old man. This is leading somewhere.*

"You *do* have plans, don't you Detective? Being fifty-eight, retirement's just two years away."

Mandatory retirement at age sixty, Truax thought. *State sanctioned age discrimination.*

"I haven't thought about it much," he lied, recalling his visions of post-retirement Armageddon, and his dwindling 401K. He still had his pension—what was left of it, but the investment bank fiasco lit a fire under the economic downturn, hastening the financial demise of major cities—cities like Baltimore.

"I see," Atkins said. "Well, maybe you'll give it some thought in the near future. Then, when CK is caught, you might consider taking an administrative position until you retire. You've earned it. And, you deserve it."

Truax took a few moments to let what he heard sink in. Administrative position; just another way of saying desk job. He recalled the one time he was assigned to desk duty. It was upon his discharge from the hospital after his first partner was killed.

The department shrink thought it best to keep an eye on him for a while, just to make sure he didn't suffer any long lasting psychological effects of seeing his partner gunned down in the street. He remembered—it was like being in a box.

"But let's move on to more pressing matters," Atkins continued. "The Cyanide Killer. Where are you on that?"

Truax fell back against the chair and breathed in the new-car smell. "With all due respect, Captain, you know damn well where I am on the case. You've read my reports."

A smile thin enough to have been drawn with an eyebrow pencil formed on Atkins's face. "Yes, I did, Detective. So did my superiors. But they want to hear it from *me*, so I want to hear it from *you*. Shouldn't be a problem for someone with an eidetic memory."

Eidetic? Who the hell talks like that?

"If you mean photographic memory, Captain, you're misinformed. It's gone. Disappeared long ago."

"Disappeared?" Atkins blurted.

The shock in Atkins's voice lacked conviction, and didn't match his expression. It betrayed him. Truax zeroed in on the deception at once. He knew, that Atkins knew, his photographic memory had faded. Years of dealing with liars, con men, and flimflam artists, told him that much. Why was Atkins doing this?

"No, Captain. I have what you might call a normal memory now. I have my good days. Get occasional flashes here and there. But it's not like it used to be."

"I didn't know one could lose a photographic memory," Atkins said.

"Why not? Memory is memory. Mine is...was...just better. It degraded as I got older. Same as regular memory, but worse."

"Worse?"

"Sure...possessing a photographic memory is like being able to run, where everyone else can only walk. But when it

29

goes, it's crippling. It becomes a liability. I have to work at it now."

Atkins shook his head sympathetically, as if being informed of someone's death. "That's really too bad. I understand it to be a tremendous asset."

"I figure it's on the same level as thirty years of street experience."

"Let's hope so, Detective. Now...CK?"

Truax squirmed in his chair. "I won't insult your intelligence with some dog and pony show, Captain. I'm at a dead end with the cyanide poisonings."

"Yes...so I've gathered. I have to tell you, Detective, your difficulties of late have me concerned. I want to offer my assistance. I want to help."

"Help?" Truax said. "Help is a relative term, Captain. Help how?"

"Why, I want to help you solve the cyanide case, of course. Provide you the resources you need. Maybe assign you a partner."

"A partner? No. No partners."

Atkins finished his coffee and stood, continuing as if Truax had said nothing at all.

"To be frank," he added, "I've given some thought to taking your other cases off your hands." He walked behind Truax and opened the office door, signaled Carol for a refill, and then eased it closed again. "They're fairly cut and dried," he said, ambling around his office, avoiding Truax's eyes. "Nothing a junior man can't handle. I feel they're a serious drain on you. Besides, I'm a little ashamed to say that the brass has taken to asking embarrassing questions. I need results, so I want you to focus on the cyanide killings. Five cases is a considerable workload in this unit, even for a seasoned cop like yourself. And then...there's your age."

Atkins paused to let his words resonate. "Not that that's an issue, mind you, but I can't help but feel a partner would benefit both you and the department; make your life a little easier, do the heavy lifting."

"I have an arrangement with the department, Captain. I thought Major Taylor would have—"

"The commander has made me aware of your arrangement, Detective, when he promoted me to command SIU. I did not get the impression that your working solo was set in stone."

Carole tapped on the door, waited a beat, and then stepped inside. She filled the mug on Atkins's desk without looking at Truax, and then left without lingering. Atkins walked back to his desk and picked up the mug, then settled himself on the edge.

"I received a call from the FBI yesterday," Atkins continued, "Special Agent in Charge of the San Diego office—Kaitlin Donahue. Seems they have a similar case out there, and she thinks there may be a connection between theirs, and ours. She wants to send an agent to compare notes, and to assist as necessary."

Truax balked. "The FBI—"

"Agent Donahue made a compelling point. She said that when their homicides stopped about five months ago, ours started up a couple weeks later. The cases bear a striking resemblance. She thinks it may be the same Unsub."

"And what do *you* say, Captain?"

"I say you need some help with this one. You've been chasing this guy for four months. The Feds have been tracking him for the better part of a year, but I'm not ready to bring them in. Not yet. They want to know what we have, so you can expect a call from Agent Donahue. You're to fill her in. I'm going to reassign your other cases so you can focus on this one, and if you're no further along in a week or so, I may engage their help—whether you like it or not."

CHAPTER 5

Sixty-foot oaks lined both sides of the single-lane country road leading to Bamboo Billy's—trees that mingled with the deepening purple of the evening sky, to bring premature night to all below.

Steering out of a left-hand curve, Harvey spotted a neon Billy behind an ancient oak, lounging in a neon hammock, and sipping a neon drink. Harvey shifted into second and veered into the lot, his eyes fixed on the computerized marquee.

"Ladies' Night," it announced, its orange and blue letters blinking and rolling and exploding across the screen. The parking lot was packed, and he was hard pressed to recall a Sunday night crowd like this anywhere.

Easing off the gas, he idled past the entrance and allowed the side exhausts of his fire-engine red '65 Stingray to play its throaty tune. Rolling through the parking lot, he found a space at the far end, and backed the classic in. Slipping the 4-speed Hurst shifter into first, he killed the engine and pushed the door open just enough to activate the dome light.

He pasted down a tuft of windblown hair and removed his wire-rim glasses, tucking them in the breast pocket of his cocoa-brown sports jacket; a jacket he seldom wore, but tonight it went with his jeans.

He slid from the car and checked the upper-half of his reflection in the driver's side window, then felt for his wallet and cigarettes before heading toward the front entrance.

Music floated on the cool night air, heightening his excitement and putting an edge on his anticipation. He recognized the tune and began singing along, just loud enough for only him to hear. He didn't care to embarrass himself before total strangers.

Ummm, you're a crazy bitch, but you fuck so good duh-duh-duh duh duh. When I dream, I'm doing you all night—

Shelling out a five-dollar cover charge, he declined the re-entry stamp. Ink on his wrist brought on memories of high school dances, and standing alone in the corner of the gym, afraid to talk to girls, and followed by the eventual humiliation at the hands of class tormentors. He stepped through the door and found the place larger than he had imagined.

The decor was Pacific Islander. Dotting the floor were artificial palm trees and life-sized mockups of burly pirate-men and half-naked pirate-women, armed to the teeth with cutlass and black-powder pistols, unmoving beside seascape walls, or rappelling from the imaginary rigging of a Man-O-War. This was a club, not a dive or biker bar as he had pictured, and knowing that drained the anxiety he felt moments before.

Music blared from everywhere, and on the left, three barmaids patrolled the main bar, each endowed with all they needed to attract a man of their choosing. With low-cut tropical print tops and short denim cutoffs, each conjured vivid debauchery in Harvey's mind, and although it had been only a week since Stacy, his Need returned to the forefront, diminishing the chaos surrounding him.

The place was at capacity and no one moved easily. Threads of people weaved through the crowd like ants in an ant-farm, one behind the other; each carrying drinks or food or a smoke, each waiting their turn, each looking for an opening. As one thoroughfare closed, another opened. The scene was as dynamic as it was serendipitous, and when the opportunity presented itself, Harvey seized the moment.

Sliding sideways between two women, he stepped to the bar and glanced back to gauge their looks. Both were young, in their early twenties, and one had what today's kids considered a hip hairstyle, although two-tone black & blonde didn't appeal to him. The other was a tad hefty, wearing a mid-drift blouse that allowed an ample roll of fat to protrude. Both displayed an excess of face piercings.

They stood apart from others, but not by their choice. They were freaks; outcasts because of their looks, laughed at by others who considered themselves part of a superior caste: The beautiful people. He remembered how it felt, having judgment pass on him when he was as shunned as the very women he now pitied. A wave of anger washed over him.

He thought about his English-102 class, and the girl who took his virginity. He remembered her. He remembered his humiliation.

All through high school and his first year at the university, he remained a virgin, but not for lack of trying. He never let on, especially to the only three friends he had, although they suspected. When they began to tease him outwardly about being cherry, getting laid became paramount, and dominated his waking hours.

The girl in his English class, the skinny one with the stringy blonde hair and heavy eye makeup, had been checking him out. He'd look away at the last moment only to glance back seconds later to see if she was still looking. His self-consciousness brought with it self-doubt: Was she staring at his hair? His clothes? His glasses?

In spite of his shortcomings, his uncertainty still allowed for the possibility that she may want him. He calculated that his odds were better with her than with a pretty girl, and when he spoke to her about a poetry term paper, she made it easy for him.

She invited him to her off-campus apartment for some collaborative internet research. Twenty minutes later she was riding him. He released upon entering her like an adolescent boy having a wet dream, but the real humiliation came when his ejaculation dissipated his erection. She stopped and leaned back, an amused smirk on her lips. "Your first *time*?" she said, and tossed her head back— laughing at him.

The memory still inflicted pain after all these years, so he dismissed it as he would inner-city homeless. He ordered a beer and began scouting the area around him. To his right clustered a group of women. One of them was a tall delicious brunette. He liked tall. He liked brunette. He eased himself within earshot.

The digital music pumping through the speakers had everyone yelling to be heard, even when standing at arm's length. Harvey strained to eavesdrop on the brunette's conversation, listening for something he could use, some telling information about her: her name, where she lived, where she worked. And as he listened, his eyes devoured her.

She looked all of twenty-five, her dark hair stopping mid-way down her back, her eyes a scintillating blue. She was smartly dressed in basic black and, more importantly, unescorted. She had an air about her that said 'intelligent,' and Harvey liked that. Intelligent women were preferable to the ones who carried their brains in their shirts...at least some of the time. But when he thought about it, intelligence didn't really factor in when they were lying on a stainless-steel table.

He finally gave up trying to listen. He couldn't hear much anyway. Just her name. Kara. He liked that name, and he imagined staring deep into her dead blue eyes, calling her by name, and fucking her for all he was worth.

He doubted she even noticed him. They *never* notice him. But that wasn't important. What *was* important was the Need pulling at him.

As he focused on her, he began fading into the crowd and becoming forgettable, his best feature. Since Stacy was so fresh, he thought it best to shadow this one. Wait for her to leave and follow her from a safe distance, learn her movements over a short march of days. He'd wait for Friday, and if her movements were consistent, he'd take his time and not give in to his Need's impulsive nature. He'd wait for her. Maybe he'd follow her. Maybe all the way home.

He continued to slip back into the crowd, away from Kara and her friends. When he was three deep in bodies, she turned and looked directly at him. He froze. Suddenly she rushed toward him. She extended her arms as she closed on him, only to run past him to a man who appeared to be mostly chest and biceps.

Invisible, Harvey thought.

Throwing her arms around the man's thick neck, she leapt onto him. He wrapped gigantic hands around her waist making it seem even smaller, and lifted her off the floor without effort, her radiant smile and unheard laughter telling Harvey everything he needed to know.

Taking her wouldn't be as easy as he thought.

He returned to the bar and ordered a last beer as the couple playfully engaged each other—laughing and touching, kissing and petting. It gave him a boner. He considered the pros and cons. There were more of the latter than the former, the man being the primary con. And there were many women here. He didn't need to risk bodily harm going after Kara. He'd be wise to forget her and come back another time. But then, there was his Need.

Forty minutes later, Harvey pulled up to his mother's house in Green Haven, a quiet little community nestled between Sloop and Eli Coves, just twenty minutes north of Annapolis. The neighborhood was old as neighborhoods go, just off Mountain Road and made up of summer homes formerly owned by Baltimore's 1920s rich. Though the years, the community expanded, developed, improved; tripling in size to seventeen-thousand or so. Harvey lived here—with his mother.

Too many beers caused him to struggle with the Vette as he rolled into the driveway. Angling it to a precarious stop, he killed the engine, shutting down its finely tuned exhaust. It would surely wake his mother if left running.

The house was a four bedroom Cape Cod, with white asbestos shingles and a chocolate brown roof. Light shown through the two-tone yellow-checkered curtains hanging about the kitchen window; curtains his mother peered through before letting them fall closed.

"Jesus, Mom…" Harvey said, switching the ignition to Accessory.

A Classic Rock station from Westminster filled the passenger compartment of the vintage Vette, and the cool night air spilled through the half-open driver's side window as he wrestled with his choices.

Should he go with the easiest but least desirable of options? Just walk in the door and deal with whatever his mother had in store for this, his latest transgression? Or should he silently flip her off from the car, back out of the driveway, and check in to The Doll Motel over on Crain. There might still be a vacancy if he hurried. The Doll filled quickly after the bars closed, mostly with married men and the single women they entertained, women for whom they provided a river of booze.

He winced, remembering the sounds of that place from years ago, and the one and only time he had taken a woman there. It was back before the time of discovery, back before the time of seeking the dead.

He recalled lying with her on an overly used mattress, listening to the drunken laughter from the parking lot bleeding through the gaps in the door. He remembered the pounding headboards against paper-thin walls that accompanied the moans of women in ecstasy; moans that were perhaps facsimile, produced for the sake of their one-night benefactors.

He had hoped that wasn't why she was with him, and hoped it would become more. He knew he was nothing special to look at, he was barely a face in the crowd, a fact he'd readily accepted, save for those rare occasions when a woman like the one he was with, for reasons known only to her, showed an interest in him. And maybe that was it. She was as plain and nondescript as he. Maybe that's what she saw in him.

Harvey glanced again toward the window and made his choice. He crawled from the Vette and strolled through the kitchen door at 2:45am, hoping his mother was in her bedroom.

She was not.

The Rockwellian image of the silver-haired woman in curlers, standing in the center of the living room, wrapped in her well-worn flower-print robe, stood in direct contradiction to the venom spewing from her mouth.

"Well, it's about goddamned time you were coming home!" she screeched, clutching her robe to her pear-shaped body. "What? You couldn't find one of your bar whores tonight?"

"For Christ's sake Ma," Harvey slurred. "I ain't got no bar whores."

"That worries me even more! What the hell's wrong with you! You never date! You never call girls! Are you queer?"

Harvey stayed silent and his eyes narrowed, saying what he didn't dare. Who the hell was *she* to talk to him like that? After all he did for her!

"Ya know Ma…" he said, keeping his voice low, believing it helped to control his shaking hands, and that would, somehow, keep them from her neck. "Sometimes you really piss me off!" Taking a deep breath, he shoved his hands into his pockets to quell the rage he kept in check. "I think it's time I moved out."

His mother's condescending laughter cut through the air like a blaring trumpet. "You can say that to me after living in my house for how long?" she snapped. "Thirty-five years? Well that time has come and gone! You fool yourself, thinking I need you here. And that's why you stay. But I don't! I can take care of myself. You're a full-grown man...still living with your mommy! So why don't you move out? Or don't you have the balls!"

Without another word, she switched off the light and stormed out of the room, leaving Harvey standing in the dark quivering with rage. Slowly, he regained a semblance of composure. Throwing his shoulders back in defiance of a woman who was no longer there, he mumbled hushed obscenities to himself as he turned and climbed the stairs to his room, enduring each cynical creak, of each mocking step.

Pushing open the door to his room, he switched on the overhead light, and after a bit of rummaging, slid the first porn tape he could find into the tape player. It would not quell his Need, but it would crowd out tantalizing images of his hands at his mother's throat.

CHAPTER 6

Monday morning found Truax back-tracking the killings in the order of occurrence; his first stop, a small Section-8 apartment complex in Rosedale on the east side. Pulling onto the lot, he watched a small group of teenagers, kids who should have been in school, scatter like roaches when the lights come on.

Open-air drug market, he thought. *The way they took off, I may as well have blown in here with a siren. So much for driving an unmarked.*

There were more cars in the lot than he expected to see on a work day, that is, until he realized most were untagged, broken-down junkers, some with flat tires, and others up on blocks; unregistered wrecks, long overdue for the junk yard.

At either end of the parking area sat unattended dumpsters, lids jacked open with overflow erupting in stench and white plastic bags; a surplus of which stacked three high and three deep on all sides. And then, there were the rats! Rats in the daytime! Well-fed rats, sniffing the air in his direction and regarding him as little more than a nuisance. He considered calling the Health Department on the spot, but as it were, he'd let it wait. It wasn't a rat that poisoned Dorothy French.

Closing the dash-mounted laptop, he opened his hardcopy file on the French woman.

African-American female, age fifty-nine, five-foot nine-inches-tall, one-hundred and ninety-seven-pounds. Never married, and living alone on government assistance. Has one son, currently incarcerated at Jessup for murder. Been there since he was sixteen.

Truax climbed from the car and made his way for French's apartment, contacting the superintendent as he went to gain access.

"When you guys gonna release the apartment so's I can rent it?" the super said, a diminutive white man with an overhang that suggested he was about to give birth. "You guys are costin' me money!" he continued, running his chubby fingers through thinning hair.

Truax gave no reply.

"C'mon!" the super continued. "She's been dead for fuckin' four months! How long you expect me to wait?"

Truax offered a pitiless smile. "This is Section-8 housing, right?"

"Yeah?"

"Government subsidized?"

"Yeah! So what!"

"So you're getting paid if someone lives here or not. I suggest you keep quiet," he said, his tone as menacing as it was soft, "before I call the Health Department and shut this pigsty down."

The super appeared to collapse into himself, his skin turning a pasty white.

"Okay...Okay! I didn't mean it personal. I was just askin'."

His disposition turned friendly, as if he'd known Truax for years, a practiced defense against familiar police pressure. "So how you like being bald?" he asked. "Shavin' your head an' all, I mean. I been thinkin' 'bout doin' it myself."

Truax gave him a cursory look. The greasy gray strands clumped together in sparse coverage hadn't seen shampoo in weeks. "It could only help," he said. "I'll lock up on my way out." Truax stepped into the apartment, dismissing the super as he closed the door, and allowing him to believe that he had dodged a Health Department bullet.

The studio apartment was nearly spotless, such as it was, and the filth that was the outside world did not reach this place. But there was sorrow here.

The single bed and the scarred wooden nightstand and the faded lamp, all spoke to a lonely existence; the small kitchen nook with its hot plate and single place-setting, the utensils of metal and plastic, symbols of life alone; the only apparent comfort—a fat ceramic chef in a white chef's hat. From its location atop a central shelf, Truax thought it important to her. A family heirloom perhaps, maybe handed down from her mother.

The solitude permeating the small room passed through him like a chill from a drafty window. He would find no leads here. No clues. But he didn't really expect to. They had already found all there was to find. His purpose was insight, to understand her existence, discover the kind of woman she was. He hoped that immersing himself in what she left behind might reveal whatever it was, that made her a target for CK. What was it about Dorothy French that put her in the cross hairs of a serial killer? What was his reasoning? Why, did he kill her?

CHAPTER 7

Checking the local papers was part of Truax's morning routine, but a community paper, *The Pasadena Observer,* published only on Wednesdays and Saturdays. Today was Wednesday, and that's when he saw it.

> ### *Cyanide Killer Claims 5th Victim.*
> ### *Police Stymied.*
> ### *By Manny Munroe - Staff Writer*

"Great. We don't have the forensics back yet and this guy's fingering CK. Cowboys like this don't wait for official word. They just make it up as they go along."

He leaned back and rubbed his eyes and wondered if Atkins had seen this yet. Then he decided that instead of trying to predict what Atkins thought, he'd just have another cup of coffee. Before he could get out of his chair, his cell phone rang.

"Truax."

"Em, hello...Detective Truax? My name is Kaitlin Donahue. I'm the Special Agent 'n Charge o' the San Diego field office. I'm hopin' I might have a wee bit o' yer time."

The voice was that of a young woman with all the musical nuances of an Irish dialect.

D.B. Corey

"Of course, Agent Donahue. My captain told me to expect your call."

"Ah! That is wonderful. An' how might you be doin' dis fine mournin'?"

"I'm good. How may I help you?"

"Well, I'm supposin' you heard from yer captain that we have been investigatin' a string o' homicides similar to yer own there in Baltimoure. I understan' them to be nearly identical to the ones here in San Diego. Would you mind tellin' me a wee bit o' what yer seein' over there?"

"Of course. The victims are always women. Their ages vary; some in their thirties, and another group in their mid to late seventies. Nothing in between, so far. The killings began with the older group. The victims die of cyanide poisoning, industrial grade stuff, and the composition is identical from victim to victim. The homicides occur in a variety of venues around the city, but so far, only in the suburbs. To be honest, we're having a problem nailing down a consistent MO."

"Aye, from what yer Captain Atkins was tellin' me, I taut we'd be seein' a similar ting. The homicides here follow the same pattern as you describe."

"So, tell me, Agent Donahue, how many homicides are you attributing to this serial killer out your way?"

"We have six, spaced several weeks apart, and as you said, the ages vary."

"Cyanide?"

"Aye. High quality. Kills in seconds. Painless as well."

"I know how the FBI is about disclosing information, Agent Donahue, but can you share some specifics? You know, as a professional courtesy, I mean. As it stands now, you're just a voice on the phone, albeit a pleasant one."

"Well tank you, Detective Truax. That is very kind o' you. An' I'm sure you know, like yerselves, we do not go about disclosin' specifics, but I can see no harm in givin' you a wee bit o' information...in the spirit of agency cooperation, that is. Is there anyting in particular you would like?"

"Yes. Can you tell me the concentration of the toxin you've been seeing out there?"

"Yeah sure," Donahue replied. "Tis 250 parts per million. A significant concentration, indeed. Enough to kill someone of one-hundred-tirty-five kilos. About tree-hundred US pounds. Death is instantaneous."

Truax nodded to himself. That was the correct answer, and he recalled when he asked Barry Johnson exactly what 250 ppm was equal to.

"250 milligrams," Johnson had told him. "To give you a comparison, a table spoon of salt is roughly 17,000 milligrams, so you can see how potent this stuff is. 250 mg. ain't a lot."

"Thank you, Agent Donahue," Truax said. "That's what we're seeing here also. I expect you'll be in touch?"

"Aye. I'll be talkin' with yer captain about assignin' an agent for fact findin' an' the like. Maybe we can catch up to dis scoundrel."

"Yes, Agent Donahue. Maybe we can at that."

"Tank you fer yer time, Detective Truax. You've been most helpful."

"Sure. Glad I could help."

"An' if there's anyting you might be wantin', please don't hesitate to call. This is me cell phone. You can reach me here, day or night. Please feel free to call."

The week passed quickly, with Friday, as all the days before, ending like that Monday, leaving Truax with more questions than he started with, and asking those same questions about Harriett Brennermann and Rosa Neunyo; women of the same ilk whose lives mirrored that of

Dorothy French. Older women, ordinary women, women with no families and modest lifestyles...if one considered living hand to mouth, modest.

What connected them? What did they have in common other than living in the same part of town? They didn't know each other, didn't share a doctor or a grocery store, didn't even attend the same church. They were unlikely targets for a repetitive killer, women he'd never expect to *be* targets, now dead by CK's hand. He left nary a clue to his identity, or indication of motive as to why he singled them out.

And then there were the others: Emma Baumgartner and Stacy Culver. Both were attractive young women full of life, women with dreams and a future, women thought to be more of CK's murderous work by Captain Atkins, by the brass, and by the media—but not by him.

He could easily follow the pack mentality and seek a single killer. Maybe he'd get lucky. Maybe not. More than likely, not. If he caught one, the other would still be out there. Maybe disappear only to resurface some other time, some other place. Sociopaths can't help themselves. They can't deny who they are...*what* they are.

Yes, the victims were all women, and yes, the potency of the cyanide used to kill each one matched exactly—as if the killer mixed up a big batch of poison, much like a painter might mix together different shades of the same color paint. The matching composition of the various kills was a fact held close to the vest by the department, and not for public knowledge. And like the others, Baumgartner and Culver weren't robbed, assaulted, or raped.

Many factors matched, more than not, actually. He could see why his captain and the others felt this was CK and CK only. But thirty years of police work and a nagging gut, told him otherwise.

The locations of the two groups differed, as did the victims and the methodology. French, Brennermann, and Neunyo were solitary kills, discovered alone, and positioned with care at the spot where they died. Baumgartner and Culver died with an audience, sprawled lifeless and undignified where they fell. The dissimilarities were too great to fit a single MO.

No...the Baumgartner and Culver killings were copies committed by a killer looking to hide in CK's shadow. A smart killer. A killer, smarter perhaps, than CK.

On the heels of animal-like rutting, a wail of ecstasy crested above *La donna è mobile* resounding throughout the lab. Spent and unmoving, Harvey lay on Jamie, half on, half off. Pinpoints of light danced inside his eyelids and he gasped for air like a drowning man.

With his blood surging through his veins at twice the normal speed, he found himself delighting in his first dual orgasm. He couldn't help but wonder if she was as exciting when she was alive.

A story from his childhood bible class found its way to the forefront of his consciousness. The story of Samson.

Miss Daniels, the parish spinster, sat at a desk stacked with ungraded assignments, *Judges 16:1-22* scrawled in yellow chalk, high on a dust-streaked blackboard behind her.

She told of how Samson destroyed the temple with his great strength, and how Delilah stole that strength when she cut his hair. Harvey laughed to himself between gasps. *A haircut didn't steal Samson's strength,* he thought. *Delilah fucked it outta him.*

He inhaled deeply, reducing his heart rate which he believed to be somewhere near the frequency of a trip-hammer. The sweat pouring from his body moments before dried on his skin as the air-conditioning cooled him. Pushing himself up, he locked his elbows over the dead girl. He discovered green flecks in her hazel eyes, a pleasing feature he hadn't noticed in his haste, and found it enjoyable that he had left them open. He breathed easily now and allowed himself a moment to appreciate her.

Soft of skin, clear of complexion; her youthful features betrayed her age. Harvey estimated her more toward sixteen. Seventeen maybe, but no older. Had she been alive, he would go to jail for statutory rape. But dead? Rape was not a consideration.

His legs no longer threatened to buckle, so he straightened and pulled himself from her. His hair weighed heavy with sweat, poking out in several directions at once, and he ironed it flat with the palms of his hands. Sliding his wire-rims back onto his nose, he grasped the green scrub bottoms gathered around his ankles and returned them to his waist.

Pulling the drawstring tight, he adjusted the matching top. He leaned over and gently kissed Jamie on the forehead, then considered a cigarette as he checked the ever-vigilant clock on the wall. *The day shift will be here in a couple of hours*, he thought. *Better skip the smoke and start her autopsy.*

CHAPTER 9

Late Tuesday afternoon, Truax found himself at home on a call with Atkins. Angling the phone from his face, he deftly muted a persistent yawn. He had spent all Monday night in Squad going over witness statements and waiting for the toxicology report on Jamie McPherson; a report he had put a rush on over twenty hours prior. He was sleep deprived. Nothing unusual for a cop, but now, for him, it came with a toll.

Because of the heightened awareness due to CK's activities, any suspicious death engaged SIU. After he got the Friday night call from Anne Arundel County Homicide, Truax interviewed the patrons and employees of Bamboo Billy's into the wee hours of Saturday morning. He cut them loose one at a time after questioning, and just before dawn, let the unquestioned go after instructing them he would be in touch. While maintaining his belligerence regarding the merits of a partner, he had to admit that a partner would have made the interviews much easier, not to mention, faster.

Eyewitness accounts were similar, and corroboration of the McPherson girl's tenacious drug use was easily attained. Pending the finding of toxicology, his initial conclusion was that she had OD'ed, and when the samples of her fluids hit the forensics lab Monday morning, he put a rush on the tests, staying up all night waiting on the results. Even with The Special Investigations Unit being part of Homeland Security, it seemed a "rush" still took over a day.

"LOOK Detective!" Walters had screamed through the phone. "There's me, and there's Browning! Cutbacks! Maybe you heard of them! If you can't wait, then maybe I should pass it to the next shift, and it'll go behind whatever they were working on yesterday. Or, maybe YOU'D like a crack at it! It ain't that hard if you know a little something about ion-exchange chromatography."

Truax backed down, swallowing the bitter pill of being bested. He didn't know shit about ion-exchange chromatography, and he didn't want to know, but he didn't want to piss off the forensics techs, fearing they might place his stuff at the low end of the priority list for spite.

Maybe he should take them to dinner. Joe Flacco—the Ravens' quarterback—did that with his offensive line. It worked out pretty well for him.

His gut said the McPherson girl wasn't poisoned. No pink skin, no almond smell. The autopsy report supported his initial impression, mentioning nothing of stomach mucosa, or greenish black hue. And...there was no mention of the ME's concern of hydrogen-cyanide stomach gasses; gasses that could have killed him, or at the very least made him damn sick.

No, he didn't think the McPherson girl was poisoned, and when the forensics report finally made its way to him, it verified his hunch. She died of a drug overdose, not cyanide poisoning, and that was good...or so he had thought.

"Jamie McPherson wasn't poisoned, Captain," Truax said, shifting the phone to the other ear.

"Well, it doesn't matter anymore, Detective," Atkins said flatly. "The top of the food chain is up my ass and

Mustang that had arrived just seconds before him. He liked Mustangs. They were affordable muscle cars, but he liked his Vette more.

And who wouldn't, he thought.

He estimated the walk back to the club to be a quarter-mile. He was miffed, feeling entitled to park closer, because he had been in on the Sunday night party before it became popular. But since that played to nothing, he decided that he'd get there earlier the following week.

His forty-minute wait in line was far from painful. The weather was warm and the women dressed accordingly: jeans and halter tops with free-roaming breasts, cheek-revealing shorts with four-inch stilettos, and snug fitting tube tops that left nothing to the imagination. Some gals wore so little, they may as well have been naked. Harvey considered his time waiting in line, well spent.

Inside, music pounded. The human mass moved to the pulsating rhythms like a photosynthetic organism feeding on light and sound; a shapeless form ebbing to and fro, absorbing the slow-of-foot at the boundaries of the dance floor, only to redeposit them once again a moment later.

Harvey stared wide-eyed. Never had he seen so many off-the-charts women gathered in the same place. And their bodies—the way they moved—each more delicious than the one before. His Need was with him.

Threading his way through a maze of overheated bodies, he reached the bar closest to the door and ordered the first of the evening's beer. Halfway through his second, he spotted her, sitting on a stool at the far end of the bar, that same girl from before, the one with the beautiful blue eyes and long dark hair; the one with the Godzilla-like boyfriend. Kara. He remembered that her name was Kara.

He watched her, biding his time, and looking for the monster-boyfriend. Several men came and went, talking to her, placing their bids to court her for personal gain; men boisterous in their affect and ill-mannered in their style; disrespectful with their four-letter vocabularies and narcissistic demeanor. He watched them come and he watched them go, and then, when there was still no sign of the boyfriend, he blended with the mass of humanity surrounding him, drifting like a piece of wood in a slow-moving creek, edging ever closer, until he was directly behind the stool where Kara sat.

Her hair ran down the middle of her back, jet-black curls churning over a white halter top. Her jeans were designer, the maker's logo embroidered above the left rear pocket in blue and white, and her waistband stressed down revealing the top of a red thong and the better part of a scorpion tattoo.

She sat sideways to the bar drinking bottled water through a straw, talking easily to a man sitting to her left, her body language espousing she knew him well as she leaned toward him.

Harvey seized the opportunity and slipped on to an empty stool on her right. He did not draw her eye, and was close enough to smell her perfume, to hear her conversation.

"Yes, Kara," the man sitting with her said, "it *has* been too long. So how *are* you? And how's Jade? I bet she's getting big."

"Too big, Earl," Kara replied. "She's trying to talk now. Babbles all the time. I don't get a minute's peace."

"Oh you love it and you know it. Does she say any words yet?"

"Yes," she said with a smirk. "She says Da-Da, much to my chagrin. And don't you dare tell that shithead brother of yours. He never spends any time with her, and if he knew that, I'd never hear the end of it."

"Yeah, Kar...I guess not." Earl shifted on his stool. "I'm really sorry it didn't work out between you and him, but he's always been more about himself than anyone else."

"YOU'RE sorry? I drank so much that night, I don't even remember sleeping with him. But ya know? I wouldn't change it now even if I could. Jade brings pure joy into my life. Who needs her shithead father anyway?"

"Yeah," Earl agreed, "she's a cutie, alright. And, you know...I could always stand in for him...some night...if you ever wanted."

"HA! Don't you even start with that shit! I love you Earl, but like a brother-in-law, even if I didn't marry that asshole brother of yours."

"Whoa Kar! I'm only kiddin'! You're too special to me to screw stuff up." Earl broke eye contact and looked around the bar. "So," he said, changing the subject as fast as he could, "who's watchin' Jade tonight?"

"My neighbor, Audrey. We take turns baby sittin' for each other. She has one a little older than Jade."

"That's convenient. Oh...and where's the big man?"

"Ray's gonna meet me here, but we're not hangin'. I'm just here to make arrangements for Amy's bachelorette party this Friday night."

Harvey's ears picked up. It was time to pay closer attention.

"Amy's getting married?" Earl asked.

"Yeah! Do you believe it? To a really nice guy, too. I warned her against it, but she's going through with it anyway." Kara tossed her head back and laughed, bumping into Harvey. Reflexes turned him away from her.

"She's not pregn—" Earl cut his words. "Oh, Kar," he said, throwing a hand over his mouth. "I'm so sorry. I didn't mean—"

Kara's hand waved off his apology. "That's okay, Earl. Shit happens, ya know? Besides, it's not like it's a disease or anything. Oh!" she said, thrusting out an arm, pointing. "There's Ray! Listen Earl, I gotta run. Great seeing you again. And *please...* don't tell your brother I said hi."

"You too, and I won't. C'mon. I'll walk ya over. I want to say hi to Ray."

Kara stood to leave and Harvey did not move, carefully keeping his face obscured as he watched her from the corner of his eye. She finished her water in several long pulls and disposed of the bottle. As she walked away, Harvey thought about his lab schedule for the coming week. Friday worked for him.

CHAPTER 11

Truax dragged himself from bed Monday morning feeling sluggish and drained; not like being tired, more like being sick.

Atkins's directive to meet with him first thing had a hint of finality to it, the undertones of which allowed him only short bursts of restless sleep, resulting in his lying awake in the dark, listening to his own thoughts, and the sound of the night.

I'm too old for this...not knowing, he thought, and debated whether he should prepare for his meeting with Atkins by buying a pack of cigarettes, or taking a shower. He chose the latter.

He lathered his head and face with shaving cream, the mentholated kind that would give him the only tingle he was apt to feel that day. He removed the small mirror propped up on the shower caddy and cleared the haze with a quick rinse under the showerhead. Replacing it at the precise angle that afforded him a steamy reflection, he set about the delicate surgery of dragging a month-old razor across his scalp.

Following a shower that didn't do for him what it usually did, he brushed his teeth, and donned his glasses to see if his shaving had missed anything. Inspecting his face, he realized that in the past couple of years, he'd traded the hair on his head for the hair on his ears, and as he took the clippers to them, he remembered Bill Cosby's bit about aging, and finding hair growing from his ear.

"Are you lost?" Cosby asked the newly discovered ear hair.

Truax allowed himself a chuckle. He loved Cosby.

He dressed in his standard work uniform: a white shirt, freshly cleaned and pressed from the Asian dry cleaners a couple blocks over, a print tie, blue, and without a single coffee stain, and a dark blue sports jacket, one of the trendier two that he owned.

He'd discovered that not having to deal with hair gave him an extra fifteen minutes in the morning. That meant an extra cup of coffee, and that was always good. But it was especially good today. He gathered up his hardcopy files on the cyanide killings and started from the kitchen before noticing the BlackBerry cell phone on the counter. He had almost forgotten about it. Atkins gave it to him by way of leaving it on his desk with an attached note.

"Every detective is getting one of these. I want you to learn to use the Apps: BlackBerry Messenger, Google Maps, Navigator…They're all pre-loaded to make it easier for you. We're going to be using them a lot so get used to the idea. They're the tools of Today. They'll allow me to know where you are, and to contact you without having to use a phone...a phone you seem to prefer not answering."

The tools of Today, Truax thought, clipping the phone on his belt. *Technology...Something else to learn. Something else to hate. Emails and the Internet are bad enough.*

When the cell phone came out, that's all it was. A phone. He knew how to use a phone. But now a phone wasn't just a phone anymore. It was a goddamn computer. Emails and texting and instant messages weren't enough. Now there were Apps and GPS and Meeting Place. The technology was too much to keep up with, so he didn't try. It was easier not to use it and get his ass chewed out. Much easier.

He pulled the front door shut behind him and slipped into the Crown Vic, turning away from the waving figure standing in her front yard next door. As he drove off, he pretended not to hear when Miss Ida called out to him.

Other than Carol, the only person in the anteroom was a young woman with her nose buried in an Austin Camacho novel. A woman he'd never seen before.

Truax started for a chair, but Carol gave him the high sign. "He's waiting for you Moby," she said, an apologetic timbre to her voice.

A chill ran down his spine and what little hair he did have bristled. Had it been longer, he was certain it would have stood on end. But what he didn't understand was the sudden fear he felt.

Part of a cop's makeup was his fearlessness. Hardened criminals had little effect on him, but this young commander had managed to do what ruthless killers could not.

Truax was afraid. Afraid for his job. Afraid for his existence. Afraid for what he knew, and afraid for what he did not. That Atkins had no feel or understanding of the job made it that much worse. Atkins could fire him and think nothing of it.

A little knowledge, he thought. *More dangerous than none at all.*

Truax straightened his back and strode toward the office with head high. If he was on his way out, he was going out with the dignity that a lifetime of police work afforded him. He stopped outside Atkins's office, straightened his tie, and tapped on the door.

Atkins regarded Truax standing in the doorway and let him wait, and at that moment, Truax recognized that Atkins was using his uncertainty against him, much like he had done with the suspects he interviewed. Several seconds elapsed before Atkins stood and pointed a slender finger at the wing chair opposite his desk. Truax slipped in and eased the door closed behind him, reminiscent of a teenager sneaking in at dawn.

The office was nondescript. Small, about 10 X 10 with the usual office appointments; among them, several training certificates and a degree in law enforcement—paper accolades declaring station and authority. On the desk sat photos of Atkins's wife and two daughters. They presented a glimpse of a life outside this room, their inconspicuous placement beguiling Truax to seek them out, just as he might strain to overhear a whisper.

Atkins eased his lanky frame into his oversized leather chair, scooting it forward in childlike bursts, and Truax chastised himself for the grin that got away from him. Atkins brushed at a wayward lock of blonde hair before leveling dull green eyes at Truax.

"I'm assigning you a partner, Detective," he said flatly, "and I want no argument from you. Do you understand?"

Truax expelled a silent breath, relieved at not being fired.

"But Captain, I have an agreement—"

Atkins slammed both hands on his desk, startling Truax, his cheeks turning a bright crimson and showing nothing of the pain now lancing up his left arm.

"THAT agreement, has outlived its usefulness," he bellowed. "People in this town are dropping like flies and the higher-ups are on my *ass*! The Cyanide Killer is making fools out of us. Out of *ME!* They want him apprehended! They want results! Something that seems to elude you!"

"But Captain, I'm sure it's not CK."

"I don't care *what* you're sure of, Detective! Knowing who it is *not* isn't worth a shit! I won't carry a cop who's not pulling his weight, and right now, that's YOU! You've lost your edge! Your last four cases went cold while you chased nonsensical leads with miniscule connections to the CK killings. I gave you a break relieving you of them."

"Now just a minute Captain!" Truax shot back, the center vein in his forehead suddenly prominent. "I worked every viable detail! I—"

"I'M NOT FINISHED!" Atkins roared, silencing Truax.

"Your recent work is unacceptable! It's haphazard! Ill-defined horsesh—" Atkins bit off his words and the very air crackled with a tactile charge. "I'd furlough your ass right fucking now if we weren't spread so damn thin! You're getting that partner I promised you."

"Captain, please—"

Atkins shot a pale finger through the air like a weapon. "DON'T!" Atkins's voice pitched high and broke from anger, quivering as he spoke. "Don't say another...fucking...word!"

Atkins moved toward the intercom, but his eyes did not. They stayed rooted on Truax, daring him to speak, daring him to move, and with the same accusing finger from the same outstretched hand, stabbed at a button on the intercom after a single glance.

Carol's voice drifted into the office like a warm summer breeze, infusing the air with calm and giving no indication that she, or anyone else within earshot, heard the screaming that came from the office.

"Yes, Captain?" she replied.

"Carol," Atkins said, forcing down the wobble in his voice. "Please...send in Agent Vecchio."

CHAPTER 12

Special Agent Frances Vecchio of the Federal Bureau of Investigation strode into Atkins's office with all the confidence of a runway model.

From under a light-gray, pinstriped, business suit, a scooped white blouse revealed a subtle hint of cleavage, a tantalizing display that drew Truax's gaze, long before it found her face. His attention drifted southward, and with the carnality of a dirty ol' man, Truax did what dirty ol' men do. He undressed her with his eyes.

She looked to be in her early thirties, and allowing for the short two-inch heels she wore, he estimated she checked in an inch or so shy of six feet. Slender of build, with her thick black hair twisted into a tight bun on the back of her head, he half expected her to don a pair of horned-rimmed glasses to complete the librarian persona. As he examined her features, he tried to decide if he thought her pretty or not.

She possessed an olive complexion. *Classic Italian*, Truax thought. But her lips were a bit thin for his liking; something he could see fit to overlook, if it meant getting laid. Her nose had an unfortunate bend, ambling ever so slightly to her left, and her dark brown eyes—eyes so dark they were nearly black—sat a little too close together, making her appear cross-eyed, depending on how she looked at him.

His gaze followed a natural downward course, and he gathered in her body with all the usual male bias. *Cher-like*, he thought. *With a better rack*.

"This is Special Agent Vecchio, Detective Truax. She is the FBI liaison from the San Diego office we've been discussing. You spoke to her SAC, Agent Donahue, last week. I discussed the situation with her and agreed to enlist the help of the Bureau on this difficult case. Agent Vecchio will assess information gathered on the cyanide killings in order to assist in CK's apprehension. She'll be riding shotgun on your investigation. "

"You're going ahead and bringing in the Bureau?" Truax exclaimed. "We're Homeland Security! Why are you handing the case over to the FBI?"

"I'm not *handing it over*," Atkins snapped, glancing toward Vecchio. "And you'd do well to remember your place, Detective! Agent Vecchio is here to verify the commonality between their killer and ours, and assist where necessary. She is here on loan. Now, if you'd prefer I assign you a *permanent* partner, I'm sure I could make that fly with Major Taylor."

Truax thought so too, and as a thin smile bordering on provocation formed on Atkins's face, Truax realized that Agent Vecchio was a lever that Atkins could use to force him behind a desk, if not out completely.

"No...no Sir. Agent Vecchio and I will get along...just fine."

"Very good, Detective. Now, get Agent Vecchio settled into the desk next to yours and bring her up to speed. You have your work cut out for you. The two of you, I mean."

"Yes Sir," Truax grumbled, and like a boy burdened with babysitting his little sister, jerked his head for Vecchio to follow and walked out; not bothering to wait, leaving her standing where she was.

D.B. Corey

CHAPTER 13

Vecchio watched Truax step through the door and turned to Atkins with a puzzled expression.

"Not the friendly sort, is he?"

Atkins shook his head slightly. "He's having some issues. You're to...assist."

"Of course, Captain."

Vecchio turned to watch Truax shuffle down the hall in a huff, and Atkins took the opportunity to let his eyes wander her body. As her attention returned to him, he raised his eyes to meet hers.

"So tell me, Special Agent," he said, "are you learning your way around our fair city?"

Vecchio flashed an inviting smile. "Oh, I'm feeling my way around," she said, gesturing with a sweep of her hand. "Staying in a hotel near the beltway," she continued, turning back to him.

"But I need to find a month-to-month furnished rental. The bureau is watching expenses, as your department is, I'm sure. If this drags out, a hotel stay could get expensive. Those extended stay accommodations are more reasonable—better to check out early than to foot the bill for the high-rent district."

"Yes, of course," Atkins said, his eyes dipping for an instant. "Well, please feel free to use the department's computers. Carol out there can help you as well. And dare I say…I imagine you'll want to eat during your stay?" He flashed a smile. "Reisterstown has some of the best restaurants in Baltimore. Actually, I was considering showing you around, perhaps taking you to dinner—you know, just to help you acclimate to the area. Maybe a couple of drinks…"

Vecchio could almost feel the heat his body threw off. Glancing toward the photos of his wife and daughters, she wondered what over-compensation his desk provided him as it gobbled up a good quarter of the room.

"I have to be honest with you, Captain Atkins," she said, her smile running from her lips. "I think I would be uncomfortable with that…as long as you continued to call me 'Special Agent.' Please, call me Frances."

Atkins's grin formed like a stop-action film, finishing with the whitest of smiles. "Very well, Frances."

Her dark eyes warmed. "So Don," she said, "Why don't you pick me up at my hotel around eight?"

CHAPTER 14

Vecchio varied her pace between a fast walk and a slow jog to catch Truax before he reached his desk, the movement inside her shirt creating approving looks from the male detectives, and posture adjustments from the females.

Truax gestured toward the desk next to his with little enthusiasm, and dropped into his chair. Vecchio heard him mutter something along the lines of wishing it was farther away, and pretended not to hear. With eyes bearing down on her from every direction, she tried to appear indifferent to the looks, both lecherous and condescending.

Hanging her suit jacket on the back of her chair, she sat and crossed one long leg over the other, tucking her skirt beneath her knee. After a minor bit of desk keeping, she pressed the power button on the laptop docking station in front of her. The monitor crackled to life and presented the Computer Locked window.

She pressed Ctrl-Alt-Delete and up popped the logon screen. 'Guest,' was already entered into the UserID field, but the Password field required an entry.

"Shit!" she muttered.

Truax kept his nose buried in Stacy Culver's case file, and did not look up when he heard the clicking of plastic keys and another, "Shit!"

"Well, Detective?" Vecchio asked, her annoyance seeping through. "Are you going to help me? Or do I have to hack my way into this computer?"

"Just hit the Enter key," he said, the instruction coming at a near whisper.

Vecchio regarded his weak response as a message to her, as if his assistance might be construed as some sort of limited acceptance.

"Guest has no password," he continued.

"Oh…" she said, and pressed the Enter key. "Oh! Okay! That worked. Thanks Moby. I *can* call you Moby, can't I?"

He gave her a withering glance, but said nothing.

"O-kaaaay...so, would you like to know about the case I'm working in San Diego?"

Truax glared from his monitor. "*Your* case? Why should I give a shit about *your* case? You came here because you think *your* killer is *here*, so why in the world would I want to know about *your* case? Correct me if I'm wrong, but you're here to evaluate and assist *if necessary*, right?"

"Well, yes."

"Then why are you blathering about your case?"

"I...I just thought—"

"Please! Frankie! Don't think! Just observe...like you're supposed to."

"It's Frances, Moby," Vecchio said. "Frankie is a boy's name."

"Whatever. I'm not interested in your case or your name or getting to know you. I just want to get through this thing as quickly and as painlessly as possible. Suppose we can do that?"

"Very well, but even if you're not interested in my case, or my name, or getting to know me, I still need a look at your files. Just the most recent murders, please. The young victims. I'm up to speed on CK's previous stuff."

"Oh, you are, are you?"

"Well, yeah," she replied. "You see, I *am* interested in *your* case." She separated out several strands of long hair with a pair of turquoise fingernails, and began twirling them in tight circles around her fingers.

"Fucking women!" Truax mumbled. "Shouldn't be cops."

"I'm sorry..." she said. "I couldn't hear you."

"Nothing!" He rolled the mouse across the pad and pulled up a file from the department's server. "Ok, if you're so up to speed on his older victims, tell me the name and sex of the last one: age, location of the body, and the concentration of the poison."

"I didn't know there was going to be a quiz," she quipped, her near-black eyes boring into his with a practiced seduction.

He averted his eyes from hers as a school boy flinches from the gaze of a pretty girl. "Well? Do you know? Or don't you?"

Vecchio smiled. She swiveled her chair to the side and leaned back, her long legs still crossed, and her light-gray pinstripe skirt riding high up on her thigh.

Truax's gaze dipped, but for only an instant. She closed her eyes and her breathing became Zen-like, almost as if she were asleep. Then, she began to speak.

"Rosa Neunyo. Female. Age, seventy-one. Responding units reported finding her on a bench. She died from potassium-cyanide poisoning. 250-parts per million."

Vecchio opened her eyes and locked on his, produced a half-smile, and waited.

Truax moved to the next victim and then the next, continuing his bombardment and reacting with increased frustration as she answered question after question, putting her considerable powers of recall on display.

As she bulls-eyed every pertinent piece of information he asked for, a flash of admiration slipped through his stone façade, and became visible to her for just a moment, before he shut it down.

"Well," Truax said, "it seems you are, 'up to speed,' as you say."

"I've had lots of time to study these files. Moreover, I have a photographic memory. It comes in handy in this line of work."

"To say the least," Truax mumbled. "You'll find the case files under MSP/casefiles/truax/active. From there, just pick the case file you want. French, Brennermann, Neunyo."

Vecchio clicked several keys before switching to the mouse. "The Baumgartner file is locked, "she said. "And Culver. May I have the password?"

"Stick with the ones I gave you."

"But I know about those. I just *showed* you that. I want a look at the recent cases. The younger victims."

"Those are unrelated."

"Unrelated? Those are the files I want to see. Your captain—"

Truax's eyes flashed anger and his features hardened as he cut her off. He lowered his voice and bored deep into her eyes, any pretense of cooperation gone.

"Look Frankie, as far as I'm concerned, I'm lead in this unholy partnership, and although I'm pretty sure you aren't stupid enough to go over my head, your insinuation rubs me the wrong way, see? From where I sit, it smacks of disrespect and insubordination. Those cases are off limits to you until I say otherwise. Understand? You're supposed to observe and evaluate. Stick to that. Leave the cop stuff to me."

"My name is Frances, Detective, not *Frankie!*"

"Yeah, you said. Now just do what I tell you, and we'll get along. Got it?"

Vecchio's dark eyes narrowed as her Italian got up, but she kept the impulsive urge to lash out in check. One need be blind not to see his resentment for her, and it would do her more harm than good to aggravate him. She needed him, and it would make her situation more difficult if he ignored her, or worse, cut her out. Best to let it go. For now.

"Sure, Detective Truax," she replied. "I '*got*' it."

CHAPTER 15

The aluminum wing chair that paired with Truax's desk served several purposes. Presently, it acted as a hanger for his dark blue jacket, and a perch for his behind. With tie loosened and sleeves rolled to the elbow, he pondered the differences between the murders, staring at the map he'd stapled to the roll-about bulletin board that he used for such things.

The map displayed the Greater Baltimore Metropolitan area, encompassing Baltimore, Howard, and Anne Arundel Counties, as well as the cities of Baltimore and Annapolis, where pushpins marked the scenes of all five cyanide killings, with the most recent fifth pin representing Stacy Culver, added only a moment ago.

There were three pushpins clustered together in and around the Middle River area, a blue-collar section of town about forty-five minutes east-north-east of Baltimore City. These represented Dorothy French, Harriett Brennermann, and Rosa Neunyo, the older poisoning victims. The pin representing thirty-three year-old Emma Baumgartner, the first of the younger victims, sat miles to the north.

Taken by itself, it seemed CK might be branching out, but when Stacy Culver was killed, her position on the map was farther away still, from both the original older group, and the Baumgartner murder, forming a pattern of sorts.

The two younger victims were not only miles from the older group of three, but they were miles from each other as well, effectively expanding CK's perceived comfort zone. But inconsistencies in age and location weren't all that troubled Truax.

The police found each of the older victims lying prone, each on a bench. One at a bus stop outside a bowling alley, one in a small park near the neighborhood library, and one in an open-air strip mall. All three died near their homes, all three with their bodies positioned with care, almost as if the killer went the extra mile to make their last moments peaceful, unfettered.

The younger victims received no such consideration. Baumgartner died in the parking lot of the Irish Tavern, on Harford Road, in full view of an audience, while the Culver girl, also surrounded by people, collapsed onto the grimy carpet inside Wurlitzer's nightclub. If all the murders were the work of CK, why the careful attention to some, but not the others? And why the drastic differences in age and location?

A copycat?

The click-click-clicking sound of two-inch heels on linoleum tile interrupted his ponderings. He turned to see Vecchio sauntering toward him. She wore her hair in a ponytail that reached the middle of her back, a man's blue button-down dress shirt under a tan blazer, and a black mid-thigh skirt. Her shield hung from her left hip, her weapon, her right, and he thought her pretty today.

"Afternoon Moby," she said with a wry smile, slowing to a stop.

"Afternoon my ass," he said, lifting himself off the chair-back. "It's Thursday. Where the hell you been? Not that I give a shit."

"Apartment hunting. Yesterday and today."

"*Apartment*? How long you planning to stay?"

"Until we catch this bastard, or we know he's no longer in the area. I needed something furnished, and had to secure an extended-stay rental."

"Hold on, Frankie."

"Frances."

"Yeah, that. I was under the impression you would be here for a week or ten days to collect Intel. Now it sounds like you're planning to apprehend CK. Am I missing something here?"

"Well if the opportunity presents itself, I'd like to assist on the collar. Couldn't hurt my personnel record."

"I see," Truax grumbled. "So you're *not* here just to compare notes. Are those your orders? Or is it your personal agenda."

"My SAC told me to play it by ear," Vecchio replied, injecting a bit of swagger. "If we get close, she wants me to stay with it. If I can help you catch him, why shouldn't I?"

"Well, for one reason, I don't *need* your help. I'm a big boy. I can do it all by myself."

Vecchio cast her dark eyes to him. "You don't have to be condescending. I know you're capable."

"More than *you*. I been doin' this a long time."

Vecchio's stance softened. "And that's why I want to stay," she said, childlike. "I've reviewed your record, Moby. I know I can learn from you. And I want to. I don't really care about the credit. Keep it. I just want to be a part of this, if you can see your way clear to let me."

Truax was taken back. An FBI agent was asking him to teach her, and the vaunted arrogance of the FBI was nowhere to be seen. This was a real switch.

"So," Vecchio said, shifting gears. She directed her attention to the map and its five pushpins, focusing on the cluster of the three centered in Middle River. Then she turned toward Truax, keeping her eyes locked on the map, before cutting to him. "What do we have here?"

Truax fought the urge to flip the board over, to hide his hard work from her prying eyes, and roll the whole damn thing back into the corner where it came from. But even he knew that was ridiculous. Better to tolerate this interruption to his life and make the best of it. The sooner he—the sooner *they*—solved this crime, the sooner he'd be rid of her.

Reclaiming his position on the chair-back, he began pointing to the map, glancing at her legs, and explaining the meaning and placement of the pushpins. He shared his theory on the differences in the murders, and how he believed there were two killers at work, a second one copying the first.

Vecchio stood and listened without interruption, taking in every point as Truax explained. She began tracing the outline of her jaw with the slender, turquoise fingernails of her right hand, as her left rested on a protruding hip.

When Truax finished, he studied her reaction, trying to read her body language—a pleasing event that he was beginning to look forward to.

She said nothing at first, reflecting inwardly, as if drawing mental images of the murders and pondering the liminal state between victims and places. Then, she turned to him.

"You know," she said, "that the first three were killed in the same area might just be coincidence."

"Coincidence? There are no coincidences in this business. I'da thought they'd have taught you that in FBI School."

"We learnt to avoid forming opinions, Moby. Especially early on. Its possible CK is testing the waters, so to speak. Getting a feel for what to expect, or how events would unfold. You said you didn't care about my case, but varying his MO here, mirrors his behavior in San Diego, so from my perspective, his MO is at least similar. That's why

I want to see those files. There could be a lot of reasons for the differences in his MO. Maybe he's trying to throw us off his trail, or something else we haven't considered. Could be a lot of reasons, the least of which, I believe, is a copycat killer."

Truax let her jabber fade into the background like so much white noise. The word "learnt," a word commonly used by Americans educated by under-educated parents, a word with a backwoods slant, was not something he expected to hear from an FBI agent of Italian descent.

But there was more to it. Truax perceived something fleeting in those near-black eyes. Something she didn't want him to know. It was there for just a moment and then it was gone. Fear was alien to Truax, and the thought of bodily harm, or even death, did not affect him the way it did others, yet a sliver of fear sliced through him like a chill: The fear of being deemed inadequate, and of missing what was right in front of him.

Truax began sifting through what little he knew about Vecchio—her photographic memory and short temper, the overstated sexuality that clung to her like expensive perfume, and now this folksy speak. Or was it something else? It seemed that lately, Agent Vecchio was just chock full of surprises.

CHAPTER 16

Strobe lights flashed, and the disco ball above Billy's dance-floor fired swirling, pencil-thin beams across the room. Music pounded, and the scrum of bodies on the dance floor appeared as clustered silhouettes, moving in unison to teeth-rattling blasts from mega-watt sub-woofers.

Harvey threaded his way through the mass of bodies, jinking this way and that, evading boisterous drunks and tray-wielding waitresses, scanning the crowd as he moved. It was almost midnight. Kara was here somewhere, and his Need was with him.

A blinding white light powerful enough to overcome the dance-floor lighting systems panned across the room. A few seconds later it disappeared, only to reappear once again, this time in a different location, and this time, centering on Kara as she made her way to the bar. Several strides later, the light vanished.

The light continued to hop-scotch its way toward his location, and Harvey saw it was the flood lamp of a hand-held video camera. Looking to the clubs many large screens mounted above the dance floor, he saw images of the crowd, laughing and dancing and having a good time.

This is new, he thought, and then, there he was, on the big screen as the light enveloped his space. Turning his back, he moved at right angles away from the light, careful to avoid another direct hit while tracking Kara to the main bar.

Kara coasted to the side of the bar nearest her. Harvey swung around to the right, weaving between people, never losing sight of her for more than a split second. Blending into the crowd, staying on the fringe, he saw her say something to one of the three bartenders. A moment later, the barkeep returned with a bottle of water. Kara handed her a bill and gestured for her to keep the change. Grabbing a straw, she headed back into the crowd. Harvey's eyes followed her as he stepped to the bar and beckoned the same bartender. The one with the waist-length hair.

"Water!" he yelled above the music.

"Which one ya want?" the bartender called back.

"What?"

"We have Dasani and Aquafina," she said. "Which one ya want?"

"Two? Let me have one of each."

The bartender dug into the cooler and came up with two plastic bottles. "Run a tab?" she asked.

Harvey answered by tossing a ten on the bar and walking away. He set course in the same direction taken by Kara. He located her minutes later, standing around a café table with several other women—the bachelorette party, he presumed. He wandered in close, and when he determined that Kara's water was Dasani, he backed off and tossed the Aquafina, still unopened, into a nearby trashcan.

Slipping back into the crowd, it was a simple task to spike the water with cyanide powder. Unscrew cap, pour contents from the miniature vile into bottle, insert straw, and stir. It couldn't be simpler. Like a recipe straight from the *Food Network*. Now all he need do was wait for an opening.

The music shifted gears to a high-energy tempo. The five women standing around Kara's café table began gyrating in place. Seconds later they grabbed each other's arms and struck out for the dance floor. Harvey found himself staring at Kara's water, sitting on the side of the table closest to him, straw jutting from the opening.

Harvey smiled to himself as he cased his surroundings. In a meat-market like Billy's, it was commonplace for males, looking to bed females, to loiter at the edge of the dance floor like wildebeests around a Serengeti watering hole. They clustered around the abandoned café tables littered with half-finished drinks, crumpled napkins, and dirty ashtrays, lusting after the women as they danced, only to scatter like jackals when the Pride returned. It was not that way with Harvey. He was a ghost. Not even a face in the crowd. His Need was with him and he did not hesitate.

Strolling to Kara's table, acting as if he belonged, he placed his bottle next to hers, hovered for a moment, and left, taking her bottle with him while leaving the tainted one. No one noticed. No one cared. *They're all wrapped up in their own little worlds*, he thought, and now, all that remained was to wait for her to drink her water and die, just like Stacy. Then he'd go to work and wait. Kara would be along soon enough.

The music blared, Kara danced, and Harvey became impatient. He knew that women would dance as long as the DJ continued to string songs together. Until he played one they didn't like, or they had to pee, they'd dance. But Harvey had to get to work. He glanced at his watch. It was approaching 12:40 in the morning. He was already late, but if he were *too* late, there would be questions. He might not be able to stay for Kara's departure.

Ten more minutes, Harvey thought. *I'll wait ten more minutes.*

One song ended and another started without a pause. Kara broke from the small cache of dancing bodies that were her friends. She walked back to the table, and another woman followed. The rest of the Pride arrived moments later.

Harvey breathed a sigh.

Finally...

The women laughed, gesturing with their hands, and there were hugs all around. Kara capped her bottle of water, stuffed it into her oversized shoulder bag, and gave everyone a final kiss on the cheek. She scurried past a disconcerted Harvey as a string of panic wove its way through him. She didn't drink the water—and there was no Plan B.

CHAPTER 17

Harvey tore through his usual ritual of changing into his scrubs, securing his personal effects in his locker, and heading to the lab. He trotted through the big double doors to find Doctor Ahmad Rabbani, the second shift pathologist.

"Ahmad!" Harvey called. "Sorry I'm late. How'd things go tonight?"

"Things were being as usual, Harvey. Two autopsies only. You'll be finding them in the cooler. There's nothing for you presently."

"Yes...well, good. I hope it stays that way."

"Are you being OK, Harvey?" Ahmad asked. "You are anxious about something, yes?"

"Yes. No. It's nothing, really. A problem at home."

"You're mother, Harvey? She is troubled?"

"No. It's...the house. Some plumbing problem I think. That's why I'm late."

"Ah! Well I am hoping you fix the problem. So, I will be going now."

The two MEs exchanged cordial good nights, and a half hour after Rabbani left, two auto accident victims rolled in, both pronounced DOA at Mercy Hospital.

Harvey completed the first of them in smart fashion, finishing in the record time of three hours. He glanced at the clock. Time had flown.

5 a.m. Where the hell is she?

Harvey had completed one autopsy and he fully expected Kara to arrive in the middle of that, if she finished her water after she left the club, that is. He couldn't know when she would come to him now, and he couldn't leave more than one autopsy for overflow, otherwise McGovern would want to know why.

If he started the autopsy on the 2nd accident victim, and Kara came in, he couldn't just stop. He'd have to finish his work, but that didn't mean he couldn't have her.

Salacious thoughts interrupted his thinking. His Need was with him. If he stopped working long enough to enjoy her, he'd want to take his time. Not rush it. Savor it, like a fine wine or a two-inch steak. He'd have to clean her up afterward, and if he enjoyed her longer than he should, there was no reason why the dayshift couldn't finish her. Not if he were very careful. Very thorough. He was a jumble of nerves.

No, that would be stupid.

He couldn't be sure if he had removed every trace of his essence, and if he missed something, someone might find it. Scrutinize it. Then the questions would start.

No. Too risky.

He paced, looked at the clock, and paced some more. His mind was racing, a mishmash of conflicting scenarios. He decided to leave the 2nd autopsy for the next shift. When the clock hit 5:45, he went for a smoke. Not so much for the nicotine fix, but to look for the transport that should bring Kara to him.

D.B. Corey

CHAPTER 18

Truax stirred three sugars into his second cup of coffee before sitting down at the kitchen table.

Turning to the crime beat section of last Sunday's *Baltimore Sun*, he considered skipping it altogether, since tomorrow was Sunday again. Before he could decide, the kitchen phone rang.

"Truax. *Ah—bonjour, Maman...oui, très bien...*Mama, you really should speak English. You need to practice. *Maman, ton anglais ne s'améliorera jamais si tu ne l'emploies pas...*no, Mama, seventy-nine is not too old to learn. Yes, your English is getting much better. No, I haven't had any cigarettes. So, what's the weather like in Montreal? It should be nice up there now...mid 70s? It's pronounced 'rain,' Mama...well, yes. I was thinking of visiting in a couple of weeks. Weeks. *Semaines*."

The cell phone sitting on the kitchen table interrupted his conversation.

"Hold on a minute, Mama, I have another call...*un autre appel.*"

Switching phones, he answered.

"Truax."

"Morning, Moby. Hope I'm not disturbing you."

Truax recognized Atkins' voice, and his heart rate jumped as pressure began to build between his temples.

89

Hearing from Atkins on a Saturday morning had all the earmarks of a ruined day, so he mustered a one-word response.

"Captain."

"I need you in today, Moby. AA County Homicide's working a woman found dead in her kitchen. Thinks she was poisoned. Says it's got the earmarks of the Cyanide Killer so they passed it to us. I want you and Vecchio to check it out."

"Right away, Captain." Truax felt the pressure subside. He fully expected some kind of ass chewing. For what, he didn't know. Atkins never needed a reason of late, but today, his tone was not condescending, and that was a plus. "In her kitchen you say?"

"Yes. Neighbor found her."

"Then I doubt it's CK."

"For God's sake!" Atkins snapped. "Can't you at *least* wait till you're at the scene before making a call like that?"

"Yes, Sir. Sorry. I'll get the address from dispatch and be on the road in half an—"

"Don't bother with that. Vecchio is on her way to pick you up. Just be ready when she gets there."

Atkins hung up before Truax could respond. He snapped his cell shut, closed his eyes, and let the back of his head bang into the wall several times.

The sonofabitch didn't even do him the courtesy of calling *him*, before calling *her*. Expelling a frustrated sigh, he picked up his wall phone from the table.

"Mama, I have to go to work. Let me call you later, okay? Yes, I know its Saturday...11:30 Mama, same as there...Mama, I'm a cop...*police...oui!* Yes, I'll be careful. *Ne pas* s'*inquiéter. Au revoir...*Love you too, Mama. Bye."

Twenty-minutes later a horn blared. At the curb sat an unmarked department Crown Vic. Truax peered through the window giving little thought to it being Saturday, or to wearing a coat and tie on a weekend. It's what he always wore to work. That didn't change, just because it was Saturday.

He threaded a tie through his collar as he trotted toward the curb. Vecchio was out of the car and leaning against the trunk waiting, the three-inch heel of one stylish boot anchored in the Vic's rear bumper. Other than being the first Saturday he had occasion to work with her, it was also the first time he'd seen her in a tight pair of jeans. Her legs looked even longer, if that were possible. With her thick black hair pulled into a ponytail, and the top two buttons of her shirt undone, he thought her pretty today.

Maybe he *was* becoming a dirty old man...but so what! It was one of the few things he had left to look forward to at his age. He was only a man, after all, and looking down her top only made him that much more so. Besides, it was her choice to wear the kind of tops she wore, the kind that drew the masculine eye, so it was tantamount to giving him permission. And if she had a problem with his leering, then she should blame herself. After all, it was her own fault.

But even that eye-popping cleavage didn't change his perception of her. He felt she was holding something back. He wasn't buying the notes-taker bit. She wasn't just someone sent by her betters to gather information. She was here to solve a crime. He felt it in his bones.

Vecchio turned as Truax neared the car, and something about the way he stared at her caught her attention.

"What?" she said.

"Nothing. You're driving."

"Yes it is something. You're staring at me and now I feel self-conscious."

"Never seen you in jeans before."

"It's the weekend. And since you brought it up, I've never seen you in anything besides those same ratty jackets you always wear. Don't you own anything new?"

"We're not going to a damn party, Frankie. C'mon. Let's go."

"*Frances*, Moby!" Her hand shot into the air. "It's *Frances*, damn it!" And with one last non-obscene flick of the wrist, she climbed behind the wheel.

The drive to the crime scene took a shade over thirty minutes and Truax enjoyed every second of it. The business suits Vecchio wore during the week did nothing for her, and various fantasies jockeyed for position in the front of his mind. But they were distracting, so he shut them off, and filled the time with small talk to gain some insight. *Hold your enemies closer*, he thought.

"So, Frankie, how'd you draw this assignment?"

"The SAC thought it'd be good experience for me."

The word 'experience' caught his ear. Adjusting the seatbelt, he twisted in his seat to face her. "What do you mean, 'experience'? How long you been an agent?"

"Graduated Quantico three months ago."

"Three *months*? You're a *rookie*?"

"The term the Bureau uses is First Office Special Agent."

"I don't care *what* they call it. You're a rookie, plain and simple. Zero experience."

"That's part of why I'm here, Moby. To gain experience. But you won't—

She loosed a fluster sigh. "Oh, never *mind!*"

Truax knew something wasn't right with her. He couldn't believe that the Bureau would send a rookie agent fact-finding on such a high profile case. But he wouldn't get to the bottom of it by alienating her.

"I'm sorry, Frankie. I didn't mean it the way it sounded. So...why don't you fill me in on the case you're working back home."

Vecchio gave him a look. "Oh, so *now* you want to hear about my case!"

"I was rude the other day. Lost my temper. I'm under a lot of pressure with this case and I'm no spring chicken anymore. I'm sorry."

Vecchio softened. "Oh...it's OK. Maybe you haven't noticed, but I get a little hot under the collar myself, sometimes." She grinned, and they both had a good laugh.

"The vics are the same there as here," she began. "Identical. Older women, younger women, the composition of the poison is exactly the same, and then, everything just stopped. It's like he just closed up shop and relocated. Agent Donahue picked up on it and contacted Captain Atkins. So here I am."

"How'd you guys get wind he was here?"

"Come, come, Detective. You're Homeland Security. We both get our Intel he same way—Law Enforcement Information Sharing Service."

"Yes, of course," Truax said.

And that's a street that goes both ways.

CHAPTER 19

Truax spoke with Detective Welford of Anne Arundel County Homicide when they arrived at Kara Templeton's apartment. Vecchio stood beside him and listened after Truax introduced her. Welford filled them in.

"Found her hanging from the refrigerator door," Welford began. "Her hand was jammed in there pretty good. I had to help Johnson free it."

"Who made the poisoning call?" Truax wanted to know.

"Johnson." Welford nodded toward the field medical examiner in the kitchen. "Said her coloring was wrong. Duty Officer said to pass it to you guys. I was just about to interview the neighbor across the hall. She called it in. You want to handle it?"

"If you wouldn't mind, can you take a preliminary?" Truax asked. "Vecchio and I will follow up."

Welford gave Vecchio a long look.

"Sure, Moby. I'll wait for you next door. Nice to meet you, Agent," he said to Vecchio, and turned to Truax with a grin.

"I see things are looking up at SIU."

When Welford left, Vecchio said, "What did he mean by that?"

Truax smiled. "Don't be so naive. He's just giving you a backdoor compliment, that's all."

94

Electronic strobes painted the small room with light as cameras recorded the scene, and several techs tagged and bagged anything of import. There was no evidence of break-in or assault, nothing was disturbed, and all was as it should be—except for the dead woman lying on the floor.

Without way of announcement, Truax caught the field ME's attention by tapping on the doorjamb. A slender man of six-feet, looking like he should be teaching chemistry instead of heading a field forensics team, halted his jotting of notes, turned, and smiled. A lock of fine black hair fell across his glasses and he tossed his head to send it back where it came from. The word FORENSICS was blazoned across the back of his smock, and his sleeves were rolled to the elbow. He didn't offer his hand.

"Good morning, Detective," Johnson, said.

"That's what they tell me, Doc," Truax replied.

"So who's your friend? New partner?"

"Let's not get ahead of ourselves, Doc. This is Special Agent Vecchio. FBI. She's here to— well, let's just say she's here."

"Oh? Well, it's very nice to meet you, Agent Vecchio."

Vecchio raised an eyebrow, smiled, and nodded.

"So, Truax asked, taking a quick look around the kitchen. "Is this how you found her?"

"Pretty much, except her left hand was jammed in the top shelf of the refrigerator door up to the wrist. Must have tried to catch herself when she began losing consciousness. Welford and I freed it. Laid her down. Other than that, the body hasn't been touched."

"Okay. What's your call?"

"Unofficially? She died of cyanide poisoning. Dead no more than three or four hours. The neighbor called it in."

"Yeah, Welford told me." Truax lifted the forensics sheet. "She's got a pinkish coloring. Is that why you think cyanide?"

"That, the vomit, and this."

Johnson pulled a plastic bottle of commercially sold water from an evidence bag. "Dasani, he announced. "Found it in the sink. How's your sense of smell, Moby?"

"Not bad for an old fart."

"Okay," Johnson said. "Take a careful whiff of this, and tell me what you think."

Truax took the empty bottle and inhaled cautiously with three short whiffs.

"Almond." He passed the bottle to Vecchio who examined every inch of it.

"Yep. Very faint. I doubt she detected it. And even if she did, it may not have concerned her. Anyway, we'll know more after her autopsy. Tox will be able to nail it down, but I don't think they'll come up with anything different."

"Probably not. Damn! If this is CK, I'm fucked."

Johnson cut to Vecchio who rolled her eyes.

"Why do you say that, Moby?"

"Atkins."

"Ah!" Johnson replied. "Say no more."

"You heard?"

"Everyone has. It's no secret he's on the hot-seat, and shit rolls downhill. Right into your lap."

Truax produced a belligerent smirk. "Don't I know it. I wonder why he's changing his MO. CK, I mean. This kill; it's the same as Baumgartner and the Culver girl, but different as night and day from the other three."

"The 'Why' is your part of the puzzle," Johnson said with a grin. "I'm more of a 'What' kinda guy myself."

Moby returned the smile, but his heart wasn't in it. It seemed the bad guys never took a day off. He was worn down, and as far as he was concerned, doing something for thirty years was long enough for anyone to be doing anything.

He glanced Vecchio's way, and thought that maybe Atkins was right. Maybe a partner would make it all easier to take. He thought about mentoring Vecchio, training her, stealing her from the Feds. She was obviously smart enough, and she came equipped with a photographic memory, one like he used to have. He smiled inwardly. *Maybe it's not such a bad thing. And God knows I could do much, much, worse.*

"Make sure I get the report, Johnson."

"You got it, Moby, and I'm ready to release the body. The EMTs are going to transport her to OCME since they're already here. You done with her?"

"Yeah, go ahead. I'm gonna look around a little."

Johnson called in the EMS team and Truax waited until they removed Kara's body before examining the kitchen. He noted the highchair with the baby's formula bottle lying on its side. He noticed the baby's water bottle on the counter, and the pot on the stove that she used to heat the baby's formula. He found that curious. Nowadays most women use the microwave. He guessed she probably didn't trust it for the baby. Sometimes the old ways, are the best ways.

He opened the refrigerator with a pen from his shirt pocket. Inside, he didn't see a single bottle of commercially sold water. Just eggs, milk, Enfamil, a two-liter bottle of diet soda, some yogurt, and the other things one might find in a single woman's fridge.

Maybe it was her last bottled water, he thought.

He checked the trashcan for packaging and empty bottles, and reflected on the Tylenol killings of the early 80s as he poked around. He found no water. The kitchen cabinets told the same story. Then he took a quick check around the apartment, ending with the smaller bedroom. Vecchio followed him in.

Four enormous plaster letters, hand-painted in green pastels, hung juxtaposed in organized chaos against a yellow wall, angled precariously beside a poster of *Sponge Bob Square Pants*; a proclamation of love and motherhood, heralding the name of the room's owner—Jade—to all who entered. Above the crib, a colorful Disney mobile spun in easy circles.

"The baby's room," Vecchio murmured.

They headed across the hall to talk to the neighbor. Entering the apartment, he found Welford taking a statement from a woman holding a small child on her lap. Truax would ask her the same questions that Welford did. It was standard procedure to question witnesses and suspects repeatedly to see if their stories stayed consistent. Then, he'd compare the answers, verifying everything with Vecchio and her big brain.

He quickly conferred with Welford, and Vecchio listened in. Then, after Welford left, he turned his attention to Kara's neighbor.

"I know you've been through this a couple of times already, Miss," Truax said, "but would you please tell me again what happened?"

Audrey shifted Jade to her other knee, wiped fresh tears from her eyes, and began.

"Kara went to a bachelorette party last night. Her best friend is getting married next week and she is—was—the Maid of Honor. My daughter Annie and I watched the baby in her apartment. We were asleep when she got home around 1am. I left Annie sleeping on her sofa and walked back here. This morning, around 6:30, I heard Annie knocking. She said Kara was playing on the refrigerator. I walked over and found her like...like..." A silent tear rolled down her cheek. Truax gave her a moment.

"Husband?"

"No, she didn't marry Jade's father. He's an asshole."

"I see. Did she bring anyone home with her?"

"No! Never! She wasn't like that. And I resent you asking—"

"I'm not passing judgment, Miss. These are routine questions. Nothing more."

Vecchio raised an eyebrow and shifted her weight from one leg to the other.

"Did she bring anything home? Food maybe? Or maybe had something delivered?"

"I don't think so. She seldom ate anything at night."

"Did she use bottled water?"

Audrey stopped, and thought for a moment. She came up empty.

"Bottled water? No. She had one 'o those filters on the faucet. You know...those attachments that purify the tap water?"

"I'm familiar with them. So how did she get along with the baby's father?" *The asshole,* he thought.

Audrey rolled her eyes. "He's a jerk. Never takes the baby when he's supposed to. But if you're asking me if they fought? Sure. But no more than any other estranged couple."

Truax added a line to Welford's notes. So far, everything jived. "Can you tell me where the party was last night?"

"Bamboo Billy's. It's a club not far from here."

"Would you happen to know who was at the party?"

Audrey rattled off the people she knew were there, and Truax jotted down their names.

"You said Annie stayed at Kara's overnight?"

"Yes."

"Do you mind if I speak with Annie?"

"Speak with Annie? Why? She's only three years—"

"It won't take long. You'll be here."

"Yeah...sure. I guess."

When Audrey called Annie, Truax watched a little girl in Scooby-Do pajamas shuffle out from the relative safety of her bedroom, the music of the *Wiggles* coming from somewhere within. When she sat down on the couch next to her mother, Truax got down on his knees facing her, and sat back on his heels. He placed his hands in his lap, and softened his features.

"Hi Annie. My name is Moby. That's a funny name, isn't it?"

Annie's dark hair hung in twin ponytails and her eyes sparkled blue. She answered with a shy smile that formed a dimple in each cheek, but scooted closer to her mother and her thumb went into her mouth. Audrey promptly pulled it back out.

"It's not you," Audrey said to Truax. "Besides her father, the only other man she ever saw this close up was Santa, and he made her cry."

Truax saw the fright in the child's eyes and decided not to push her.

"Frankie?" He motioned her down next to him. "A little help if you please?" Vecchio was there in an instant. Annie relaxed, and Truax stood, giving Vecchio the go-ahead.

"Annie," Vecchio said, "can you tell me what you saw at Miss Kara's house?"

Annie looked up at her mother.

"Go ahead, Annie. Tell Miss Frankie what you saw."

Annie turned a pair of wary eyes on Truax, displaying all the trust one would give a used car salesman, then looked back to Vecchio.

"Miss Kara swang from the fidgadater door," she said, "and went to sleep."

"Why did you go into the kitchen, Annie?" Vecchio asked. "Were you hungry?"

"Yessss. And Miss Kara told me somtin."

"She told you something?" Vecchio repeated. "What did she tell you?"

"She told me 'bottle'."

"Bottle?"

"Yessss."

Jade began to fidget and cry, Annie looked up, and Audrey began bouncing Jade on her knee. It did little to appease the child.

"I think she's getting hungry. Can we go next door? I want to make her some lunch."

"Sure. We'll go with you." Truax got down on one knee. "Thank you, Annie. Only a big girl could be so much help."

Without another word, Annie slid off the sofa and ran back into her room as fast as her little feet would carry her. After Audrey made sure that her apartment door would not lock, she started across the hall to Kara's apartment with Jade on her hip. Truax and Vecchio trailed her by a couple of steps. As they went, Truax's mind was working.

Bottle…bottle…she must have meant the poisoned water bottle Johnson found in the sink.

When they stepped into the kitchen, Audrey placed Jade in her highchair. Fetching a clean bottle from the dishwasher, she filled it with formula and sat it in the pot, still sitting on the stove. She turned the burner on low.

"Why not use the microwave?" Truax asked the question, but was pretty sure of the answer he'd get.

"Oh...Kara never trusted it for the baby. Always heated her bottle on the stove." Jade continued to cry and held her arms out toward the counter.

"What sweetie?" Audrey asked.

She turned and saw that Jade was reaching for her water bottle. "Oh, you want some wa-wa?" She placed the bottle on the tray.

Jade picked it up and, once she found her mouth, began to drink. Audrey continued.

"I'm sorry Annie couldn't be of help, Detective, but she's just little, and…"

Audrey saw that Truax had stopped listening.

"Detective?"

Vecchio's head snapped around when Truax didn't answer.

"Moby?"

Truax ignored both women. His eyes were fixed on the sink and the flashing red LED on the water filter. He glanced over to Jade happily drinking from her bottle, and saw the water level decrease with each swallow. His eyes shot back to the faucet and the flashing red warning light, then again, back to Jade's bottle.

Something ate at him, gnawing away at his insides like a parasite. If Kara didn't trust a microwave to heat her baby's milk, would she give her water from a dirty filter? Especially when she had a bottle of commercially filtered water?

Truax exploded across the room startling both women. In a blur he lunged at the highchair, and Jade.

"NO!"

Audrey stood in stunned disbelief as Truax slapped the half-sized bottle from Jade's hands and sent it flying across the kitchen. Vecchio froze not knowing what to do. Truax snatched up the startled child, knocking over the highchair, and sprinted to the front door, leaving the two women, mouths agape in the kitchen.

Running outside, he saw the ambulance with Kara's body turning the corner two blocks away. Then he spotted Johnson getting into his car.

"Johnson! JOHNSON!"

"Yeah, Moby…What?"

"Do you have a poison kit?"

D.B. Corey

"A poison kit? No, I don't usually carry—"

"Get the paramedics back here, NOW!" He turned and nearly knocked Audrey down after she overcame her hesitation and followed him out. He grabbed her arm hard enough to leave bruises. "Did she use vitamins?" Truax shrieked. "B-12! DID SHE HAVE ANY B-12?"

"B-12? I have some, but why—"

"GET it! Right NOW!"

Suddenly panicked by the intensity of his outburst, Audrey rushed back into her apartment with Truax on her heels. Vecchio, hearing the exchange was already in the bathroom, ripping open the medicine cabinet and rifling through the medication. She found the bottle of vitamin B-12 capsules.

"Dump them in the sink," he commanded Vecchio, shoving the baby into Audrey's arms. "Hold her! Open her mouth!"

Grabbing several capsules from the sink, Truax broke them open. Seeing Audrey struggling to get Jade's mouth open, he forced the baby's jaws apart with the thumb and forefinger of one hand, and poured the powder into her mouth with the other. Jade cried and squirmed and tried to spit it out.

"HOLD her! God-DAMN IT!" He dumped water into her mouth and clamped her jaw shut, closing off her nose at the same time and forcing her to swallow.

Audrey stood horrified holding a writhing Jade in her arms. She turned the child away in an attempt to protect her from a madman.

"What in the HELL are you DOING to this BABY?" she screamed.

Truax's light gray eyes bored into her like a drill. His face hardened, but his voice did the opposite, commanding her attention. "This child will be dead in minutes," he said softly, "if you don't hold her still."

Audrey's mouth dropped open as if the muscles holding it closed had suddenly vanished. She did as ordered and Truax gave Jade another dose. The paramedics arrived moments later.

"Treat her for cyanide poisoning," he ordered, "and HURRY!"

The medics hustled Jade to the living room and held an inhaler of amyl nitrite under her nose. They followed up with dosed, intravenous injections of sodium nitrate and sodium thiosulfate.

Afterwards, they hurried her to the ambulance and rushed her to the hospital. As they pulled away, Truax watched from the doorway and ran his fingers across his bald head, a nervous habit that replaced his old one of reaching for his cigarettes without thought. Until lately.

When they walked back to the kitchen, Truax picked up the water bottle, unscrewed the top and gave it a sniff. There was the faint aroma of almond. He screwed the lid back on and tossed it in a zip-lock baggie he found in a drawer, then began patting himself down for the pack of cigarettes he knew he didn't have.

"Jesus, Moby," Vecchio said, shaken to the core. "How the hell did you know?"

Truax turned and leveled a pair of tired eyes at hers.

"I'm a cop, Frankie. I'm supposed to know."

CHAPTER 20

Truax had Vecchio drop him off at Squad, and then sent her home to change clothes.

"We're going out for a drink," he told her, "so wear something appropriate, like me."

"But I don't *have* any clothes older than I am," she jabbed, a thin smile forming on her face. Truax ignored her attempt at levity.

Squad was no longer empty. Unusual, but not unheard of for a Saturday. Four of the eight desks now had cops behind them. Truax made five.

He tried to ignore the clicks and clacks of keyboards, the one-sided phone conversations, and the undercurrent of complaints as to why the Orioles couldn't seem to win a ball game; although the latter had him wanting to add his two cents, and served to remind him that he'd rather be other places. But he wanted to check Vecchio's story concerning her case. There was something she wasn't telling him.

He accessed the Information Sharing Service and located the case in San Diego regarding the cyanide killings. All was as she said...almost. Vecchio said the victims were the same as here, but there was no mention of younger victims. He had to wonder why she omitted that small fact, but he wouldn't ask *her*.

He pulled her business card from his wallet and began to dial the San Diego office before reminding himself it was Saturday. He doubted Donahue would be there, but decided to give it a shot anyway.

"FBI. This is the Operator. How can I direct your call?"

"Agent Kaitlin Donahue, please."

Several clicks lead to several rings and a voicemail system.

"Dis is Agent Donahue. I am out o' the office at present. Please leave a wee message and I will return yer call when I can. For emergencies, please dial the Duty Agent on-call at 800—"

Not much sense in that, Truax thought. He decided to take her up on her offer to call anytime...day or night. He took that to mean weekends as well.

He retrieved her cell number from his phone and pressed Send.

"Detective Truax!" the pleasant voice said. "An' how might the world be treatin' you today?"

"Agent Donahue, I'm fine. And yourself?"

"I am doin' well, tank you. So, what might I be doin' fer you, Detective?"

"Well, I was discussing your case with Agent Vecchio."

"Yeah sure, an' how might the two of you be gettin' on?"

"Fine, Agent, fine. As I was saying, we were discussing the San Diego case, and she said something that caught my ear. Can you tell me the ages of the victims of your case?"

"Em...let me tink. As I recall, they were older, an' younger. Tirty or so, an' sixty or so. Why might you be askin'?"

"I did a little research on your case. There was no mention of any younger victims."

"Ah! Well! We don't go about tellin' the Press everyting, Detective. An' I suspect neither do you."

"No ma'am, we don't. But I wasn't talking about the Press. I got the info from the service."

"Ah. Well, I'd be guessin' not everyting you read on the service is accurate, Detective. The information 'tis only as good as the data inputted, 'tis it not?"

"Yes, ma'am. That's true. "

"Very good. So, 'tis there anyting else on yer mind, Detective? I *am* rather busy at the moment."

"Actually, I was wondering about the number of cases Agent Vecchio has worked, and if any of them were homicide cases. She seems a bit...green, if you will. Maybe too inexperienced to be working a case of this magnitude."

"Agent Vecchio 'tis a bright lass, Detective, an' I tink if you'll be givin' her a wee chance, she might be surprisin' you. Besides, I understan' you to have a wealth of experience in these matters. Surely you can be passin' a wee bit o' that vast knowledge on to a young associate, can you not?"

"Yes, ma'am. I suppose I can."

"Very good, den. Now, will that be all, Detective?"

"Yes, ma'am. Thank you, very much."

"No worries, Detective. Tink nottin' of it."

Just as Truax ended the call, another came in. He caught it on the first ring.

"Truax."

"Detective Truax, this is Doctor Balum from Arundel Hospital Center."

"Yeah, Doc. What can I do for you?"

"Doctor Johnson asked me to call and update you on the little girl. Looks like she's going to be fine."

"Hey, that's great, Doc. Thanks for letting me know."

"It's my pleasure. You know, that was some pretty quick thinking. The B-12 slowed the cyanide binding long enough for the paramedics to get to her."

"Will there be any neurological or cardio issues?" Truax asked.

"Don't think so. The exposure was minimal, thanks to you. You did a hellofa job, Detective. You saved her life."

"All in a day's work, Doc. I'm sure you've done the same yourself."

Doctor Balum changed gears and asked an off-topic question. At least, it seemed off-topic to Truax.

"You are of French descent, are you not, Detective Truax?"

"French-Canadian. Why do you ask?"

"Most people wouldn't know to use B-12, but in France, they use hydroxycobalamin as an antidote for cyanide poisoning. It's a form of vitamin B-12. It binds with cyanide to form cyanocobalamin, rendering it harmless."

"Well, that's all very scientific-ey Doc," Truax said, "but the B-12 was all I had available."

"Which prompts me to ask," Balum said. "How did you know to use it?"

Truax thought for a moment, willing his mind to retrieve the answer from memory.

"Funny thing, Doc," he said, "but I can't seem to remember."

CHAPTER 21

The squad-room belonging to The Special Investigations Unit was housed within the one-hundred-year-old, two-story brick, State Police Headquarters building in the middle of Pikesville Maryland; a medium sized town about twenty minutes northwest of Baltimore as the crow flies. A 4 X 8 sign sitting to the right of the entrance bore the Maryland State flag, a hybrid motif of yellow and black, and red and white, based on the Coat of Arms of the founding Calvert and Crossland families, and adopted by George Calvert, the first Lord Baltimore.

Below the emblem, an index listed the various parking areas and office locations. Vecchio swung the unmarked sedan through the small brick archway that led to the west side of the main building to get Truax.

Dropping into the passenger seat, Truax glanced over. She had changed into a tan summer suit and white shirt, but elected to leave her hair in the same ponytail from earlier, and Truax found himself wondering what she looked like with her hair down.

"What's that you're wearing?" Truax asked.

"What? This?" she said, tugging at the lapel of her jacket.

"No. You smell nice. What is it?"

"Oh! My perfume! Christian Dior. You like it?"

"It's OK, I suppose. Smells expensive."

"It's not as bad as some. I have some stuff at home that—"

"That's OK, Frankie. I don't need a lineup. Just wanted to tell you."

They chatted on and off for the rest of the thirty-five minute drive to Bamboo Billy's, talking about aspects of the case. The ages of the victims came up.

"So..." Vecchio asked. "Why'd you call Donahue? Checking up on me?"

"You heard from Donahue..."

"She likes me, Moby. More than you do. Thinks I have a future."

"I like you, Frankie..."

"Frances."

"I just wanted to verify the ages of the victims. There was an inconsistency."

"And I'm it. Is that what you're saying?"

"Don't go getting all emotional on me. The facts were inconsistent. That's all."

"Well, the next time you feel the need to verify something with Donahue, I'd appreciate a heads up. OK?"

"Fair enough."

Vecchio pulled the Crown Vic onto Billy's parking lot and Truax became all business. He entered ahead of Vecchio, and stopped inside the door to take in the surroundings. It was just after five. Too early for a doorman.

A handful of locals sat sprinkled around the main bar. Neighborhood men. Some in baseball caps, others in tank tops, and one old geezer in a pair of plaid Bermuda shorts so loud, Truax swore they emitted light.

Most drank beer, with one or two sipping straight whiskey. The rear bar saw no action at all save that of the wait staff running here and there carrying this and that, reminding Truax of island locals preparing for a hurricane.

The bar-backs were stocking the coolers with cases of beer, and the band was in the process of assembling their equipment on stage. Other than that, the place was empty in proportion to its size. Ambling to the bar, the two cops grabbed a couple of stools.

"What'll it be?" the perky bartender asked, offering a genuine smile and a nametag that read 'Georgia'.

Truax leered at the willowy five-foot platinum-blonde, dressed in the club's standard uniform for female employees: a blue-and-white tropical print shirt, gathered and knotted in the front, and a pair of cutoffs that appeared more like paint, than fabric.

Truax knew she was at least twenty-one. She had to be to work a bar, but to him she looked about fifteen, except in the chest.

When he didn't reply to the bartender's greeting, Vecchio thought him paralyzed by lechery, and shot him a look before speaking up.

"I'll have a bottle of water," she said. "And a menu."

"Make that two," Truax managed.

"Sure thing," Georgia replied, her bright green eyes darting to Vecchio. The young barkeep dug her hands into the cooler. "We serve two brands. Aquafina and—"

"Dasani," Truax injected.

"Huh," Georgia said. "Neat trick. How'd you do that?"

"X-ray vision," Truax replied.

Georgia smiled and placed the bottles on the bar along with two menus. "I'll give you guys a couple of minutes," she said. "Be right back."

Vecchio poked Truax in the ribs with her elbow as Georgia walked away. "You can reel your tongue back in now," she chided as she scanned the menu, then added, "And besides being too young, she'd probably cause you a seizure."

"I don't know what you're talking about," Truax mumbled.

He lifted the Dasani to eye level and rotated it slowly.

"You're the one with the picture memory," he said. "What was the batch number on the water bottle in the apartment?"

Vecchio looked up from her menu and closed her eyes. "AUG2209 K2 1285YC06235VV355-dollar sign." She opened her eyes again and continued perusing the menu, scrolling down the lunch specials with her index finger.

The number matched the bottle in his hand exactly, and a twinge of jealousy ran through him.

"Now we know where the water came from," he said.

"I think I'm going to have a bar burger," she replied.

"Whoever killed this girl, screwed up."

"What?"

"I don't think she was supposed to die at home."

Vecchio closed her menu and turned to Truax. "Why? Just because the other victims died somewhere public?"

"Actually, yes," he said. "That's *exactly* why. She was supposed to die here. Last night."

"C'mon, Moby. That's a stretch, even for you."

"Think about it. All the victims ingested the poison and died on the spot, the older women in solitude, but the *younger* women died while patronizing a bar or a club. Had Kara not taken her water home, she would have as well. The killer didn't foresee that, which tells me the women from the bars were targets of opportunity. Singled out, maybe because of their looks."

"Yeah? So?"

"So the others were along in years and not so pretty. They had no connection to each other that we could find.

The only similarities between them were their age. They led a solitary existence, had no family and struggled financially. They died outdoors, and the killer afforded them a degree of respect. I believe the killer may have had their trust. Maybe he cared about them, or maybe he just liked watching them die. Who knows? We thought at first that he selected his victims at random, but I'm beginning to think maybe not. We have two sets of victims. Assume different motives, and you have different killers—to my way of thinking."

"You can't be sure of that," Vecchio said. "You can't be sure it's not CK...I mean *absolutely* sure. You're just speculating."

"That's the job, ain't it? Speculation? We got nothing other than two distinct groups of victims. Different as night and day. And as far as I'm concerned, we're chasing two killers."

"Well, what about the poison? Why does the concentration of the cyanide match exactly between *all* the victims?"

Truax picked up his menu and pretended to begin reading. "I don't know. A leak, maybe. Or the killers are a team."

"Well," Georgia interrupted, upon returning. "Have you two made up your minds?"

"Tell me, Miss..." Truax glanced towards the nametag pinned just above her left breast and allowed his eyes to linger a bit too long. "Georgia...how many bottles of water does a place like this go through a night?"

"Depends," Georgia said. "A couple of hundred on busy nights. People nowadays switch to water an hour or so before leaving. They know your friends are waiting just down the road."

"My...*friends*?" Truax said, feigning ignorance.

Georgia produced a comforting smile, as if reassuring a child who'd guessed the wrong answer to a parental question. "C'mon. Only two types of people ask questions like that, and you two don't look like no bottled-water salesmen."

"It's his clothes," Vecchio injected with a wry smile. "Isn't it."

Truax cut off any reply. He'd been made. It had happened before, but never by a girl who looked all of fifteen-years-old.

"Is the manager here?" he said. "I'd like a word with him."

"Her," Georgia corrected. "Ms. Rice." She picked up the phone and said a few words. She turned back and asked for their IDs, said a few more words, and hung up. She pointed to a hall that ran down the front side of the room and directed them to the last door. Truax nodded and pulled out a ten.

"It's on me," Georgia said with a smile.

He gave her a wink and thanked her again, and left the bill lying on the bar.

The door was ajar when they arrived at the manager's office. Truax tapped and they heard a woman's voice inviting them in. They stepped into a large, well-equipped office with the usual appointments: a desk, filing cabinets, a computer, and a wall safe that hung open.

There were stacks of money piled on the desk by denomination: ones, fives, tens, and twenties. There was another pile of bills—hundreds—but that pile was much smaller. The manager glanced up and noticed the pair eyeing the cash.

"Well, if you can't trust the cops," she said, "who *can* you trust?"

She smiled and gestured for them to wait. She finished adding a column of numbers to the whirring sounds of an old paper-tape adding machine. In this day and age of computers, Truax thought it a nice touch.

"Yes, Detectives," she said, punching the tally button a final time. "How can I help you?"

"Ms. Rice," Truax started. "We would—"

"Please. Call me Sandy."

"Yes, ma'am. We want to ask you a few questions concerning the murder of a young woman." Truax produced a picture of Kara Templeton and handed it to the club manager. "She was here last night for a bachelorette party. Do you recognize her?"

Sandy looked at the photo. "She was murdered? Oh...how sad. I've seen her here a few times, but she's not what I would call a regular. I don't know her personally, but you might check with the girls. Maybe they can help you. They should all be here by now."

"I noticed you have video screens around the room," Truax continued. "Sporting events and such?"

"Yes. And other things."

"Other things? Like what?"

"We use them for closed-circuit video. I have a videographer take video of the crowd. The customers love seeing themselves on the big screens."

"Do you make recordings?" Vecchio asked.

"Yes. We play them back during Happy Hour, before the band starts, or when the DJ is on break. Things like that."

"We'd like to see them," Truax said.

"Sure. Any particular day?

"Last night."

Sandy Rice smiled. "No problem. Wait here a sec."

She stepped into a small back room adjacent to her office and returned moments later with a VHS tape and handed it to Vecchio.

"You still want to talk to the girls?"

"Yes," Truax said.

Sandy called the wait staff into the office and Truax showed them Kara's photo. A tall, dark-haired woman spoke up.

"I know her, Detective. She and her boyfriend sit in my section whenever they're here."

Truax walked her into the hall to question her away from the others.

"Tell me about the boyfriend," Truax said.

"There's not a lot to tell. Nice looking guy. Freaking huge! Dark hair. Quiet. Doesn't drink a lot."

"Does he seem like the jealous type?"

"No, I wouldn't say that. She'd flit around the club talking to all sorts of people. She was friendly like that. He'd just talk to friends and wait for her, or he'd walk over and join her. I don't think I ever saw him get mad."

"She was divorced, right?"

"No…don't think she ever married her baby's father. I met him once, but he didn't come here regular. She used to complain he didn't spend enough time with the baby. What an asshole!"

Truax smiled inwardly to himself. What was it about women, and that word? Especially when it came to their Ex's.

Two of the other women said they knew Kara, and he questioned them separately as he had the first woman. They all said basically the same thing: pretty girl, well liked, can't imagine who would want to harm her.

Truax thanked everyone for their time and passed out his card, stipulating that they should call if they think of anything else. Walking out of the office, he said to

Vecchio, "I think we've got all we're gonna get here. Let's call it a night."

Vecchio unlocked the sedan and climbed in behind the wheel. Truax took in the gathering Saturday night crowd before opening the passenger door, and as he got in, Vecchio slid the key into the ignition.

"Hold on a minute, Frankie."

"*Frances*, Moby...pl-eeeease!"

"Look at the customers and tell me what you see."

"I see a lot of people that will probably end up in bed with one another, or sleeping it off in the pokey."

Truax turned toward her and grinned. "Anything else?" he said.

"Not really. Just a bunch of folks out for a good time."

"Yeah, but if you'll notice, there ain't many couples. Groups of women, groups of guys...singles."

Vecchio shrugged her shoulders. "Okay. So?"

"Makes for a good hunting ground. Killers are creatures of habit. When they find something that works, they tend to stick with it. In this place, there are a lot of witnesses. Cyanide works very fast. Maybe too fast for him to get away without being spotted.

"Whoever poisoned the older victims didn't like witnesses and stayed secluded. Away from others. My guess is whoever killed the girl this morning gave her the poisoned bottle, switching it with another maybe, and hightailed it out. Even if someone saw him give her the bottle, odds are good they wouldn't think twice about it, and he probably wouldn't hang around to watch her keel over."

"No, this isn't the first Cyanide Killer. Here, we're dealing with someone new. I'm sure of it. Forensics be damned."

Vecchio turned the key and brought the big V8 to life. "I don't know, Moby. Sounds pretty farfetched to me."

"Farfetched? Haven't you been paying attention? It's the *only* thing that makes any sense!"

"Well, you'll never convince me of that."

"I don't have to convince *you* of *anything*. You're here on loan."

"OK...but what about Atkins?"

Truax fastened his seatbelt.

"Fuck Atkins."

CHAPTER 22

Vecchio drop Truax off at home after he told her to keep the Crown Vic for the rest of the weekend.

"It's the partnerly thing to do," he said, a touch of sarcasm seasoning his comment.

On the way back to her hotel, at about a quarter to eight, her cell phone rang. She pulled it from its holster thinking Truax had come up with yet another theory. She was wrong.

"Vecchio," she answered.

"Hello Frances. It's Don Atkins."

Her voice turned pleasant. Alluring. "Yes, Don. I knew it was you."

"You did? And how did you know it was me? That renowned, FBI power of deduction, I presume?"

Vecchio giggled like a high-school girl. "Well, I'd like to take that kind of credit, but the truth is, it was Caller ID. I saved you in my cell."

Atkins paused before speaking. "Well," he said. "I'm flattered. It's not every day an attractive woman saves me away in her phone."

"You're worth saving," she said, allowing a bit of vixen to creep into her voice.

A longer pause. Atkins's breathing became noticeable over the phone. "I don't know what to say," he replied.

"Well," Vecchio said. "Why don't you start with why you called?"

"Yes. Of course. I'm afraid you caught me off guard. I didn't expect that kind of a—"

"That's okay, Don. I do that sometimes. I'm sorry. I am glad you called. I neglected to thank you for a wonderful dinner the other night, and for the drinks. I hope your wife didn't mind."

"My wife? Oh! No…it was no problem. Showing out-of-town folks around comes with the territory. She's okay with it."

"That's good, because I'm sure there will be occasions where we spend evenings together. Working, I mean. And I wouldn't want them to cause you trouble at home."

Another pause. "No. No trouble at all."

"Good," Vecchio replied. "So…how can I help you?"

"Help? Oh…yes. I was calling to see how the investigation is going. And to see how you and Detective Truax are doing. He can be…difficult, at times."

"The investigation. Well, Don, it seems that Detective Truax feels there is a copycat emulating the Cyanide Killer, and this latest murder we're investigating just has him all the more convinced."

"Yes…I was afraid of that. He seems obsessed with the theory there is a second killer, in spite of forensic evidence suggesting otherwise. I am at a loss as to why he's off on this tangent, but I suspect personal issues may be interfering with his better judgment. What's your take on his mind-set?"

"Don, I don't think it's my place to pass judgment on a fellow—"

"I'm not asking you to pass judgment. I'm trying to gage his mental state. He's been under a lot of pressure lately, and this case is under a microscope. He's my most senior detective, and I don't want him distracted any more than he is. You can appreciate that, can't you?"

"Yeah. Sure, but I don't see—"

"Frances. As I told Agent Donahue, part of the reason I agreed to allow FBI's participation in our case was not just due to the spirit of inter-agency cooperation. OK. She believes your killer and ours are one in the same. I get that. But I have to worry about my city, my cops. Truax is under a lot of pressure as I said, and this is the hottest case we've had in decades. Truax is my most experienced investigator regarding matters such as these, but he doesn't want it.

"Oh, he hasn't said as much, but he's on the downward side of his career. He's tired. But the case had to go to him or the brass would want to know why it didn't. I have another detective working in the background, but he's not as experienced, nor is he fairing any better."

"Another detective?"

"Yes. Detective Nichols. And please keep that to yourself. Detective Truax already thinks I'm shoving *you* down his throat. If he knew I had Nichols on it, he might give up on the case and just go through the motions."

"I don't understand," Vecchio said. "How does all this involve me? I'm here on a fact finding junket. If I can help connect the dots and we catch CK, all the better, but I don't see how I—"

"Frances, I believe you can ease the pressure on Truax. Give him an extra set of hands, eyes...an alternate viewpoint. But I feel he's resisting your involvement. Am I right? Or am I wrong."

There was a short silence before she answered. "You're not wrong," she whispered.

"Don't feel like this is your doing, Frances. He's been out of sorts of late, dismissing obvious evidence to chase some hare-brained theory of a copycat killer."

"But I still don't—"

"I want you to keep Nichols in the loop. Advise him of pertinent information he might not have. Share your insight as to what Detective Truax is thinking, what he's looking into."

"Don, I don't know if I—"

"I know this is a lot to discuss over the phone, so how about we talk in person. Maybe dinner at your hotel tomorrow night?"

A derisive smile found its way onto Vecchio's lips. There it was. What she'd been waiting for. Seemed it never took a man long to get to the matter of things with her. They'd beat around the bush for a short while, and then make their move. When that happened, she owned them.

She was near the age of twelve when the boys started paying attention. An early bloomer the adults called her. A year after that, around the time she began spilling from her bra, she began drawing stares from anything wearing pants.

She sensed a wanting in them, and saw a kind of hunger in their eyes. It was then she began to realize the power she possessed. She began learning how to use it, and when she turned thirteen, the realization of that power registered in earnest.

Her best girlfriend's father, the man next door, a man of more than forty years, began showing new interest in her when she visited their house, jogging downstairs when he heard her come in, holding long conversations with her about school, about boys, about things she liked.

After that, she noticed that he would appear at his front door whenever she was outside, or she'd see the curtains at his front window pull back, only to be released when she turned to look. She decided to test her theory.

On a Friday night, when she was fourteen, she asked if he would get some beer for her and her friends, and meet them in the woods behind the elementary school down the street. There were no friends, and she had no intension of meeting him or taking his beer, but she watched from a distance as he showed up at the designated spot, six-pack in hand, and waited for her.

It was then, she knew. She knew she could get whatever she wanted from boys. From men. And she didn't have to spread her legs to get it. All she needed to do was make them *think* she would.

"Dinner tomorrow?" she repeated. "I'd love to have dinner with you tomorrow."

CHAPTER 23

Harvey couldn't understand why Kara didn't show the day before, and as he began his shift, he tried to make sense of it. They wouldn't have taken her to a hospital; the cyanide would have killed her long before the EMS team arrived.

Maybe she didn't drink the water. Maybe she threw it away. Shit. Who knows? But one thing he did know. His Need was not satisfied. He could make another run at her, but that would be dangerous if not completely stupid. And then, there was the issue of the monster boyfriend. He didn't know if he could catch her away from him again.

Walking into the lab, Harvey found Rabbani finishing an autopsy, and when he closed, Harvey offered to move the body to the cooler so Rabbani could leave on time. The two men chatted for a few minutes before saying their good-byes, and after Harvey completed his carry-over chore, he began reviewing the intake log. He saw a name that caught his attention.

A woman named Kara Templeton had arrived that afternoon. But was it the same Kara? He didn't know her last name. It could be another woman, but Kara wasn't a name that was exactly commonplace. He noted the drawer number and headed to the back, and the coolers.

His heart raced as he pulled on the refrigerator-like handle, the one that reminded him of the old ice cream trucks that prowled his childhood summers. Pulling out the drawer, he yanked back the sheet.

It was her. His heart skipped a beat, and for the briefest of moments he considered pulling her out to complete the date he had so meticulously planned. But she was damaged goods. The Y incision and her body temperature, the pasty-white of her skin, all combined to dampen any possible arousal—Need, or no Need.

He cursed his misfortune, slid her back into her temporary tomb, and headed to the lab to check her arrival time. Pulling the intake log for the day shift, he found what he was looking for.

1:30 in the afternoon...what the hell kept her? The cops? No, something's wrong here. Homicide wouldn't hold her body that long. She must have had the water later. It's the only explanation.

Then, as if someone had turned on a light, another thought plowed through his mind. His hands began to twitch.

The day shift ME did the autopsy. He drew actual specimens. Legitimate specimens! *And now they're on their way to Tox. The lab techs will discover the difference in the poison and implicate a second killer. They might even retest the previous victims, and if they don't use the bogus specimens I already sent, if they secured new specimens from organ slices, they'll realize that someone has tampered with the samples. They'll start an investigation to find the break in the evidence chain, and that will eventually lead to me. I have to do something to intercept Kara's specimens! But what? What can I do?*

CHAPTER 24

Harvey agonized over the question of how to swap Kara's specimens before Tox discovered the discrepancy in the poison that killed her, and after much thought, admitted to himself that there was just one thing *to* do. He had to swap them. There was no other way.

He'd have to gain access to the specimen cold storage, but there was more to that than telling a simple lie. The real problem was that he wasn't authorized. Toxicology had to sign the specimens in to maintain the evidence chain, so to pull this off, he had to convince the lab tech to swap the specimens for him—without logging the change.

Tall order.

He'd fabricate a plausible story to feed the lab tech, walk over to Tox, and confess there had been a mix up. He would say that the specimens with the name Kara Templeton were actually those of a heart attack victim, Ms. Carrie Temple, autopsied at the family's request and expense.

Somehow, the dayshift confused the specimens, and it was a good thing that he—Doctor Harvey Morral—performed his due diligence and discovered the mistake. Now it must be corrected, or the family may get wind of the error and accuse OCME of incompetence.

Simple enough. And believable.

He waited until 4:45am before making his move. On a normal night he'd run the specimens over immediately after finishing his autopsies, usually 4am and 8am, give or take. Tonight, Tox should be busy doing their thing at 4:45 and wouldn't be expecting him. If they were busy enough, and if he could make them believe the SNAFU could cost some poor pathologist his job, then maybe he could convince a lab tech to do his bidding.

It had to work, because if it didn't, he'd better get used to wearing international-orange.

He placed the genuine CK specimens he had earmarked for Kara in a lab transport cooler and walked them over to the toxicology lab. He badged in and set about locating the lab techs; there were usually two during the week, starting on the Sunday night mid-shift. But tonight, they were nowhere to be found.

Harvey explored the lab, an open area consisting of counters, cabinets and the instruments necessary for toxicology work. The techs were not there, so he meandered into the back where a handful of offices and storage closets were. It was the only other area where they could be, if they were still in the building.

The section was dark. He ambled toward the back, looking to turn on the lights, and checking office doors as he went. He found every one of them locked. No surprise there, since the area housed the admin and management offices, and the entire section was unoccupied outside of daytime hours. As he neared the end of the hall, he thought he heard sounds, voices coming from the last office on the right.

The office was dark when he reached it, and he thought perhaps his imagination was playing tricks. He twisted the doorknob and it turned, so he opened the door. Stepping in, he slid his hand along the wall and found the switch. He snapped on the lights.

Two startled faces stared back at him. He had located the two lab techs: her, bent over the desk, and him, buried inside her.

Harvey realized, as they did, that theirs was a career ending infraction. Of that there was no doubt. But more importantly, and to their good fortune, they had just solved Harvey's problem *for* him.

CHAPTER 25

Loose gravel crunched under the soles of Harvey's shoes as he ambled across Bamboo Billy's parking lot. Thanks to the extra-curricular activities of his two oversexed colleagues, the problem of swapping Kara's specimens was now behind him, and he could turn his attention to the mistake that put him in that position to begin with.

The Cyanide Killer's MO was getting his victims to ingest poison. Harvey knew now, that ingestion wasn't altogether foolproof for the way he operated.

The Cyanide Killer didn't care to hook up with his victims after he killed them, leaving them lying on a bench for the police to collect. When they ingested the poison, they died and that was that. He was done with them. But the Need Harvey suffered had to spend the quiet time with his kills afterward. He had to return to OCME to be there for them, so there was no way for him to coax them; no guarantee they would die within the predefined window between their poisoning, and when Homicide released their body.

That Kara took the tainted water with her from the club to die at home emphasized that. He hadn't anticipated that particular wrinkle. For ingestion to work, they had to swallow their stuff on the spot, like the first two: Emma and Stacy. Without that, there was no controlling the timing, and timing was the one element he needed to control.

The only way he could figure to get around the problem was direct injection, but that was riskier than spiking an open drink and getting the hell out. How would he pull it off? How would he inject her without her suffering pain from the needle prick and drawing attention? He couldn't very well have her scream for help and then drop dead in front of a crowd.

That just wouldn't do.

The insertion point was no problem. He could inject her anywhere through her clothing. The responding units weren't going to undress her at the scene and comb her body looking for the cause of death, although he wouldn't put it past some of the EMTs he'd run across. A couple of those guys didn't look too stable.

No, examining the body for COD was the medical examiner's job—*his* job. So, he either had to numb her somehow to avoid her screaming in pain, or catch her alone. The latter seemed like the only feasible plan at the moment, but a single fly remained in the ointment. He had to have the stones to actually walk up and jab a freaking needle into her; maybe not so easy a thing to do. Maybe if he were a physician instead of a pathologist—

He forked over the cover charge and walked to the bar. He had to think this through. But whatever he came up with, he'd have to decide soon. He had failed with Kara, and his Need beckoned again. Worse this time. Hungrier, and more demanding.

He took up station and caught a bartender's attention; a petite little thing with an ample chest and long platinum-blonde hair. He ordered a beer and studied her as she bent over the cooler, losing the bet he made with himself when her breasts didn't get in her way.

"So, what's your name?" he asked, throwing a five on the bar. He already knew the answer from her nametag, but he wanted a better look at her. Asking a question guaranteed another thirty seconds or so of conversation.

"Georgia," she said, collecting the bill. "And yours?" She dried her hand on the back of her jeans before offering it.

"Harvey," he replied, taking her hand. It was cold from the cooler. Cold like death. An increase in blood pressure stiffened him. "Keep the change," he said, his eyes driving down the deep plunge of her top.

Georgia smiled and leaned in just a bit, giving him a better view to guarantee a bigger tip for the next time. "Thanks," she returned.

"So...tell me, Georgia," Harvey said, his eyes sweeping back to hers. "What nights are you here?"

During the next three hours, Harvey found it increasingly difficult to divert his eyes when Georgia scanned the bar, looking for thirsty customers. Direct eye contact wasn't his style, and he wanted to look away each time, but his Need didn't allow it. His focus centered only on her...her figure, her features, her hair, the way she moved. Everything about her.

The hunt had begun and so he left; just before the bouncers began clearing the club.

He parked his Vette on a small unlit lot serving a florists shop across the street, killed the engine, and made himself comfortable. Leaving the driver's window open, he lit a cigarette and turned the radio down to a whisper. He figured he had about a thirty or forty minute wait.

Twenty minutes later, at 2am, a gaggle of unruly women in tropical print tops and very short cutoffs left through the front door, and even with the sounds of insects filling the night, their voices carried on the cool air. Laughing and talking, they compared notes on the night's take in tips, and the customers they'd sleep with on the first date—not all of them men. The group began to break up as they headed for cars sprinkled around the parking lot, each one's path slightly different from the others', and as they crossed the asphalt they faded into the dark, but even with the minimal lighting Harvey could see none of them had long platinum-blonde hair.

A bouncer stood momentary vigil just outside the front door, then ducked back inside as the women approached their vehicles. Nearly thirty minutes later, when Georgia emerged, the bouncer did as before and watched until she was within several feet of her car. Then he stepped back inside.

Complacency is a wonderful thing, Harvey thought. The bouncer didn't bother to wait the extra ten seconds it took for her to get into her car, where her relative safety was assured.

Georgia backed her silver Malibu from its space beside a tree-lined perimeter consisting of tall scrawny pines and thick stately oaks; trees that had seen fifty years or better. Steering toward the lot's entrance, she came to a full stop before entering the empty country road.

Looking both ways, she eased the car onto the highway and accelerated slowly. Harvey started his engine and pulled out after giving Georgia a ten-second head start, keeping a reasonable distance between them. Twenty minutes later, she pulled into an apartment complex in Severna Park. He followed.

She went to the center of three buildings set in a horseshoe pattern, and Harvey drifted to the far side of the lot and parked. He waited several seconds before disabling the dome light and climbing from the car.

He watched as Georgia strolled from her parking space to the entrance of her building. Her easy and unhurried gate suggested that she was unconcerned regarding possible danger. Odd, Harvey thought, since the garden apartment design included no security doors. Anyone could enter.

Georgia pulled up short, stopping beside a cluster of aluminum mailboxes embedded in the brick wall. She inserted a key and opened a door. Removing nothing, she relocked the door and trotted up the steps, disappearing into the darkness enveloping the stairway. Several moments passed and Harvey saw the windows light up in an apartment on the second floor. He smiled and lit a cigarette. Before climbing back into the car, he took note of the area. At 2:50 in the morning, no one was about.

And there was even a bench.

On the drive home, Harvey pondered the obstacles: The How When and Where. The How had to be direct injection. He couldn't spike her drink as if she were a customer standing at the bar. She was the barkeep and wasn't allowed to drink while working. Besides, any water or soda she might sip was far from his reach, sitting on the shelf at the bar's center, and probably there by design. He simply couldn't get to her that way.

The When dictated the Where, simply due to time constraints, and to have the time he needed with her. As it was now, he'd have to take three hours on the front end of his shift to get to her when she left work around 2:30, 3 o'clock. He'd have to catch her on Billy's parking lot, since waiting for her at her apartment added another thirty minutes. Plus the 2 to 3 hours the cops would hold her body. Another thirty-minute drive downtown to OCME...it was too long. She'd get there too late for him to enjoy her.

He had to wait for her at Billy's. Homicide would hold her for a couple of hours, then a transport contractor would drive her in. She should get to him about 6:30 in the morning, giving him just enough time.

He wanted a minimum of thirty minutes with her, and he'd simply work the overtime to finish her autopsy, but more importantly, he didn't want another Kara. He regretted killing her for no reason. It was wasteful. He should have planned her better, and as it stood now, the situation with Georgia was nearly the same. She was a problem without a solution and he should abandon her altogether. Find another. But his Need wanted her, and that's all there was.

He pulled up to his mother's house and climbed the back steps. No lights were on and that was good. He didn't need any crap from her. Once inside, he pulled a two-liter bottle of soda from the fridge, and poured some in a small glass. He took it to his bedroom and closed the door. He thought about Georgia and her magnificent tits. Implants, he was pretty sure, but he'd know for certain after her autopsy.

CHAPTER 26

Truax spent the better part of two days interviewing Kara's friends. From the list the waitress gave them, he located and questioned all the girls at the bachelorette party. All told a similar story: Kara was friendly, she talked to everyone, and everyone loved her.

The same held true for the boyfriend, Ray. One of Kara's friends said he was, as they used to say, like a mole on Marilyn Monroe's face—just happy to be there. He was an easy-going guy who showered her with affection and never held expectations of her, and although they'd been dating just a short while, Kara's friends could see he was a keeper. He adored Jade and was more involved in her life than her biological father, whom they described as a no-count loser.

According to at least two of her friends, Jade's father refused to marry Kara after she became pregnant, ignoring the pressure from his father, a church-going man of conviction. He stayed with her, but after the baby was born, he began to drift, staying out nights and running with women. Kara had enough and threw him out. She insisted he stay in Jade's life, but even that was too much to ask.

Now that Kara was dead, he was responsible for the child—something her friends saw as a catastrophe. Interviews with the two men turned up solid alibis, and when criminal background checks came up clean, Truax ruled them out as suspects.

Back at SIU, Truax pulled the autopsy reports on all the victims. With the original three murders, food was the vehicle used to administer the poison: a chicken tender, a piece of candy, a miniature éclair. Comfort food. Since the victims died within minutes, the ME found the whole of the item in the victims' stomachs. Items they could eat in a single quick bite.

The dosage was lethal, engineered to kill immediately. Instantaneous death, painful, but short-lived. Kara's stomach, on the other hand, was empty. Water was the delivery system; a liquid, same as Baumgartner and Culver. This was a major departure from the established MO, but the dosage was the same. Truax pondered the change of method as he settled in to view the club's video tapes. He was looking for footage of Kara, and anyone she may have interacted with that night.

While the tape rolled forward, Truax called up the crime and autopsy reports on Kara, printed hard copies, and added them to The Cyanide Killer's folder. Starting with Kara's file, he worked backwards. It took a couple of hours to re-familiarize himself with the details of CK's earlier kills, some of which he actually remembered, most of which he did not. But in any case, he wouldn't remember what he didn't see, and he hoped he might find something he missed earlier.

If Kara was CK's work, then her murder should fit his pattern, and perhaps suggest a connection. In every case he'd ever worked, the killer had some kind of connection with the victim, but with The Cyanide Killer, there was none.

After three hours of reviewing tapes from the club, Truax removed his glasses and rubbed his eyes. He had spotted Kara just once, crossing the room and heading to the bar. The video shifted and caught the backend of her transaction with the bartender, a young woman he had yet to interview. He picked up the phone and dialed the number of Sandy Rice.

"Hello?"

"Ms. Rice, this is Detective Truax. Do you have a minute?"

"Of course, Detective. What can I do for you?"

"I found Kara Templeton on the video tape that you provided. She ordered something from a bartender I don't recognize, working the main bar. Can you tell me who she is and how I can contact her?"

"I do, but there were three women working the bar that night. Can you describe her?"

"Long dark hair is all I can tell you. Very long. Down to her a— Down to her behind."

"That'd be Dora. Hold on, I'll get you her number."

Truax listened to five rings before Dora picked up. He knew right away that he woke her.

"H-Hello?"

"Miss Mathews?"

"Who is this? Alfie? Is that you?"

"No ma'am. This is Detective Truax. Special Investigations Unit. Do you have a minute to answer a few questions, please?"

"Who—who is this?"

"Maryland State Police, ma'am. I need to ask you a few questions."

"I'm sleeping. I work nights."

"This won't take long. Just a few—"

The line went dead. Truax dropped the handset into the cradle and reminded himself again—why he didn't conduct phone interviews.

The trip to Dora Mathews's apartment took forty-five minutes. It took another ten of pounding on the door before she answered.

"I'm Detective Truax," he said, brandishing his ID. "We spoke on the phone...until you hung up on me."

"I remember. I'm sorry. I work late."

"Yeah, you said. May I come in?"

"Do you have a warrant?"

"I can get one, if you want."

Dora shrugged and closed the door to remove the slip chain. Truax stepped inside to find a petite Dora, the dark circles under her eyes aging her by twenty years. She wore only a pair of panties and an unzipped sweatshirt, and her long dark hair reached all the way down her back. Truax kept his eyes above her shoulders.

Hip-Hop was playing from somewhere, and empty wine bottles were strewn about the living room. A naked man lay passed out on the floor. The one ashtray in the room overflowed with cigarette butts, and beside it, a small white dinner plate with a crack pipe and rock cocaine. Crack.

He turned his gaze on a withering Dora, but said nothing about the drugs.

"Just a few questions, Miss."

Dora's eyes cut to the dirty glass pipe, and back to Truax. "Yeah. Sure. What do you want to know?"

"You worked the main bar at Billy's last night?"

"Yeah...I guess."

"That's what Sandy Rice told me. Did you, or didn't you?"

"Yeah. I worked it."

"A young woman ordered a bottle of water from you."

"A lot of chicks order water."

"This one was murdered."

Dora staggered back a step and the color drained from her face.

"Murdered? When?"

"She got the water from you near the end of the night. Her name was Kara Templeton. Did you know her?"

"Kara? Kara's...dead?"

"Do you remember?"

"Yes...I remember."

"What else do you remember? Anything odd? Unusual? Anything at all."

Dora found the sofa with her hand and sat down. She looked to the naked man on the floor, and back to Truax. She reached for the glass pipe, but then thought better of it.

"I remember...just after she walked away, a man ordered water too. He couldn't take his eyes off her. We serve two brands, but he didn't seem to know which he wanted, so he bought both."

"Could he have been ordering for himself and someone else?"

"I don't think so. He ordered 'a' bottle of water at first. He only bought both when I asked which one he wanted."

"After he bought the water, which direction did he go?"

"I can't be sure, it was so busy, but now that you ask...I think he followed her."

Dora gave Truax a description of the man. It matched fifty percent of the men who lived in Maryland. Adding the characteristic of "nothing special," didn't give him much more to go on.

He checked with forensics, and they confirmed finding a single, unopened bottle of water in the trash—Aquafina. Not the brand that killed Kara. But they did say that the condensation on the plastic removed any prints that may have been there.

It was like he had learned nothing at all.

CHAPTER 27

Should he employ a direct frontal assault? Or take her from behind...

Harvey pondered that during his two days off; that, and the other nuances connected to a face-to-face, do-it-yourself, murder. Considering his failure with Kara, he decided Georgia required more personalized attention.

The frontal approach had obvious drawbacks. If something went wrong and Georgia survived, she could identify him. But on the other hand, she'd let her guard down since she knew him from the club...or at least, knew his face. He was a customer, after all. But still, jamming a cyanide-laden hypo into her flesh isn't quite the same as waving hello. Switching Kara's water bottle was easy. Injecting a needle into someone required a bit more sand.

Then there's the problem of the entry point. If he were to mimic the CK homicides, he couldn't afford to vary the MO too much. A little here or a little there would be dismissed as minor variance. But a puncture wound is not a minor variance. It's a glaring departure from CK's established patterns. Therefore, the wound must be small—virtually invisible, but more importantly, it must go unnoticed by the field forensics techs.

He ruled out intercepting Georgia at her apartment, and although the bench located on the apartment property was in keeping with CK's MO, it would take more time than he had.

She wouldn't arrive at the pathology lab until his shift was nearly over, so what would be the point? He had to inject her on the club parking lot when she left work, and considering the risk, he felt a dry run was in order.

Wednesday nights were nearly as popular as Fridays at Billy's, mostly because Pasadena's young professionals liked to blow off a little mid-week steam, let their hair down, and cut loose with a few drinks.

Harvey pulled onto Billy's lot about 1am, and located Georgia's Malibu. He called the second shift ME, Ahmad Rabbani, to say he was running late; that his Vette wouldn't start, and that he'd be there as soon as possible. Parking his car down the road, he waited an hour before slipping into the trees surrounding Billy's lot.

The moon was half-full, pooling a soft light onto the parking lot, but the copse of oak and pine surrounding the lot blocked its light, keeping the interior of the small thicket pitch black.

He moved slowly and tread carefully for fear of incurring an inadvertent facial scratch, or the loss of an eye, courtesy a low-hanging branch.

He inched closer to the lot, silently picking his way through tangles of underbrush. Dim light from the parking area trickled in past the massive oaks, managing to penetrate several feet into the woods. It was of no concern. His dark clothing ensured he would remain invisible.

Georgia's car sat within a few feet of the tree line, and Harvey positioned himself behind a large oak several feet away. The woods provided him the advantage of seeing from the dark into the light, whereas Georgia had the opposite perspective. She could not see in. As she approached, he shallowed his breathing and stood deathly still.

The bouncer seeing to her safety had already returned to the club with Georgia still several strides from her car. Harvey watched her walk around the front, and his whispered breathing rang in his ears, sounding much like the raspy gasps of a fat man climbing the stairs. His heart pounded, courtesy of the adrenalin flooding his system, and the pitch black enveloping him did little to alleviate his fear of discovery. He never felt so alive.

As Georgia slid the key into the lock, she didn't look up. She didn't look around. *And why should she?* he thought. She'd done this a thousand times. And a thousand times, she'd had no reason for concern.

Because Georgia had backed into the space, an approach from the trees was the only sensible approach. The driver's side door was farthest from the club, and her car acted as a barrier blocking any view.

Harvey sequenced through the events in his mind and visualized each step in real time.

As she pulled the door open, he imagined rushing her. He was so close, it would take only seconds, and even when she heard the noise he was bound to make, she would hesitate, human nature being what it was.

Next, her mind's inability to process the sudden and unexpected would lead to denial and she would freeze; her subconscious unwilling to believe what was happening. By then it would be too late. He would inject her with the poison, turn, and leave the same way he came in, secure in the knowledge that she would be dead before she hit the ground, or at the very least, before she could return to the club. Then all he need do was head to work. She would soon follow in a body transport.

Reaching for a cigarette, he smiled as her engine groaned to life. The small section of parking lot directly in front of the Malibu became awash with light and the car rolled forward, headed for the entrance. When it turned the corner and its taillights faded from sight, Harvey strolled from the woods as casually as a guy who had just taken a piss behind a tree.

CHAPTER 28

The Dog Days of summer: That's how the locals refer to August in Baltimore; the canicular part of summer when the humidity skyrockets due to the proximity of the Chesapeake Bay, and you could almost see the water in the air.

This Saturday night was one of those nights. Harvey stood near the trees, in the shadows, on the small Florist's parking lot across from Billy's. He lit a cigarette and waited for the first of the wait staff to leave. He knew Georgia should show herself about twenty minutes later.

He had parked his car on a neighborhood street two blocks away, keeping it out of sight, but within easy walk of the woods. As the doors opened and a familiar gaggle of women flocked from the club, Harvey crushed his cigarette under the toe of a black Puma and checked his watch.

Once the staff cleared the lot, he began his trek for the woods; walking up the single lane county road away from Billy's, and then crossing over, only to double back on the other side of the road when he was sure no one was around.

He had refined his plan since Wednesday's dry run. Tonight, he brought a ski mask. As the time approached for him to position himself, he dry swallowed two pills; a mild sedative to calm his nerves, a necessary modification given his unexpected excitement of the other night. He scanned the immediate area as he neared the point of ingress into the woods. Seeing no one, he darted in.

The sticky August night brought with it a symphony of woodland sounds; crickets and tree frogs chirping and clicking, and the continuous ratcheting up and down of cicadas presented an auditory parabola to the ear.

The temperature must be up there, he thought, knowing the insects would drown out any noise he made as he moved through the brush. *If she screams, I doubt anyone more than ten feet away will hear her.*

Still, even with the rainforest-like environment drowning out most noise, snapping twigs and rustling leaves were inconsistent with insects, and anyone who was paying attention would take note.

Georgia hadn't parked in the exact same space as Wednesday. She was several spaces closer to the club, but it was still near the large oak where he would wait. If anything, this location made it easier, and as before, she had backed into the spot.

He'd given considerable thought as to where to inject her. Ideally, he'd like to hit an artery without leaving a visible puncture wound, but even with a small-bore syringe, there'd be a *little* blood. That's the first thing the forensics investigator would look for. Stabbing a needle into uncovered skin? He may as well hang a sign saying, "LOOK HERE!"

A better option would be to inject her through her clothing. Cyanide kills within seconds, and once the heart stops, there is no blood pressure. No blood pressure, no bleeding. And while a minuscule amount would absorb into the cloth, he could avoid its detection by pushing the needle through a breast.

She wore a push-up bra to entice her male customers and maximize her tips, a must if she wanted to make any real money. The inner lining would absorb the little bit of blood the puncture would produce. No cop or field forensics examiner would dare remove her clothing at the scene. They'd be brought up on charges. He decided he'd go that route.

He leaned easily against the trunk of the big tree until laughter sliced through the heat-fueled sound of insects like a cell phone ringing in a theater. He peered around the tree and saw Georgia heading in his direction. Easing back, he pressed himself against the coarse bark of the massive trunk, and his heart made itself known. A trickle of sweat ran behind his ear and down his neck, and he thought that maybe the sedative wasn't working. Second thoughts began to surface. Could he go through with this? He wasn't so sure now. He peeked around the tree again. There she was, walking slowly. Unaware of him. O-fucking-blivious.

She wore a different uniform. Knee-high black leather boots, a too-short black skirt, and a tropical print top cut so low it barely contained her. Her long platinum hair bounced in time with her step as did her breasts, hatching vivid fantasies in Harvey's mind.

He had to locate the bouncer. If that Neanderthal didn't follow his established pattern and remained on the lot, it would ruin his timing. He should be retreating into the club any second now, so Harvey stretched his lanky frame to the limit and leaned around the tree. He saw the entrance door closing and nothing else. Assured the bouncer would not be in play, his eyes returned to Georgia.

She continued to her car and Harvey licked the corner of his mouth, watching as she drew closer. Her beauty captivated him and all doubt, all hesitation, vanished. He was going to have her.

Harvey could tell where Georgia was from the sound of the gravel beneath her boots. He pulled on the ski mask and fished the syringe from his back pocket. Taking a calming breath, he removed the protective cap from the needle.

Georgia made the turn around the front of her car and coasted to a stop beside the driver's door. She inserted the key. Harvey stepped from behind the tree making no sound, having cleared away the dried twigs when he arrived. With the night alive with insects, the snap of a twig would slice through the night like the report of a high-powered rifle.

Georgia opened the door and Harvey took a step.

She tossed her purse inside and Harvey took a step.

She straightened up, and Harvey rushed her.

CHAPTER 29

Harvey didn't remember emerging from the woods. He didn't remember jumping into his Vette, or making a hasty departure from the neighborhood. He didn't remember turning west on Route 100, nor did he remember mashing the accelerator to the floor.

It wasn't until he saw the needle on the Vette's speedometer climb past 98 did his presence of mind return. Everything that had happened between his encounter with Georgia and this very moment came from off in the distance. Surreal—like squinting through shimmering waves of heat, rising from a blacktop highway.

He slowed to 60, trembling as he examined every mirror, looking for something flashing blue and giving chase. There was nothing, and so, he heaved a sigh of relief. But the respite was short lived. His peripheral vision caught a pair of hollow eyes staring up at him. Terror seized him and he cried out, running the Vette onto the shoulder of the highway as his heart rate soared. With the sound of gravel peppering the car's under-chassis, Harvey recognized the ski mask and erupted into a fit of nervous laughter.

Calming himself, he ran his fingers through his hair as reality took control once again. He hadn't forgotten injecting Georgia, and he hadn't forgotten running through the woods, or having to stop and pick up the ski mask when a branch ripped it from his head. He hadn't forgotten his indecisiveness, waffling over leaving it or not, or his forcing himself to go back the three steps to fetch it. He hadn't forgotten any of those things. To him, those events weren't real, as if occurring in a dream or a fantasy. As if they hadn't actually happen. Then he remembered something else, and panic hit him like an open hand across the face.

He launched himself from the seat, steering with one hand and searching to find the syringe with the other. He slid it into his back pocket as he ran from the woods, but he didn't remember that either. As he crossed a small two-lane bridge, he tossed the needle through the open passenger window into the brown murky waters of Furnace Creek.

Harvey's hands had stopped shaking by the time he arrived at work. He focused on Georgia, and anticipated her arrival within the next three hours. He thanked Rabbani profusely for covering until he could get there, and said he would return the favor upon request.

"And I'll have to get that damn Vette fixed this week," he yelled as Rabbani hurried out the lab's double doors. "That's the second time it stranded me. GUESS I OWE YOU—" Rabbani disappeared into the hall "—two favors."

Harvey watched the door swing shut. His thoughts returned to Georgia and the stirrings in his loins. What's it been now? A month? Five weeks? He couldn't remember. It seemed longer than that, but it was too damn long in any case.

He figured that in three hours' time, all of that would be forgotten. He picked up the shift log, trying to become interested in the day's goings on, but dropped the clipboard on the desk and began to pace.

Maybe a smoke.

CHAPTER 30

The flashing colors of the emergency lights atop patrol cars had changed throughout Truax's years in Homicide. First, they were red. Years later, they were blue. Now, they were a combination of both. But they were always present for the same reason. Somebody was dead.

Truax coasted off the single lane county road to the entrance of Billy's parking lot, and pulled next to the blue-on-blue, Anne Arundel County patrol car blocking the entrance. Truax flashed his SIU credentials and the police sentry cleared a path through a small group of curiosity seekers. He pulled into the first space he came to, climbed from the car, and approached the spot where Georgia's body lay.

Truax identified himself to Corporal Amos, the officer in charge of the scene; a large man with a potbelly to match. Crouching down, Truax slowly pulled the forensics sheet from Georgia's face.

"I know her," he said, his deteriorating memory teetering on the edge of recollection, the hint of a name, repeating over and over in his mind like a skipping record. "Spoke to her last week," he said. "G…G something…"

"Georgia." Amos filled in the blanks for him. "Georgia Parsons."

"Yes," Truax repeated. "Georgia."

"She's the lead bartender," Amos continued. "One of the bouncers found her when they locked up for the night. Wasn't hard to see with her layin' in the middle of the parkin' lot like she is."

"What do you have, Corporal?"

"She just left work. They tell me she's one of the last to leave. Has to tally the night's receipts and get them to the owner. The owner locks the safe, comes back in the mornin' to go over the numbers and then gets the money to the bank. I'm thinkin' maybe they thought she had the money with her."

"They...Corporal?"

Amos gave Truax a look that said his statement was self-explanatory and he shouldn't have to clarify it to a detective, of all people. "Whoever killed this girl. Probably thought she had the night's take."

Truax ignored Amos's expressed insult, put on his glasses, and guided his flashlight over Georgia's body. There were no visible marks, but the pink coloring of her skin was hard to miss, even under a flashlight.

"Witnesses?"

"Just a few of the staff...over there," Amos said, gesturing toward the front door of the club. "Most of them were already gone."

Truax glanced over to a handful of employees gathered together—sylphish women in tropical tops matching Georgia's, and large men in light blue tee shirts with the word SECURITY in bold black letters across the back; an irony not lost on Truax.

"I got their names and contact info for you," Amos said. "Figured you'd wanna talk to them."

Truax replaced the sheet with care and stood to face Amos. "Anything else?"

"That's her Malibu up there." He nodded toward the car. "Her purse is on the passenger seat and her keys are on the ground next to the car. Door's still open. Looks to me like that's where she was attacked."

"Did you check her purse?"

"Yes."

"Anything missing?"

"Don't think so. It was unopened. Inside there's a wallet with a couple o' small bills, an envelope with over five-hundred in twenties, makeup, mirror...all the usual chick stuff."

"And because you don't think anything is missing, you believe this to be a robbery..."

Amos shrugged. "Well, I figured—"

"Thanks for your help. Where's the forensics investigator?"

"Over there." Amos gestured with a half-hearted wave toward a white van.

Truax said nothing more and walked toward the unmarked field forensics unit. Amos followed. He stopped short of joining them, but stayed within earshot just the same.

"Hi, Moby," Barry Johnson said, looking up from his clipboard and ignoring his report for the moment. "Looks like our friend is back."

"That's what my captain thinks, but I'm not so sure. Doesn't fit the established MO. Hey, Barry. Got any cigarettes on you?"

"Cigarettes? You know I don't smoke. And besides, I thought you quit."

"I'm starting up again. So, what're your thoughts, here?"

"Can't be sure till the tox report comes back, but judging by her coloring, and that bit of foam around her mouth, I'd say it was cyanide. You really don't think this is CK's work?"

"Not a chance. Listen, I'm done with the body if you want to release it. I'll wait for the ME's report. If you need me, I'll be interviewing the staff."

"Yeah. Sure thing, Moby."

Truax gave Johnson a half smile and a pat on the shoulder before walking to the small group of club employees. He checked faces against the names on the list Amos gave him and verified phone numbers. Because it was almost dawn, he released everyone except Sandy Rice.

"Please stay available for questioning," he told them as they dispersed to their cars, then he asked Sandy Rice for the night's video tapes, avoiding any familiar chitchat.

Before following her in, he watched the transport van with Georgia's body leave for OCME. It was a thirty-minute ride to the city and he knew the ME would get samples to Tox within the next few hours. But he still had a two-day wait before he received the complete autopsy and forensics reports.

Two days was an eternity for him, and if he weren't SIU, it'd take even longer. Homicide Division had to wait a week or more, and DNA results took three or four for a rush order. Baltimore's murder rate was on the rise and OCME had their hands full, but high profile SIU cases like this one took priority; a small consolation, for which he was thankful.

Georgia's death was the second killing connected to Bamboo Billy's, coming after Kara Templeton's murder last Saturday.

Pretty ballsey, Truax thought, *returning to commit another murder.*

It was rare, but not unheard of. Just the same, he would put a couple of plain clothes officers in the club for a couple weeks. Atkins would be all over this.

While he waited on the tox report, he'd use the two-day lag time to interview the staff. Witnesses know things that they don't know, they know.

Maybe somebody had it out for Georgia. Or the club. Or the owner. Maybe someone on the staff pissed somebody off. Maybe they barred someone, or refused to serve someone because they were drunk. Maybe somebody stole somebody else's girl. Maybe the band sucked. There were a hundred reasons to target this place.

There was some kind of connection. He could feel it. And he had to find it. But for now, he decided to get some sleep. He doubted he'd see much of that for a while. It was just something else that made being him, suck.

The Jerr-Dan tow truck carrying Georgia's Malibu followed the body contractor's van out of the parking lot and headed toward Baltimore, just as Vecchio pulled up in a white Toyota Celica. Truax waited next to his squad car while Vecchio climbed out.

"Hi, Moby," she said across the Celica's roof. "Sorry I couldn't get here sooner. Was on a date."

As she emerged from around the car, Truax thought her decidedly attractive, having one of her pretty days, tonight. Her black hair was down in a full natural wave that framed her face, and bounced when she walked, and the tiny hook in her nose was hardly noticeable anymore. He had to admit, he was getting used to the idea of a partner. Especially one who wore her tops cut low and her jeans skintight.

"Well, Frankie," he said, "far be it from me to ruin your social life."

"I got here as fast as I could! Maybe if the department would give me an unmarked to use…"

"Why don't you just check one out from the Bureau?"

"I tried. They say they're all spoken for."

"DC?"

"Same. So I rented this, but it doesn't come with lights or a siren."

"Yeah…well, maybe the Bureau just don't like you."

Vecchio threw a frown his way, her dark eyes sparkling in the light from the flood lamps.

"Anyway," Truax continued, "it's not like you *have* to be here. You're just observing, right?"

"Is there anything you want me to do?"

"Yeah. Give me a cigarette."

"But I don't smoke."

"Then go home."

"Home? But Forensics is still—"

"You want to help them gather evidence?"

"Well, no. Not really."

"Thought not. You can help me interview witnesses later today if you want, but we're done here. Nothing more to do. Go home. Get some rest. Maybe go to church. We'll hit the bricks around dinner time. We should catch people at home."

"Are *you* going home?" she asked.

"No. I'm going back to Squad. I want to schedule a couple of undercover guys here for a couple weeks, and then go and watch some TV." He waved the evening's video from the club. "Got a new batch of footage to peruse."

"Want me to help?"

"No. Do what I tell you. Go home. You can help me later."

Vecchio shrugged. "Aren't you even going to tell me what happened? What you found?"

Truax said, "If you want to know what happens at a crime scene, be on time."

"But I just told you—"

"Not my problem, Frankie."

"Well, if this is what I can expect when I get to a crime scene, maybe next time I'll save the gas and just call."

"Whatever feels right," Truax said.

Vecchio shrugged. "Okay, Moby. Then I guess I'll see you later."

Truax said nothing, climbed into his cruiser, and backed out of his parking space. Pulling up beside Officer Amos, he told him to keep the lot closed until Forensics left.

CHAPTER 31

Harvey's mind was on Georgia's arrival, and he reached the guard kiosk before realizing where he was.

"How goes it tonight, Doc?" Bowers said.

Harvey jumped out of his skin. His lower echelons of awareness wholly controlled his movements, much like driving home from work on autopilot. Every movement was automatic requiring little if any thought, freeing his mind to think thoughts and indulge fantasies, while misplacing the guard's existence in the process.

Time and place quickly realigned, and Harvey straightened his posture to answer.

"Evening, Officer Bowers." As he spoke the words, it occurred to him he had never used Bowers's first name, and now that he thought about it, he realized he never knew it.

He hadn't actually met Bowers in the traditional sense. Bowers was just there. Social pleasantry was automatic, a returned courtesy, little more than a reply bounced back to Bowers as he walked by the guard station.

Eventually, it was a word here, a gesture there, and then a conversation over shared interests...usually the current month's *Playboy*, the only thing they actually had in common.

"Everything okay, Doc? You seem a little preoccupied tonight."

"Yes yes, I'm fine. Thank you for asking. Just a little situation with— It's nothing really. Figured a cigarette might distract me."

"That Vette giving you trouble again, Doc?"

"The Vette? What are you talking about?"

"Rabbani said you've been having a lot of trouble with it lately. I saw him in the hall as he was leaving; heard him mumble that you should buy a new car so maybe you can get to work on time."

"Oh...yes, it's been giving me a fit of late."

"Well, I hope you get her all fixed up, Doc. She's a beauty, that's for sure. And speaking of beauties, have you seen the new *Playboy*? I picked up a copy yesterday. *Miss August*. Very nice. *Very* distracting."

Harvey produced a thin smile. "No...no, I haven't. Maybe, when you're finished with it—"

"Yeah. Sure, Doc. Here ya go," Bowers said handing him the periodical. "Get distracted. She's hotter than any cigarette."

Harvey sat on the smoker's bench, thumbing through the magazine, dangling a cigarette from his lip. A breeze sent smoke into his eyes and he turned his head and blinked them clear. Taking a last drag, he flicked the butt into the night and watched the embers explode upon impact with the street, certain he'd set a personal distance record.

Having his fill of self-imposed restraint, he finally turned to the foldout and gazed at the tall willowy blonde gracing the center of the magazine. He found himself comparing the airbrushed model to the woman who was on her way to him. They were much alike, Miss August and

Georgia. Both had the kind of looks a man would kill for, both were lifeless and unmoving, and both were his.

Walking back to the lobby, he returned the magazine to Bowers just as the headlights of the body transport passed by the front door. Georgia had made it in record time. Now he wouldn't have to rush through her, or her autopsy.

Glimpsing the clock, Harvey calculated the time he could spend enjoying Georgia before rinsing away his presence, and proceeding with her autopsy. He would work over to compensate for the three-and-a-half hours he was late, and that should give him the time to do the things he wanted to do, the things he needed to do, and then, the things he had to do to appease McGovern.

Possente Amor Mi Chiama filled the lab and Harvey ran his hands down Georgia's top, removing it a button at a time, and savoring the act as he undressed her the old fashion way; the way he would have had they been lovers; the way he would have, had she allowed it.

No courting, no rejection, no humiliation...they're so much better dead.

Completing his *tete-a-tete* with Georgia, Harvey cut her open and removed several medium-sized bits of what appeared to be a whole grain Kaiser Roll from Georgia's stomach, along with a few chunks of french-fries. Then he emptied her stomach completely, discarding everything in the bio waste container scheduled for incineration.

He then substituted several vials containing biological specimens belonging to a legitimate CK victim, fluids he had extracted and stashed in the old refrigerator in his mother's garage. He labeled them as belonging to Georgia Parsons, CK victim #7, and then took great pains in the evacuation of her remaining fluids, before rinsing them down the drain, thereby following standard procedure by disposing of all liquids coming from her body—all evidence—and passing only the fluids he wanted Tox to have.

Completing her autopsy, he took care to rinse away all traces of his interlude with her one last time before completing his report, a report that omitted any mention of the tiny puncture wound in her breast, and the major post-mortem tearing he inflicted on her nether region. Satisfied he had missed nothing, he transported her to the cooler and smiled to himself.

Surprising, he thought. *Her tits were real after all.*

CHAPTER 32

Truax leaned forward in the rigid aluminum chair and pressed the eject button on the video deck. The machine responded by disgorging the cassette from its whirling innards.

He learned one important lesson from watching Billy's tape last week: Turning off the sound was a must. Classic Rock was more his style, not that nerve-racking shit they played now-a-days.

He managed to crunch four hours of people, writhing around like worms on a hook, into half the time by fast-forwarding to the sections with the bartenders.

The cameraman hadn't framed the area around the bar for any length of time. That would have defeated the purpose, he supposed. The gimmick was for the customers' benefit, not the staff's.

He slid the tape into its cardboard sleeve and carried it back to his desk. Setting the video on his desk blotter, he dropped into his wing chair, and rubbed his eyes hard, recalling his mother's predictions of going blind.

His father told him the same thing about jerking off, but in spite of all their warnings, he could still see. It was one of his few remaining senses that Time hadn't fucked with.

Tilting back on the chair's rear legs, he began sifting through what he knew about the latest killings. He knew the delivery system was similar, but not the same as CK. He knew the location of the bodies didn't follow those of CK. He knew that the club was the source of the killer's last two victims, and he knew that all this was different—too different—to be CK.

Setting aside, for a moment, that Georgia and Kara were at Billy's before their deaths, Truax considered the similarities in timelines.

Georgia died in the early morning hours after leaving work, where Kara died late morning at home. As it turned out, Kara took her poison home with her. Had she not, she would have surely died around the same time, in the same place, as Georgia.

Both time of death and location were outside of CK's *initial* pattern, so is he establishing a new one? Or are they so dissimilar they couldn't possibly be the same killer?

Such radical shifts and differences from one crime to the next made it seem as if the killer was experimenting, working out the kinks; kinks that didn't exist in the killings of the older victims.

Was that it? Was that what the killer was doing? Working out the kinks? Sure it was, and since they could find no bottled water anywhere on the parking lot where Georgia died, the killer must have used another method of delivery.

Cyanide kills quickly, and if Georgia had ingested it inside the club—from a bottle of water, like Kara—she would have had no chance of making it to her car; which every indication at the scene suggests that she did.

More than likely, she was poisoned somewhere near her car, and made it as far as she did before she died. If that's what happened, and water was used as before, then forensics should turn up the tainted water bottle. But if there is no bottle, he'd have to wait on her autopsy to tell him how she died. He believed the killer didn't anticipate

Kara taking the bottled poison home, expecting her to drink it right away. If that was the case, he had made a mistake—a mistake tonight's murder was designed to correct. A mistake he wasn't apt to repeat.

Returning the chair to its intended four-legged position, Truax tried to stretch out the tight spots that had settled in his back. Snatching the video tape from his desk he headed for the door. *Time to talk to Georgia's friends*, he thought. The first of which was Angela Morris. But before that, he wanted to collect Vecchio.

An hour later, the two cops sat on a red micro-fiber sofa that matched the red micro-fiber chair, where Angela Morris sat crying.

Gathering herself, she climbed from the chair, and then faltered. Truax lunged to catch her, but Angela recovered, rendering his assistance unnecessary. As Truax eased himself back down, Angela pulled hard on her over-sized tee-shirt to conceal her light-yellow underwear.

She plucked several tissues from a blue rectangular box sitting on a glass end table and blew her nose; the white of the paper complimenting her clear cinnamon skin.

Truax waited, allowing her time to complete her task. His next question could wait, and as she returned to her chair, he replayed in his mind what he'd learned about Georgia Parsons, pleased that his memory was having a good day.

Georgia's MVA record hadn't shown as much as a parking ticket. She possessed a single credit card with a zero balance, received her B.A. in History from the University of Maryland two years prior, and like many new graduates, couldn't find a job that paid more than the one she used to put herself through school. So she continued bartending.

That was no surprise to Truax. A girl with looks like hers could make five times as much tending bar versus working as an entry-level historian. Her school transcript listed a 3.4 GPA with a minor in physical education, and her Facebook account revealed that she loved the beach, Chocolate Labs, and baseball. She never dated men from work, wrote poetry, and wanted to publish a book of poems someday.

Blowing her nose once more, Angela settled herself, dabbing her eyes with the unused corners of the tissue. Sitting down, she clung to the crumbled Kleenex in her hands as if they were important to her in some way.

"Sorry," she whispered.

Truax offered an insincere smile and continued. "Was she seeing anyone recently?"

"No, not really." The worst of Angela's crying was over, but her voice still contained the texture of someone trying to remain brave for someone else. "But that was by choice," she continued. "You wouldn't believe the phone numbers that girl came home with. She could collect men if she wanted." Angela dabbed the corner of her eyes once more, intercepting fresh tears that threatened to break loose down her cheek.

"We didn't find any phone numbers in her apartment," Truax said, "other than those in her address book."

"She never kept them. She wasn't interested in the men that came to the club. In spite of how she looked, she was the cerebral type. Smart." Angela sniffed and blew her nose again, the emerging red around her nostrils overtaking the light coloring of her skin. "She was interested in the Arts. A good time to her was an afternoon at a museum or an art gallery or a poetry reading." A tear managed to escape before she could catch it and streamed down her face. "I warned her over and over," she said, slapping her thigh, emphasizing each word: "MAKE-THEM-WALK-YOU-TO-YOUR-CAR!"

Her tears began to run free.

"You mentioned that you last saw her about a week ago" Truax said. "Can you tell me about that?"

"There's not much to tell," Angela replied. "I had an appointment at the salon." She gestured to her hair. "Cornrows. Takes a long time. I can't expect my daughter to sit for six hours with nothing to do, so I asked Georgia if she'd watch Shawna for me. Georgia used to tease that one day she was gonna have a daughter of her own, so she could stop borrowing mine." A painful laugh found its way out. "It's an inside joke we have...we had."

"I really am very sorry, Ms. Morris." Truax said, delivering practiced empathy automatically and without effort.

"My daughter doesn't know," Angela said. "She's going to take this really hard. She loved her Aunt Georgia."

Vecchio glanced at Truax. He didn't respond, but his face begged the question.

"Oh," Angela added, her dark eyes reflecting the light in the room. "I guess you can tell we're not blood. Shawna knew Georgia wasn't her *real* aunt. Her coloring wasn't right, but she called her 'Aunt' anyway. I told Shawna she was the white sheep of the family." A nervous laugh escaped as she reminisced, and Truax knew it for what it really was—a way to dull the pain.

He offered a sympathetic smile in return and then rose to his feet. Vecchio followed suit. "I see," he said. "Well, I appreciate you seeing us, Ms. Morris. I'm sorry to have intruded during your time of loss. Please keep my card. If you think of anything, please give me a call. Day or night."

"There is one more thing," Angela said, clutching the business card in her hand.

The detectives said nothing, but looked at her with interest.

"Don't know if this is useful or not, but I used to tease her about getting knocked up by one of the hot guys at the club. She told me not to worry. That pre-marital sex was a sin. You wouldn't know it to look at her...maybe because of the way they made her dress for work...but she was a devout Catholic. Went to Mass most Sundays, even after working late at the club. But marriage was not yet in her future and she remained celibate. She was still a virgin."

CHAPTER 33

The 6am sun blasted between window and drape, striking dust motes floating in the narrow beams as the alarm went off. Truax crawled from bed and shuffled toward the bathroom, brushing his head with his fingertips, and playing with the transition from stubble to skin. Being bald was still a novelty to him, even after nearly a year.

Flipping the wall switch, he peered at a haggard version of himself in the mirror and silently cursed the crow's feet that weren't there the day before. After tending to the nature's immediate business, he remembered it was Monday.

Days could bunch together on a tough case like this, one day sliding into the next, making it difficult to remember what he did when. He figured that's what weekends were supposed to do...act like an index for the week, marking a beginning and an end. But no matter. It was Monday, and hating Mondays was always easy.

Plunging his arms into the sleeves of is plaid burgundy robe, he made his way to the kitchen. It wasn't unlike most kitchens, composed of stainless steel appliances and yellow, flower-print wallpaper, paper he'd been meaning to replace when he moved in some five years ago, but its continuing presence made its removal, that much more unnecessary.

It's a matter of time, he thought, ejecting a sigh at yet another chore undone. *Spare time. The kind of time that never comes.*

Retrieving the coffee and the half-empty packet of filters from the top shelf, he started a fresh pot. He dumped yesterday's grounds into the trash and began the too slow process of filling the pot, waiting for the water to reach the top for what seemed like forever.

Firing up the old machine, the coffee maker began making the noises coffee makers make. He traveled to the far side of the living room, pulling his robe tight around him.

He stopped adjacent to the drafty front windows, whose replacement remained the #3 chore on his list of things to do. Regarding the dark-green blackout curtains as a defensive screen, he deftly coaxed aside an edge with a single finger, peeked through a pane of silted glass, and scanned the area for passersby. But mostly, he was looking for Ida.

Spotting Saturday's *Pasadena Observer* on the lawn, he began cursing and started to the front door. He'd have brought it in when he got home had he seen it, or even thought about it. But he didn't. In his life, newspapers were for morning, and coffee.

Pulling the door open a crack, looking left, looking right, seeing no one, he ventured barefoot onto the dew-laden grass. Every morning, when his bare skin contacted the wet ground, he swore to himself that the paperboy had it out for him. He couldn't understand what was so damn hard about tossing the paper on the porch. He looked for the little hooligan to voice his displeasure, and as usual, he was nowhere to be found.

"Officer Moby? Hello? Officer Moby?" It was the Widow Ida, hovering on the stoop.

Ida lived in a small bungalow that looked like every other bungalow in the neighborhood, but hers was next door to his. When her husband died some fourteen-months ago, her attention, and her attachment, turned to him.

She came bearing gifts: a tin of cookies one day, a basket of tomatoes the next, and Truax accepted the gifts with courtesy and gratitude, so as not to bruise delicate feelings. Ida was a nickel shy of eighty, so amorous inclinations toward him—the brush of a hand, a peck on the cheek—didn't concern him. *But*, he thought whimsically, *it pays to be wary. Especially with Miss Ida. For with Ida, one just never knew.*

Pulling her front door shut behind her, she looked as if she had just come from the beauty parlor, with her many curls of blue-gray hair protected by her shear red kerchief. Waving a frail hand over her head, she descended the three steps to the sidewalk with care, clinging white-knuckled to the black wrought-iron railing, each step deliberate, each purposeful, with a slight bend to her back that suggested osteoporosis.

At the landing she settled herself, smoothed her black cotton dress, and took a beeline to the section of chain link fence closest to Truax.

Damn spry for her age, Truax thought. *If only she used a walker or something. I coulda beat it back into the house before she cleared the steps.*

"Good morning Miss Ida," Truax said, stuffing the paper under one arm before pulling his robe tighter, and re-cinching its terrycloth belt double tight. "How are you today?"

"Oh, I'm peachy!" she said with a full-tooth smile, the bright enamel bearing witness to a lifetime of care. "I haven't seen you in several days, Officer Moby. Have you been on vacation?"

"No, not vacation. Been very busy at work. You know Miss Ida, I'd love to chat, but—"

"My son has a dog. You remember my son, don't you Officer Moby? He has to give it away. Do you want a dog?"

"No, Miss Ida. I don't have time for—"

"I don't think he's old enough to take care of a dog, do you?"

"Miss Ida...he's what? Fifty-four?"

"You know, I can't remember. Let's see...I was twenty when he was born. No, twenty-five I think. Would you like to come in for a cup of tea? Officer Moby?"

"I'd love to Miss Ida, but I—"

"Oh!" Ida said suddenly, thrusting a crooked index finger into the air. "Is that my phone?"

Truax barely detected ringing through an open window. Apparently, there was nothing wrong with Ida's hearing.

She turned back toward her house. It wasn't that far away, just several strides, but he doubted she'd get there in time. Still, it distracted her attention away from him.

Truax breathed a quick sigh of relief, and a thought of locating a cigarette played in his mind. He decided that the next time he fetched the paper, he'd bring his cell phone with him. He could get her number easily enough, enter it into his phone and just press—

No, he berated himself. *That isn't right. Her husband is dead. She's just lonely. Would it kill you to spend a few moments talking with her?*

The shame he felt were reflections of childhood lessons, taught to him by his mother, on how to be a decent man. Lessons he never forgot. But shame can last only so long. Once back in the house, he forgot all about Ida, and focused instead on his growling stomach.

He locked down two slices of whole wheat in the toaster, brushing the crumbs from the reflective top of the machine, before pouring himself a fresh cup of coffee. Stirring in three spoons of real sugar, he plopped down at the kitchen table and turned directly to the sports.

Once the Orioles signed interim manager Dave Trembley through 2008, the team promptly hit the field and lost 30-3 to the Texas Rangers, the worse loss of any major league team since the turn of the century—the *19th* century. They followed that up by losing the back end of the double-header 6-3.

Not an auspicious start for Trembley, he thought. *But the up side is, it can only get better.*

The box scores were as amusing as they were depressing, and after shaking his head for the third time, and as he turned to the front page, his cell rang. It was Atkins.

"Did you see Saturdays *Observer?*" Atkins fumed, skirting the courtesy of a "Hello."

Truax didn't answer as the front page settled flat on the table—the headline took only a second to catch his eye.

Cyanide Killer Strikes Down Two at Pasadena Hot Spot. Sources at the Scene Confirm, "It's the same MO."
By Manny Munroe - Staff Writer

The early hours of Sunday morning marked the second slaying in a week for The Cyanide Killer. Anne Arundel County Police were called to a popular Pasadena nightspot around 3am, where the body of a young woman, a club employee, was discovered in the parking lot by a co-worker. Her identity is being withheld pending notification of next of kin. Sources close to the investigation report she was poisoned. "It's the same MO," [as CK] reports a county officer at the scene. This marks CK's second killing connected to the club in a week, and his seventh in total, the previous deaths

occurring as early as May of this year. Currently, the police have no leads and the killer remains at large. According to sources within the department, they believe The Cyanide Killer chooses his victims at random. The Department asks that anyone with information relating to these crimes, please call the Crime Tip Line. They will remain anonymous.

"What the hell?" Truax blurted.

As he read, his face flushed from the anger-driven blood coursing through his veins. He pushed the anger down.

"I see it, Captain. How did they—"

"This says the murder of the bartender was CK's work! YOU were on the scene! So was this fucking reporter! Now just who the fuck leaked this to him?"

"Captain I...I don't know."

"You don't KNOW? Then you'd better find *out*, Truax! Today! You HEAR ME?"

The call ended when Truax heard the nothing sound of a disconnected cell. He laid his phone on the table and fell against the chair's backrest. A compelling need for a cigarette grabbed him. His memory was good today, and it brought back recollections of another headline fiasco.

The case involved a murder-for-hire ring. He had made the mistake of discussing the ring's signature trademark with a junior detective—a double-tap to the back of the head with a .22. It was an efficient weapon for assassination, since that caliber had enough power to enter the skull, but not enough to exit. The result was two small pieces of lead ricocheting around inside the mark's head, turning his brain into Swiss cheese.

That particular piece of information hadn't been made public, until the over-zealous junior detective dropped it to a female reporter he wanted to screw. She never slipped between the sheets with the detective, but her resulting headline produced a four-fold jump in .22 caliber, double-tap murders. Now, he had a similar problem.

He bent the paper over at the fold, and then folded it again into thirds, carefully creasing it to remain that way. He placed it on the table and ravaged his desk for an old cigarette. Finding none, he headed upstairs for a shower and a shave.

The ass-chewing Atkins gave Truax played like a tape in his brain. He wasn't scoring any points, and if anything, he gave his new boss reason to relieve him of this case. It might even provide him the ammunition to trump up cause for dismissal, or early retirement, or whatever else suited his fancy. His ears were still ringing as he trudged to his desk.

It was late morning, and he found Vecchio poring over autopsy files, an activity that did nothing to improve his mood, or give him cause to warm to her further. Her diligence made him look bad, which made her look good. It was just one more thing to add to a list of things about her that irritated him.

"What are you doing..." he sniped, dropping into his chair with a grunt.

"Yes, and good morning to you too, Moby. I'm going back over the autopsy reports."

"I can see that, Frankie. Why?"

"I have a gnawing feeling we're missing something."

"Like what?"

"I don't know. That's why I'm going over them. But I noticed something I wanted to ask you about."

"Shoot."

"What do you think about this?" She twisted her monitor toward him, and in essence, invited him over. Truax rolled over to her desk and caught a whiff of her perfume. It pleased him, which annoyed him further, and he rolled back to his desk.

"What am I looking at here?" he grumbled, nodding toward her monitor.

"The same medical examiner did the autopsies credited to CK; all except for Kara Templeton. Do you find that odd?"

Truax thought a tick. "Did you see when the victims arrived at OCME?"

"Yes. Except for Templeton, all came in after midnight."

"Did you check his schedule?"

"Well, no. I didn't think to—"

"Then why don't you check that out. If he's always on the mid-shift, then it wouldn't be unusual for him to do the work."

"Yeah," she said. "I guess maybe you're right."

"If he's always on mids, I wouldn't spend any more time on him. Then we should take another look at the interviews with friends and family," Truax said. "Someone knows something. We just haven't made the connection yet, so let's get on it."

Hours passed, and reviewing written accounts of friends and family, and crime scene and forensics reports, put them no closer to developing a new lead than before. Truax was certain he was dealing with two killers. Even Vecchio reluctantly admitted his theory had a bit of merit, as if that in itself meant anything, but Atkins was adamant, pushing the one killer theory down his throat, mandating that he pursue it from that angle.

Truax thought about what his old boss, Eddie Merrick, might say about that.

"How long you been doing this, Truax? Twenty—thirty years? You're telling me you followed the orders of that snot-nose Atkins over your own gut? What the hell's wrong with you?"

CHAPTER 34

Vecchio felt as if her eyes would fall from their sockets if she didn't get away from information she had already committed to memory. She discovered no new information, and she was sure she missed nothing in the crime scene and forensics reports. She just wanted to get away from it for a few minutes.

"I've had it Moby," she said. "I have to shift off of this for a while. How about a dinner break?"

"Yeah. Sure. I'm gettin' kinda hungry too. I'll buy if you fly."

"Really? That's awfully nice of you."

"What...I can't be nice?"

Vecchio could only smile.

"What did you have in mind?" Truax asked.

"The deli down the street. Thought I'd walk it and clear my mind."

Truax handed her a twenty. "Good choice. Can you get me a cold cut sub? No mayo."

"No mayo? You on a diet or something?"

"High cholesterol. The bad kind. Doc says if I don't lower it, he'll have to put me on meds."

"Oh...I see. OK, be back soon."

She gathered her things and made it to the door when Detective Nichols bumped into her. He glimpsed her figure without trying to disguise it, and then his eyes found hers.

"Hey!" he said. "Agent Vecchio. I was hopin' I'd find you here."

"I'm here," she returned. "You must be Nichols."

Nichols face lit up. "Yeah! How'd you know?"

"Captain Atkins told me about your hair."

"My hair? What about my hair?"

"Oh...nothing. He just said it was red. I had no idea *how* red."

Nichols said nothing.

"So," Vecchio continued. "Captain Atkins asked me to keep you in the loop. I was going to call you tomorrow, but since you're here, I can pass something to you now."

"I'm all ears."

Vecchio glanced over to see that Truax had taken an interest in their conversation. She knew he was out of earshot, but that didn't keep him from watching, and she didn't want to chance that he might be able to read lips. She knew that where she was concerned, Truax kept his talents close to the vest.

"I don't want Detective Truax to see me talking to you for too long. Meet me by the ladies room in half a minute."

When Nichols strolled over to the bathrooms, Vecchio gestured to an unoccupied area of the lobby near the entrance.

"So, Agent Vecchio...whatcha got?"

"You're aware of the two women who were killed at Billy's nightclub?"

"Yes," Nichols replied. "Of course I am."

"Did you know that Truax thinks CK will hit there again?"

"No. I didn't."

"I didn't think so. He's keeping that under wraps. He's placing a couple of plain clothes officers there for a couple of weeks...he's that sure. Thought you should know."

"Damn...that sly bastard. Covers his tracks pretty good. Thank you, Agent Vecchio. I think I'll hang around Billy's for a while too, just in case. Did he tell you who he was sending?"

"Frick & Frack is how he referred to them."

"Yeah. He doesn't give up much, as I'm sure you know. OK. Thank you, Agent Vecchio. Let me know if anything else develops that I should know about."

Vecchio smiled, and walked out the door.

CHAPTER 35

Monday night wasn't a regular night out for Harvey, but this Monday proved different. McGovern had called. Asked him to work Tuesday's mid-shift; on overtime, of course. Said the scheduled pathologist had called in sick.

Harvey thought back a day to his euphoric bonding with Georgia. But euphoria, like any other drug, wears off. His Need demanded another run, but having to wait until his regularly scheduled shift delayed his next encounter at least several days. McGovern's request couldn't have been timelier, because with Monday night, came Monday Night Football.

Having another run at Billy's occurred to him, but he knew that would be just plain stupid. Considering the risk, he thought it better to change his hunting ground than return there. He recalled a bar not far from his mother's house. The Governor's Tavern, an establishment he passed daily on his way to and from work. Years ago, it was the neighborhood eyesore, a low-class dive that attracted the town's most unsavory element, but today, courtesy of its new owner, it shined up like a newly minted coin, complete with a new roof and new yellow siding.

A state-of-the-art computer sign drew the attention of all who passed, and offered an array of entertainment specials which included Karaoke, Happy Hour, and Monday Night Football. Harvey decided it was worth a look-see.

Around 9pm he came bounding down the steps smelling like a kid on his first date.

"Where are you goin' all spiffed up like a five-dollar whore?" his mother asked.

"I'm going out." He saw no reason to mention having to work as well. It would just start another argument.

"On Monday night? You never go out on Mondays."

"The Ravens are playing a pre-season game against the Eagles."

"Why don't you watch it here with me," she asked. "I've always wanted to learn football. That's all men my age ever talk about."

Harvey imagined himself sitting in the black 70s-style leather La-Z-Boy residing in the corner of the living room, trying unsuccessfully to explain football to his graying mother. What could he tell her? He found the game of no interest, and it was almost as big a mystery to him as it was to her. He only watched it in the bar because that's all they played on the sets mounted on the walls. He wasn't there for the games. He was there for the women.

"I'd rather hang out with the guys, Ma. You don't care about football. Why don't you just watch your cooking shows like you always do? I think *Emeril* has something about Cajun catfish. He's from New Orleans, right?" Harvey hustled to the door. "I'll see you tomorrow. Maybe take you to lunch."

"You're never home at night anymore," she said, changing to *The Food Network*. Emeril's kitchen filled the screen. "Can't you spend one night with your mother?"

"C'mon, Ma. I only have two nights off. Gimme a break, will ya?"

She pulled her attention away from the TV like someone who burned themselves on a hot stove. "You're getting to act like your no-count father lately," she snapped. "When he walked out, that was the best day of my—"

Harvey tuned her out, lifted the tail of his long-sleeve white shirt, and dug around his pocket for his car keys. He knew all too well about his lousy father. His mother had filled his childhood with stories at every opportunity; stories of how he abandoned them before Harvey reached his first birthday, and to hear his mother tell it, it was the best thing that ever happened to her.

But not for Harvey.

Harvey took the place of the man in his mother's life, filling the hole his father left when he ran off. She never remarried. It was sad. Pathetic actually. Shit, he wasn't even sure they were ever married in the first place. He assumed his mother had the same last name as his father— the same last name as him—but even if she didn't, what did it matter? He was all she had, and she reminded him of that, and his obligation, almost daily. He gestured with a half-hearted wave as he walked out the door, not caring if she acknowledged him or not.

An old refrigerator sat behind a cabinet on the back wall of his mother's stand-alone garage. It contained a brown paper lunch bag hidden behind an open twelve-pack of beer. The bag contained four vials of biological material from a genuine CK kill, materials needing refrigeration to maintain functionality, and too dangerous to store at work for fear of discovery.

These particular specimens belonged to sixty-seven year old Harriett Brennermann, a Caucasian female, or as Harvey liked to think of her—CK victim #2.

Carefully placing the bag on his worktable, Harvey reached high into an old metal cabinet, a dirty-white cupboard discarded after remodeling the kitchen years ago.

Pulling on one of the rusted chrome handles, he opened the door and fished out a tiny, 1 X 1 zip-lock baggie, one of the type used by drug dealers. But this one contained a healthy dose of rat poison, finely chopped to dissolve in liquid instantly. This he carefully stuffed into the small coin pocket of his jeans. Pressing closed the old cabinet door, he slipped into the Vette, placed the brown bag with the vials in the glove compartment, and locked it.

Satisfied all was ready, he fired up the engine, backed out of the garage, and headed to The Governor's Tavern. It was football night on the big screen, and if he was right, the place would reek of women.

Fifteen minutes into the 2nd quarter, Harvey walked through the front door of The Governor's Tavern. Despite the outside improvements, the inside hadn't changed at all.

The smell of stale cigarettes, beer, and something putrid fouled the air. The rectangular bar jutted halfway into the room, blocking a direct path to the other side, forcing him to correct his course to the right.

On the far side of the bar sat four pool tables entertaining several not-so-high-rollers. The sound from the game blared throughout the tavern, and one unsteady music lover tried to jam money into the jukebox. Being unplugged, it rejected his bill.

The out-of-order sign hanging across the machine bore witness to a costly lesson learned by the management long ago, when they lowered the sound on a Ravens game in favor of the jukebox. The bar owner created the sign after he witnessed a standing-room-only crowd, dissipate to nothing in the span of ten minutes.

Harvey made his way to the bar, slicing between two highly animated men dressed in purple Ravens jerseys. LEWIS appeared between the shoulder blades of the first.

The second, REED. The bartender was short and fat and probably the regular Monday night girl. Harvey was struck with how she roamed behind the bar like a precision machine, flitting back and forth, from customer to customer, tossing empty beer bottles in the trash with one hand, while slamming fresh ones on the bar with the other. When she turned her attention to him, he ordered a beer.

Tossing four ones on the worn hardwood bar, he stepped back onto a vacant piece of floor behind him, all the while scanning obscure faces of people he didn't recognize.

He preferred it that way. He didn't want to know these people. They were of a lower caste. Minor people without hope, devoid of dreams or desires beyond those of drinking themselves into oblivion.

Distasteful women with pasts but no futures; disheveled men with a singular goal to survive the workday and arrive here. He found them repulsive in their drunkenness, wasteful in their existence. His hopes for the evening waned.

Then, just as the 4th quarter started, she walked in; a stunning woman who brought a rare beauty to this unworthy place. Her hair was red, a darker shade than Kara's, and there were light streaks throughout, which couldn't occur naturally. Lean and statuesque, she wore a well-filled, pink sleeveless top with one white bra strap sliding down her near shoulder. It appeared as if someone had poured her into her white Levis, and as she walked, her scuffed, pink, three-inch heels caused her hips to move in such a way as to eliminate any need to observe the rest of her.

She ignored the bar and headed directly for the ladies' room, a term Harvey considered too lofty a title for this place, but because *she* was going there, it somehow applied. He maneuvered toward the restroom and waited for her to come out.

Eleven minutes later, the new redhead walked blindly past him, wiping her index finger under her nose and sniffing as if from a cold.

She's a cokehead, he thought. The words running through his mind were reason enough to eliminate her, but as she passed, he turned, and as his eyes caught the sway of her hips, his Need took control.

But then again, why should that change anything?

He thought it genius of sorts, mimicking her coke-addicted behavior, running his finger under his nose and collapsing his nostrils with an occasional snort. That she responded so aggressively to his mock behavior set him back. Initially, he put little stock in his bogus performance, thinking it foolish that she might respond, but then, without warning, she approached him with abandon.

"Hey!" she said, a coy smile shaping her full lips. "Can you hook me up?"

"Yeah, baby. I can hook you up. What you lookin' to score?"

She slipped in close, placing her pink painted lips to his ear. "Well, that's the thing," she said, "I don't really have any money. I thought maybe we could party."

The smell of her perfume, the warmth of her breath—Harvey knew that female addicts of lesser means had a way about them when it came to drugs. They doled out blowjobs like smiles when they needed a fix—anytime, anywhere, to get those all-important little white lines. Harvey didn't have any coke, but *she* didn't know that.

"Party?" he said. "I like to party. I got some stuff that ain't been stepped on much. High quality shit. Keep you up for days."

She pressed into him, grinding herself against his groin. "Well, baby...let's get outta here then," she said, turning full crotch-on against him. "Maybe get a room somewhere."

Harvey's Need raged. His manhood grew solid under her sexual onslaught, and for the briefest of moments, he considered taking her while she was still alive. But he knew it wouldn't be as exciting. Wouldn't be as satisfying. It would be so...normal. He dashed the thought, deciding instead to stick with what worked.

He knew he couldn't be anywhere near her when she died. He had to be on his way to OCME, so he reached into the small coin pocket on his right hip and retrieved the baggie of rat poison. Being so finely chopped, it easily passed for cocaine. He wrapped his left arm around her waist, then he slipped the poison pack into her hand on the sly.

"Take this," he breathed into her ear. "I have to pay the tab. Meet me outside. I have a lot more."

She clenched the baggie tight and rewarded him with a deep-tongue kiss—a promise of things to come—then offering a hurried smile, pushed away and took a course directly to the restroom, not glancing back, not wasting a single, precious, second.

Harvey smiled, finished the last swallow of his beer, and started for the front door.

He measured her delivery to OCME in hours, expecting her there at or about 1am.

As he passed through the front door, he stopped for a moment but did not glance back. I *don't even know her name*, he thought. *But then again, why should I care*?

Stepping onto the parking lot he angled right, navigating between rows of parked cars like a rat in a maze. He had parked his Vette near the lot's entrance off a dark side street, three rows down and several spaces in. But upon arriving at the space, the car wasn't there.

He meandered around the lot trying to convince himself he hadn't parked where he thought, but after ten minutes of searching, he conceded to the reality of it all. The classic, fire-engine-red, '65 Corvette Stingray was gone—and with it, the fluids of CK victim #2: Sixty-seven year-old Harriett Brennermann.

Harvey jumped the split rail fence separating The Governor's Tavern from the used car lot next door. He bolted in a panic-fueled sprint for Crain Highway, a busy single lane alternate running parallel to Ritchie, desperate for a glimpse of his car going down the street, or parked on a convenience store lot, or wrapped around the nearest telephone pole.

Seeing nothing, he was left with the only thing he could do that made any sense: Put as much distance between him and The Governor's Tavern as possible.

Concealed by the night, he slowed to a trot as he emerged onto the sidewalk from between two bungalows bordering Crain. His easy gate provided no hint as to why he was gasping for air.

How could I have been so stupid, he thought, *I shouldn't have brought the vials. Should've left them in the garage. Doubled back home to get them on the way to work. Fuckin' stupid!*

He made his way to a 24-hour convenience store three blocks away, a store that he knew was there, but had never patronized. Once inside, he avoided the cameras and the kid with the face piercings behind the counter, and fished a quarter from his pocket. Using his cell phone was out of the question. There would be a record.

After wiping both sides of the coin on his shirt, he held it by its edges and dropped it in a payphone before dialing Directory Assistance. When the automated operator connected him to his party, he told the dispatcher of Red Top Cabs where to pick him up. Now all he had to do was decide where he wanted to go...and what to do about his stolen car.

CHAPTER 36

Truax stuffed the change from his twenty in the top drawer of his desk, unwrapped his sub, and thanked Vecchio for making the run.

"What'd you get?" he asked.

"Just a salad," she replied, pulling a tin-foil bowl from the bag. "Have to watch my girlish figure."

"I think you have that covered," he said. He patted his stomach. "But just you wait. This'll happen to you."

"Oh no! Not me. I am determined to stay in shape. I have a small gym at my home in San Diego. Use it most every day."

Truax looked her up and down, but this time, there was no lechery in his inspection of her.

"Well, I'd say it's working, Frankie. You look good."

"Why, thank you, Moby. I try."

"So," Truax said in his best matter-of-fact tone. "What were you and Nichols talking about?"

Vecchio's eyes cut to him, but she didn't answer, electing instead to finish chewing a forkful of lettuce. She gestured for him to wait by raising a turquoise-tipped finger skyward.

"He asked me out," she replied seconds later, her voice a near whisper.

"Oh," Truax responded. "That's good...I guess."

"Moby! Is that a hint of jealousy I detect in your voice? I'm flattered."

Truax mopped the corner of his mouth with a napkin and avoided eye contact. "Don't be," he replied. "I just didn't peg Nichols as being your type, that's all. He's such a...dick."

Vecchio offered a demure smile. "Well, you'll be happy to know your powers of perception are intact. He's *not* my type. Too much Momma's Boy there, I think. Besides, I don't date people from work."

Truax grinned. "People? Frankie?"

"*Men!* I don't date *men* from work. Jesus, Moby! Can't you stop being a cop for just a little while?"

Truax grinned. "Yeah. OK. I suppose it can become annoying."

A smirk formed on Vecchio's lips. "Oh! You have *no* idea."

CHAPTER 37

The taxi that came for Harvey reeked of booze and stale perfume, its back seat blemished with something unseemly. Harvey wondered what additional uses the cab might have had, and hovering above the seat like a woman in a gas station bathroom crossed his mind.

The middle-eastern cabbie wasn't talkative, preferring not to compete with the cab's radio and the sounds of the flute-like Ney, common in Arabic music. Harvey was glad for that.

Thinking his location too close to The Governor's Tavern where he killed the nameless redhead, and considering his fuck-up in leaving Harriett Brennermann's fluids in his now stolen Vette, he decided that giving the driver a destination he could plug into his GPS would be a most stupid thing to do.

He told him he was just visiting and didn't know the address, and guided him where he wanted him to go by spouting turn-by-turn directions. "Turn here." "Straight through the light." "Take the next left up ahead," leading the cabbie in circles, using an obscure back-street route into his neighborhood within the larger development.

Now that he was less conspicuous, his thought processes calmed and approached something closer to normal; normal enough to let him forget the car, and the cops, and the dead coke addict, to focus on what he had to do to get out of the jam he had created for himself. He knew reporting the car stolen was out of the question. At least for the time being.

A classic red Vette, would stick out like a sore thumb. Maybe a chase ensues. Maybe the cops search the car. Maybe they find the fluids. No, bad idea. Besides, to report the car stolen would require a police report, and I certainly couldn't say it was at the bar where a doper was murdered. In fact, to file the report, I'd have to be at the scene, wouldn't I? How else would I know the car was gone?

But a stolen car wasn't the problem. When the cops found the biological specimens, the lab would run DNA tests in an attempt to identify the source, and the search would match Harriett Brennermann, a victim of The Cyanide Killer.

Tying him to the Vette would take only a registration search, or if the tags were missing, a search of the Corvette's Vehicle Identification Number. It wouldn't take long for them to tie him to the Vette, *and* the fluid samples. The cops would want to know what he was doing with state's evidence in his car, and why he broke the evidence chain.

Being the attending ME, there was a slight possibility he could concoct a valid reason to justify his possession of the specimens, but that was a low percentage play. He had to hope the fluids weren't in the car when the police found it...*if* they found it. Cars like that are more than just valuable. They're extremely rare, simply because they don't make them anymore, and for cars like his to just vanish without a trace was not unheard of.

Harvey stopped the cab on one of the few unlit streets in the community. It was just three blocks east of his mother's house. A breeze picked up signaling a cold front passing through, rustling leaves in the trees, and blowing bits of paper down the street.

Handing the cabbie two crisp twenties, Harvey climbed from the cab and allowed himself a bitter smile of frustration. He knew he was just fooling himself, delaying the inevitable. He had to report the car stolen at least by morning, and he had to be at work when he did—as if he discovered it missing at the end of his shift.

He considered telling the cabbie to return in an hour to pick him up, but then dismissed the thought as another stupid idea; *like carrying fluids in the Vette!* He'd have to call another cab. From a different company. Besides, he had other work to do before all that.

As he watched the cab's taillights disappear around the corner, he began walking the three blocks home, turning occasionally to see if anyone was around; anyone who could place him there at that exact time. He had to hurry. He needed to get to work. But first he had to get back to his garage and dispose of the rat poison.

CHAPTER 38

All was quiet in squad when the call reporting a dead girl in a bar came in from Anne Arundel County. It was 10:30pm, just when Truax and Vecchio were about to call it a day. The drive into Glen Burnie took 40-minutes.

Truax pulled the cruiser behind a county squad car that sat squarely in the right lane of Ritchie Highway, directly in front of The Governor's Tavern. The cops had run most everyone out, keeping them at bay on the front parking lot to preserve what they assumed to be a crime scene.

Throwing the shifter into Park, he split his attention between killing the engine and glancing toward Vecchio as she reached down for her purse. She sported a robin's egg colored blouse matching the pin striping in her java-brown suit—his favorite to date due to the shorter skirt.

"Why do you suppose they do that?" Vecchio asked, nodding to the sea of patrons adorned in purple Ravens jerseys.

Truax looked to the bar. "Do what?"

"Suck cigarette smoke into their lungs as if cancer existed only in the movies. Why would anyone choose to suffer a slow and painful death?"

Truax didn't answer.

Shifting gears, Vecchio said, "I feel overdressed. Maybe I should have worn jeans." Then she glanced at the jacket

Truax had on, one of the two he seemed to wear on a daily basis. Today it was the brown tweed. She grinned. "Shit. Anything I wear makes me overdressed compared to you."

"If you'd have gone home earlier like I told you," Truax mumbled as she sat back against the seat, "you could have. You don't have to work late, just because I do."

"If I didn't," she snapped, "I'd never complete my assignment! You tell me nothing of any worth and you know damn well you wouldn't have called me in on this, if I had."

Truax shrugged. "Eh...maybe. But it ain't my job to train you. That little privilege belongs to the Bureau."

Leaving the red and blue emergency beacons flashing, Truax swung open his door and then looked over to her. "So...you ready to take notes?"

Vecchio shrugged.

Truax climbed from the car and stretched out the kinks, surveying the area while Vecchio waited for him to take the lead. When he saw the county sergeant in charge of the scene, he nodded in his direction, and Vecchio followed him over.

Truax spotted a man sitting in the rear of the county police cruiser. He could see he was handcuffed. Folks tend to lean forward when their hands are shackled behind their backs.

"Detective Truax," the sergeant acknowledged.

"Sergeant Grisham, right?" Truax said.

"Yes Sir. Good memory."

"You'd think, wouldn't you? Whatcha got?"

"Caught him coming out of the bathroom where we found the victim" Grisham replied. "Looks like an overdose. Says he had nothin' to do with it and was just lookin'. Thought he could help."

"Help?" Truax asked. "Help do what?"

"Didn't say. Maybe he sold her the drugs. They like to hang in the stalls and snort that shit up their nose."

"Who is he?"

Grisham handed him the man's ID. "I figure we can charge him with disturbing a crime scene for starters. Probably more."

Truax read the name on the driver's license in the flashing emergency lights, and then returned his attention to Grisham.

"Do you read the papers, Sergeant?"

"No, Sir. Not much. Why do you ask?"

"No reason." Truax turned to Vecchio. "Frankie, why don't you check out the body? See if they've ID'ed her yet. I want to talk to this guy for a minute."

Vecchio raised an eyebrow. "Yeah, sure, Moby."

Walking to the car, Truax compared the vital statistics and photo to the man sitting cuffed in the back seat. Twenty-four years old, six-one, two-hundred pounds. After studying his face through the window, he opened the door.

"Mister Munroe?" he asked, leaning in. "Would you step from the car please?"

A county officer standing guard assisted Manny from the back seat without being asked, and then placed himself five strides distant, but retained a wary posture.

"Mister Munroe, I'm Detective Truax, SIU Division, Maryland State Police. Would you care to tell me why these officers found you with the victim?"

"I was in the area. Heard the call on the scanner for a 10-100. Decided to follow up on the story."

Truax watched Munroe's body language carefully as he answered, looking for the little signs that would attest to his honesty, or lack thereof. So far, he believed him, but then again, he hadn't said all that much yet.

He recognized the name on the driver's license, remembering the byline on the CK article in the morning paper; the same article that had Atkins chewing his ass out. He began inspecting his fingernails. It was a misdirection technique he liked to use during questioning. It had a way of lulling a suspect into a false believe that he wasn't really paying attention.

Without looking up, Truax asked, "Why don't you tell me what happened. How you came to be with a dead woman."

Munroe twisted his wrists in the cuffs. "Any chance you can let me outta these things?"

"No."

Munroe grimaced, then began talking.

"I'm a reporter."

"I know who you are."

"Oh..." A half smile. "OK, so as I said, I heard the call on the scanner. I was just a few minutes away and drove over. Beat the cops. I know the neighborhood. I know the bar. My ol' man taught me to shoot pool here when I was a kid. He was friends with the owner—Oscar. When I heard the call, I thought I'd check it out."

"That's all well an' good," Truax said, shifting to another fingernail, "but that doesn't tell me why you were in with the dead woman."

"Well, I was getting to that. A crowd was gathered at the front door and three bouncers blocked the entrance— nobody in, nobody out. Since the cops weren't here yet, I thought I'd get as much information as I could, before they blocked my access. I remembered a door in the back. They weren't blocking it, so I used it.

"I heard sirens and knew I only had a couple of minutes. Once the cops got here, they'd lock the place down and question everyone they found inside. I figured they couldn't know I wasn't there to begin with, and that they'd hold me for questioning. Then, all I had to do was listen.

"Mister Monroe, you are trying my patience. Get to the point."

"OK. OK...I squeeze past a group of women clustered around the women's restroom door. They were pointing and gesturing at something inside, so I stuck my head in. I saw a woman on the floor. A redhead. She wasn't moving. I thought maybe she might still be alive...those rednecks in that bar wouldn't know a pulse if it sprayed all over them."

"I don't need the conjecture," Truax mumbled. "Keep going."

"Yeah...so when I stepped inside to see if she was alive, I saw a white powdery substance around one nostril, and a short plastic straw on the floor. 'Doper,' I say to myself. Then I found the baggie with the coke. I figured she was an overdose—just another throw away junkie, and not the work of CK. Then the cops dragged me out and put me in chains. That's about it."

Truax looked at him as if expecting something more, but said nothing. Another ploy to keep him talking. Manny shifted his weight from one leg to the other and worked his shoulders.

"I didn't even touch her. And I didn't know the woman was dead until after I went in."

Truax held his hand up, spread his fingers, and examined his nails in the flashing lights of the nearby cruiser. "*After* you went in?"

"I wanted to see if I could help her, that's all."

"Do you know her?"

Manny answered without hesitation. "Never saw her before tonight."

"Your headlines have caused me a considerable amount of grief, Mister Munroe. Been getting a lot of flak from my boss."

"Detective, I do my job. Just as you do yours. I report what I hear. What I see. That's not a crime."

Field medical examiner Johnson chose that moment to emerge from the bar. Squeezing past several officers, he broke into a trot toward Truax, waving a hand above his head.

"Moby! Hey, Moby!"

Truax extended an arrow-straight index finger which projected to a point somewhere between Munroe's eyes. "Stay put," he said, and then turned to meet the field examiner.

"Johnson," Truax said in the way of a hello. "I didn't know you were here. Out drinkin' tonight?" he added with a wry grin.

"Yeah, Moby. I always drink heavily when the Ravens play. Calms my nerves."

Truax's grin widened. "So where's your van?"

"Parked around the side. Easier to get in from the back, and I can avoid this menagerie when wheeling the body out." He swept his arm in the direction of the front parking lot and its curiosity seekers.

"Makes sense to me. So, what you find out?"

"What did I find out? I found out that Vecchio looks better every time I see her. You have one smokin' hot partner there, buddy."

"Vecchio? You think she's hot?"

Johnson's eyes widened. "Shit! You *don't*? You *are* getting old."

"She's okay, I suppose, for a cross-eyed chick." Truax replied, his eyes cutting back to Munroe.

"Cross-eyed?" Johnson replied incredulously, his face contorted in exaggeration.

"OK OK!" Truax groused. "Forget Vecchio! What did you find out?"

Johnson said, "Well, at first glance, it looked like she OD'ed, but we found that the powder in the baggie and around her nose isn't cocaine. Its cyanide, so finely ground it looks like coke."

Truax drew a long breath, and deep lines furrowed his brow. "I can't catch a fucking break," he said under his breath. "You sure of this?"

Johnson shrugged, "As sure as I can be without lab testing, but I've seen enough of it lately, as have you. Check it out for yourself if you want to be sure. See what you think."

Truax knew Johnson was right. Johnson was *always* right. "No, that won't be necessary. Where's Vecchio?"

"Still inside getting statements from the women who found the body. Told me to tell you the victim has no ID on her person. No purse, no wallet, no license. Said all she had was a comb and a tube of pink lipstick. Looks like you're going to have to do this one the hard way."

"But of course! Why should things change now? Thanks Johnson. I'll meet you inside."

Truax made his way back to Munroe standing beside the cruiser. Stopping in front of him, he grinned. "So, you say you report what you hear. What you see. Correct?"

"That's right. Nothing more, nothing less."

"Well, how would you report what happened here tonight?"

"The girl overdosed. I wouldn't report it at all. Murder's my beat. Not suicide."

"She didn't OD."

Munroe's eyes widened and he straightened up, momentarily forgetting about the strain his back was experiencing. "She was murdered? That powder...It was cyanide? It was CK, wasn't it?"

"You see? There you go...jumping to conclusions. I don't like that. It's irresponsible. Irresponsible reporting gets people hurt."

"Irresponsible? What I report, I get from sources like you! Maybe *you're* the one who's irresponsible, Detective!"

"You didn't get your sensationalist CK headlines from *me*! We don't know for sure if it's CK, but now that you've put that scenario out there, reported information without merit, we have to compensate for it, work around it. I thought you people were supposed to verify your information.

"So, since I have nothing else at the moment, I'm holding you on suspicion of murder. You were seen walking out of the restroom where we found the girl's body. Preliminary findings from forensics say the powder she snorted is cyanide. As far as I'm concerned, that makes *you* suspect #1; first in line...to be the Cyanide Killer."

Even under the flashing red and blue lights, Truax thought he saw the color drain from Munroe's face. He motioned for the county officer standing guard to put Munroe back in the cruiser, and then turned toward the bar, concealing a smile as Munroe wrestled with the panic that gripped him.

"I had nothing to DO with this!" Munroe wailed, twisting and turning under the officer's vise-like grip. Raising his voice, he shrieked ever louder in an effort to reach the retreating detective.

"I didn't kill her! Ya *HEAR* TRUAX? I *FOUND* HER LIKE THAT!"

CHAPTER 39

The downpour slowed within a short fifteen minutes, eased to a fine mist, and then stopped all together, turning the city streets into slick ribbons of polished asphalt. Harvey climbed from the cab just west of the Inner Harbor, right where the Baltimore-Washington Parkway became South Paca Street; a walkable three blocks to OCME.

Reaching through the open passenger window, he handed the driver a pair of twenties and told him to keep the change. It wasn't much of a tip, just five dollars and a few coins. The cab pulled away and Harvey began walking west toward OCME, stopping at the first storm drain he encountered.

Insuring no prying eyes were on him, he removed the box of rat poison from home and poured the contents into the rushing torrent at the bottom of the sewer. He followed that with the container that would find its way to the Patapsco River, and end its journey at the point where the Jones Falls dumped into the Inner Harbor. There, it would mix with the rest of the garbage floating in the murky basin.

The following day a flat-bottomed trash skimmer would make its rounds, and patrol the waters of the harbor. Its conveyor system would scoop up the trash and debris deposited there by the storm, thereby solving one of his problems. As much as he hated rain, tonight, he thought it a blessing.

Harvey made short work of the three city blocks lying between him and his job, jogging the entire way. It wasn't until he reached the front door and focused on catching his breath, that another problem surfaced. His OCME access badge—It was in the Vette.

He pressed the afterhours call button mounted next to the front door, and a voice came over the speaker.

"Guard's Desk."

"Officer Bowers?"

"Yes?"

"This is Doctor Morral. I forgot my badge. Can you buzz me in please?"

Bowers buzzed the door and Harvey stepped in, explaining and apologizing the whole time for his absent-mindedness in leaving his badge at home.

"No problem, Doc," Bower's said. "Guys here always forget their badges. Let me assign you a temporary."

Bowers pulled out a brown clipboard. Attached to it were faded Xerox log sheets and a white photo-less badge that was a bit larger than a credit card. OCME UN-ESCORTED blared across the front in red. As Bowers filled out the log, he glanced up at Harvey.

"Sorry, Doc, but this won't get you into the garage."

"What?"

"This badge," Bowers repeated. "It won't get you into the underground garage. I can have the doors opened for you if you want. I know how you love that car."

It dawned on Harvey what Bowers was saying, and at the same time an alibi presented itself. If he were to report the Vette stolen in the morning, it *had* to be on the street. There was no way someone could steal it from the secure parking area.

"Oh! Oh, thank you, Officer Bowers, but right now, I have to get to the lab. I'll come back at lunchtime and pull it around."

"Suit yourself, Doc," Bowers cautioned. "I know if it was mine, I wouldn't even bring it into the city. Not around here, anyways."

Harvey nodded and started for the lab, temporary badge in hand. His luck was changing. Now, if questioned, he knew Bowers would verify his story as to why he left such an exotic car on the street. And all he had to say was that he got busy, and simply forgot about moving it.

His alibi was completely believable. It wouldn't be a stretch to believe he forgot about his car; mothers leave their children in hot cars every summer. As far as his badge goes, he could always amend his statement to say he must have lost his badge, and that he only *thought* he'd left it at home.

CHAPTER 40

Truax stepped into The Governor's Tavern, and the stench of stale cigarette smoke hit him.

There was a difference, he noted, between the smell of cigarettes, and the smell of *stale* cigarettes, and figured that this is what his clothes must have smelled like when he smoked. Ten feet further in, the stink of vomit and urine followed, and he wondered how anyone could drink in a place like this.

He spotted Johnson in the back-right corner by the women's restroom waving him over. Vecchio was on the far left side of the room, past the pool tables, questioning a group of women. She held no pen or paper and Truax shook his head, recalling when he could interview multiple witnesses without taking notes. He simply remembered everything they said.

When Truax joined him in front of the restroom, Johnson turned and let Truax pass. Forensics had yet to collect the baggie containing the powder, or take samples from around the girl's nostril. He squatted down next to the body, careful not to let his knee touch whatever fluids had pooled on the floor.

Pushing back the smell of piss, he sniffed around the girl's face. Even with the pervasive stench of urine, the faint but unmistakable aroma of almonds met his olfactory system. He knew right away that this was not CK's work. It was simply all wrong, and as much as he'd like to hang this on the newspaper reporter sitting in the squad car, he knew it wasn't his doing either. *But, it can't hurt to teach the little bastard the consequences of creative journalism*, he thought.

"Okay, Johnson," Truax said, exiting the restroom. "She's all yours."

As Johnson's team removed the body, Truax leaned back against the wall. He studied Vecchio from across the room, watching as she conducted her interviews.

'Give her a chance,' Donahue had said to him. So that's what he would do. Giving her her head to conduct her own interviews tonight would give her that chance. But he wouldn't make it easy for her, because watching her brought back memories of when he was a rookie, just like her; full of piss & vinegar, mistakes, and a photographic memory.

But credit where credit is due, he thought. *So far tonight, she was right about one thing.*

She is overdressed.

Truax and Vecchio stepped out of The Governor's Tavern to find the ground glistening from a recent rain. A fast moving squall line had passed over while they were in the bar, and now, a following breeze cooled the night, rippling the puddles reflecting the blue and red beacons from the police cruisers. The air had been scrubbed pure by the rain, and the fresh clean smell returned Truax to his childhood.

Summer storms, he thought, noting the southbound clouds. *Come outta nowhere.*

Vecchio took off her jacket and shook it out like a blanket. "My clothes probably stink of cigarettes, now," she mumbled, then turned to Truax. "You aren't really going to do what I think you're going to do," she said, climbing into the car. "I mean, he could sue you! The newspaper could sue you for crap's sake! And the department!"

Truax twisted the ignition key and started the Crown Vic's motor. "Why would the *department* sue me?"

"You know what I mean, Moby."

"Can't sue the department," he said. "It's government. Government's got immunity."

"Well, Moby," Vecchio said, shifting in her seat and crossing her legs. "He can still sue *you!*"

"Won't do that either," he replied, shifting his eyes to pull into traffic, what little there was at 1:30 in the morning. "He'll be too busy defending himself."

"Oh come *on!*" Vecchio exclaimed, emphasizing her astonishment with Italian hand-speak. "You don't really believe he's the Cyanide Killer...*or* your CK wanna-be."

"Don't matter what I believe, at least according to Atkins. This is the first real break in this case. Besides, I'm in such deep shit, I have to handle everything strictly by the book. No judgment calls. If I cut this guy loose and he turns out to be a bad guy, it's my ass. Atkins'll make sure I'm walking the unemployment line within 24 hours."

"Okay... So we waste time interrogating him, checking him out, verifying his alibis and whereabouts, and then toss his place, and when we're finished with all that and find nothing, we won't be any closer to the killer than we were before."

"Killers, Frankie. Plural."

"All the more reason not to waste time, and from what I saw in there tonight, we could be dealing with yet *another* copycat. Did you see how sloppy this was? Not like any of the previous murders."

"Of course I saw. But I'm not jumping to conclusions like you. And I'm certainly not going to suggest a *third* killer to Atkins. He'll have my badge on the spot. You keep that little twist to yourself until we see what the lab sends back. Savvy?"

CHAPTER 41

Harvey meandered about the lab as he awaited the redhead, his agitation level high. He considered his options, limited as they were. He couldn't clear the jumbled disjointed scenarios that bobbed and weaved in his mind, appearing and disappearing at random; images of flight and pursuit, imprisonment and sodomy—and suicide; specters of undesirable ends, rendered suddenly unimportant the moment the redhead arrived.

Jane Doe was the name on the toe tag. Harvey thought it an appropriate name for a beautiful woman unknown. He hadn't cared enough to ask her name while they were in bar, so why should he care now. All that mattered to Harvey was the probability of never again having the women he desired; the women his *Need* desired.

Her prompt arrival allowed him ample time to have her in every possible way, and the fantasy images his mind conjured up, images of her final moments snorting powdered death, turned his lust animalistic...brutal.

Visions of her pleading for help in an empty room pushed his lust past anything he'd ever experienced. He wanted to hurt her. He didn't know why and he didn't care. He was the last man she would ever have and he wanted her to know it—dead notwithstanding.

Sealing her in the refrigeration unit ended Harvey's time with her. It was an encounter he would remember, hopefully not from a prison cell. His Need satisfied, he turned his attention to the problem at hand.

In his haste to dispose of the rat poison, he neglected to remove his final set of CK specimens from the garage. Now, he had no choice but to send the redhead's specimens to Tox. If Forensics managed to collect samples of the powder from the bathroom, they would match the toxin in her blood, and Tox would include it on their reports. If that happened, he wouldn't be able to hide in CK's shadow.

That was bad in itself, but nothing about that pointed directly to him. Since he cleaned up the redhead when he was done with her, there would be no markers leading back to him. The real problem was the Vette, and the CK specimens it contained.

Walking back to his desk, he steeled himself for the phone call he had to make. The Play was about to begin. The curtain was coming up and the Players were in place. He lifted the phone and pressed the three famous numbers.

"Baltimore City 9-1-1," the female voice said. "What is your emergency?"

"Yes ma'am," Harvey said. "I want to report a stolen car."

Wispy clouds from the earlier storm drifted across the city skyline. Water vapor in the air became a prism and separated the early light, painting a vivid rainbow across a blue sky—a gift for a city waking to a new day.

The flow of traffic had picked up, signaling the onset of the morning rush hour, and as Harvey fished his Marlboros from his lab coat, he tracked a red 2009 Corvette as it made its way down Pratt. It reminded him that his odds of remaining a free man would be considered a long shot at Pimlico.

The Law of Unintended Consequences, he thought, lighting a cigarette. With all his care and all his preparation, the possibility of having his car stolen never presented itself.

Leaving his ID in the car wasn't a big deal. People leave their work IDs in their cars all the time. But the fluid vials pointed directly to him. If the cops recover the car, they will find the vials, and if that happens, it'll just be a matter of time.

His only chance is if the vials are not in the car. A slim possibility remained that the thieves would have discarded them, but he'd be a fool to hang his hopes on that. Odds are good he'll know either way. If the car is recovered and he gets a phone call, the vials probably weren't in the car. But if the cops show up at his door...

Expelling a thin line of smoke, he watched it swirl away before turning his attention to the corner of Penn and Pratt, and the arrival of the Baltimore City squad car he'd called ten minutes earlier. Because the theft occurred at a government building, they dispatched a car immediately.

"So, Doctor Morral," the officer said, reading back the information as he filled out his report. "A fire-engine red, 1965 Corvette Stingray Fastback. Mint-condition, right?"

"That's exactly right, Officer. I came out to smoke a cigarette and the car just wasn't here."

"What time was that?"

"Less than an hour ago. Just a little before I reported it stolen. Maybe thirty, thirty-five minutes ago. Do you think you can recover it?"

The officer glanced at his partner. The man had yet to utter a word, but grinned a grin that said the car was toast.

"Doctor Morral. From the look of it, these guys were pros. No broken window glass on the ground or marks of any kind. Not even tire marks. They might have used a Slim-Jim and hotwired it, not hard to do on older cars like yours. Or they may have just dragged it onto a flatbed and drove it away. Would take guys like this no more than one, maybe two minutes tops."

"So, what are you telling me?"

"Usually, one of two things happens to cars like yours. They're either disassembled at a chop shop—big money in parts for classics—or they're sold overseas. Rolled into a cargo container and shipped to some Middle-Eastern country. The Sheiks love classic American sports cars. Pay over a hundred grand for 'em. It's not like they ain't got the money."

For this part of his performance, Harvey did his best to appear disappointed with the less-than-optimistic outlook put forth by the officer. But the cop was still filling out his report, and the practiced expression of despondency Harvey had worked on in the locker-room mirror, went unnoticed. Now, what he earlier thought to be a roadmap leading the police directly to him, became nothing more than undue concern.

"You insured it, didn't you?" the cop asked.

"What? Oh... Insured. Yes. Of course."

The cop handed the clipboard to Harvey. "Please sign here Doctor Morral. Bottom copy's yours. Well, you should be all right then. At least you'll get most of your money back, but I gotta ask—why didn't you park it in the secure garage?"

CHAPTER 42

It had taken more than three days to ID the Jane Doe from The Governor's Tavern, and Truax stumbled around his kitchen wondering why it was, that getting information from a sister department took so freaking long.

The lab's excuse was that her prints were lost in the FOIS system, that it had taken days before they ID'ed her as Anya Eiffel, a career junkie who lived in a rented room in a rundown two-story row-home in Curtis Bay; a less than desirable place to live, but a great place to do business should you be a pimp, a hooker, or a crack dealer.

With the exception of the time it took to carry the widow Ida's groceries into her house, and the added few minutes he took to talk his way out of a cup of tea, he had spent most of Wednesday—yesterday—running background checks on Anya and the people she associated with.

Anya was in the system, and a visit to her probation officer Wednesday morning had turned up mostly small-time stuff: possession and solicitation and the like. And out of the hundreds of probationary cases Anya's PO handled, he had little difficulty remembering her.

"Anya Eiffel," he said to Truax, a broad grin overcoming his jowled face, "Oh yeah... I know her. Every male PO in the office knows her. A couple of 'em said they'd pay me to transfer her case to them. Some shit, huh?" He leaned in and lowered his voice to a whisper, as if he thought a hidden microphone was nearby. Truax could smell the booze through the mouthwash.

"Around here, we call her Anya Eye-Full. You know why, right? You got a look at her. I bet she looked better dead than most women do alive. Am I right? Or am I right!" Resuming his normal voice, he said, "She did a little time, and was out on probation with the condition she attend drug rehab classes, which she didn't."

The PO leaned in again and this time Truax leaned away. He didn't want the aroma of bourbon to seep into his clothes so early in the morning. "She knew she could get away with it. Knew I wouldn't violate her probation because…well, just because. She had a way about her, ya know? A real special way."

He grinned again, in much the same disgusting way he did before. "Too bad she OD'ed," he said, returning his voice to normal. "She could have done so much more with her life than piss it away giving head for a couple of bumps."

Or for her Probation Officer looking the other way, Truax thought.

By the time Truax walked out of The Division of Parole and Probation, he wanted to arrest Anya's PO for something. Anything. The man was a pig.

Truax spent late Wednesday morning into the afternoon interviewing witnesses from The Governor's Tavern, rechecking their accounts based on the notes Vecchio had typed up. Everything jived, and everything resulted in another dead end.

The one uncertainty they could clear up was that Manny Munroe, as Vecchio had said, was not the Cyanide Killer. Truax sent Vecchio, warrant in hand, to follow up on Munroe and toss his apartment. Truax didn't really believe Munroe was a killer, but he had to dot every "i" to keep

Atkins at bay until CK, or his imitator, or both, made a major mistake.

The way things were going, that seemed unlikely. Now, this last killing, Anya "Eye-Full," tossed yet another wrench into the works, and Vecchio had made it a point to mention that the murder was sloppy and unlike any of the CK credited murders to date, suggesting in her own annoying way, that there might actually be a second copycat mimicking CK.

He had to admit Vecchio could be right. There might actually be three killers, and the only upside he could see to that little development was that maybe the slayings would stop should any one of them be caught.

If that were to happen, a weasel like Atkins would hang all the killings on that one suspect whose guilt or innocence would be determined by how air-tight a case the state prosecutor could manage. But before that became a possibility, they had to catch at least one of them.

One out of three. His odds were improving.

Rubbing the sleep from his eyes, he made his way to the fridge and slugged down several gulps of diet soda, straight from the plastic 2-liter bottle. Squeezing the air out of before spinning the cap back on, he dropped the bottle into the door shelf and rummaged through several items of questionable age, looking for something appetizing to eat. He figured the run-down state of his energy reserves were due to low blood sugar, and some sort of food was in order.

He opened a plastic bag of deli ham, took a whiff, and tossed it in the trash. He was afraid to guess how long it had been there. All the bread was stale, the 1% milk didn't smell bad, but it didn't smell good either, and the last time he saw brown lettuce was the last time he had opened the crisper.

After tossing out everything that appeared abnormal, he picked up the phone to order a veggie pizza, then giving it a second thought, dropped it back on its hook. *McDonald's* he thought. *I'll pick up something on the way in.*

Once on the road, he thought he should call Vecchio to see if she wanted some dinner. Flipping open his cell, he heard the familiar tones of a discharged battery. Plugging it in to the mobile charger did nothing. The battery was gone, and with it, his cell. Now, if he was lucky, he could find a Verizon Wireless store somewhere close to a McDonald's...if, he was lucky.

CHAPTER 43

The enormous plate-glass windows on the west wall of the SIU Squad room focused the retreating sun like a magnifying glass, increasing the temperature of Vecchio's space by ten or so degrees. That's when it dawned on her why no one else wanted that desk. 6pm was brutal.

Pealing off her suit jacket, she kicked off her matching light-blue pumps and rubbed her feet together under the desk, working the muscles and pushing out the fatigue, before sliding up the cuffs of her slacks to do the same to her calves. It wasn't much of a massage, but it would do for the time being.

As she turned back to her monitor, the black and white display of Anya Eiffel's criminal record disappeared, and was replaced by the screensaver. She took it as a sign, some sort of lesser omen that urged her to make a decision. She was achy and tired, and upon glancing at the clock, wondered if she should wait for Truax, or just call it a day and go home.

Before making up her mind, she decided to call him. When his cell went directly to voice mail she hung up without leaving a message, and as she pulled on her shoes the phone on Truax's desk began to ring. *Another omen?*

Reaching across Truax's desk, she plucked the handset from its cradle.

"Detective Truax's desk, Special Agent Vecchio speaking."

"Vecchio? The FBI agent?" a man's voice said. "You're Truax's new partner, right?"

"Not to hear *him* tell it," she replied.

"Yeah… We heard all about you over here," the voice said. "'Bout time the Feds took some interest in this case."

"Who *is* this, please?" she asked.

"Oh! Sorry…this is Harry. Harry Browning. Down in Toxicology. Listen, I know Truax's case is hot, and normally I'd just email the tox reports to him, but the email server is down. Third time today. You'd think they could fix the damn thing. But I wanted to let him know that I'll be going home soon and thought he might want to come pick up a hard copy before I do."

Vecchio debated braving the downtown rush hour for a report they would certainly have first thing in the morning, if not later tonight, assuming the email system came back online.

"Normally," she said, "I'm sure he would, but he's not here and he's not answering his cell, so I'd have to say let it wait till tomorrow."

"Tomorrow? Fridays can get pretty busy around here, Agent Vecchio, but suit yourself. And for the record, I think he should know that there are significant differences in the samples from this victim...ah—Anya Eiffel...as compared to the other cyanide poisonings."

"Hold on," she said. Stretching the phone at arm's length and extending its cord to the limit, she walked around the two desks to Truax's chair, and eased herself down.

"Significant how?"

"Well, the cyanide the killer used in the Eiffel murder is nothing more than your run-of-the-mill rat poison. Not like the pure industrial grade stuff we found in the others.

218

Cyanide hasn't been used in rat poison since the early '80's. Not since the Tylenol poisonings, so this stuff is pretty old."

"Do you know the concentrations?" Vecchio asked.

"Yeah. It's more than triple what was used in the other victims. Enough to kill a horse. And there's something else you guys might want to look into."

"What's that?"

"Well, one of the supervisors from the Ordinance Road Correctional Facility swung through here last Tuesday afternoon. I thought that kinda odd. Those guys never come here. Said they were running a clean-up crew down on Ritchie Highway and one of the inmates, a brownnoser trying to chop time for good behavior, found something unusual—a paper sack with glass vials in it. Human fluids, just like the samples pathology sends over. Two vials were broken, but the other two were intact, and contained blood and vitreous humor. Eye fluid."

Vecchio leaned forward toward the phone. "These vials. You say they come from pathology? Like the type OCME uses? Did you test the fluids?"

"No, these vials were different than the ones OCME uses, but anyone can get something similar from any drug store. And yes, we did test the fluids. Both samples contain cyanide of an amount consistent with the CK poisonings. And, the cyanide was an exact chemical match."

Vecchio bolted up arrow straight, her mind now fully engaged.

"Prints?"

"Sorry...no."

"Okay. You say they found this on Tuesday? On Ritchie Highway? *Where* on Ritchie Highway?"

"Where?" he asked. "They found the sack in the grass median...about four blocks north of The Governor's

Tavern. The bar where your latest victim was murdered. Interesting...don't you think? Agent Vecchio?"

"Yes, Harry. *Very* interesting. And as far as the tox report on Eiffel, I think Detective Truax would like to have it ASAP, so I'm going to leave now and come pick it up."

"When will you be here?"

"Forty-five minutes. Maybe a little longer."

"I'll wait," Browning said.

"One last thing, Harry," Vecchio added, picking up the solitary pencil on Truax's desk, "You didn't happen to run DNA tests...on those fluids, I mean."

"As a matter of fact," Harry replied, "we sent samples to the FBI DNA lab in Jersey when they came in. It's standard procedure for unknown biological human samples. Don't have the results back yet, though."

"When do you think you'll get the results, Harry?" she said, tapping the pencil's point against the desk blotter.

"Well, it's almost 6:25," Browning said. "Tell you what, Agent Vecchio. An old college bud of mine runs the swing shift over there. He should be on by now. Let me give him a call while you're on your way over. Maybe he can shed some light."

Vecchio started for the door, and ran into Nichols.

"Agent Vecchio..."

"Detective."

Nichols looked around Squad. "I don't see Truax. You here alone?"

"So far. He's not here and he's not answering his cell, so I'm going home."

"Only an old codger like him would leave a woman like you, alone."

Vecchio smiled.

"So," Nichols continued. "I see that CK struck again. Some dive in Glen Burnie. You and Truax were there. I'd say he was wrong about CK hitting Billy's again."

"Excellent deduction, Detective Nichols. I'd have to agree with you."

Nichols beamed.

"But nobody's right about everything, and in this case, Truax was wrong. But, he got lucky. Caught a suspect in with the dead girl. Arrested him on suspicion."

"I heard. But what do *you* think, Agent?"

"What do *I* think? I'm just out here comparing notes. And like Detective Truax reminds me on a regular basis—it doesn't *matter* what I think."

"Yeah. That sounds like something he would say. But you don't really think CK would let himself be caught with one of his victims, do you?"

"Good point! No. I don't! Plus the guy Truax arrested is a local guy. Truax says Atkins is always up his butt and he had to arrest somebody. Since the guy was caught with the body, that was good enough for him. But between you and me? I think he's going off the deep end here. I don't have a lot of confidence the suspect has ever even been to San Diego, or that he ever killed anyone. But I'm going to chase that down first thing tomorrow."

"Let me save you the trouble. I'll run it down, Frances. May I call you Frances?"

Vecchio nodded, and then loosed a dazzling smile.

"Good. Feels less formal this way. So, since you don't believe the suspect in custody to be CK, what *do* you think?"

Vecchio stepped toward Nichols, close enough for him to smell her perfume, feel the warmth her body threw off. She saw him flush.

"I think CK is trying to throw us off. This one was a diversion to keep us busy, nothing more." She shifted her hips and leaned in a bit, drawing Nichols closer. "I just got a call from Forensics," she whispered. "It came to Truax's phone, but he's not here. So I answered it. I spoke with some guy named...shit, I forgot his name."

"Walters? Browning?"

"I don't remember."

"I thought you had a photographic memory, Frances."

"For faces, places, events—but not for names or numbers. For some reason, they don't stick. I'm sorry."

"Eh, there aren't that many lab techs across the three shifts. I'll find out who called. So what did he tell you?"

"He said that Jane Doe—the dead girl in the Glen Burnie bathroom—was a junkie. But this time she snorted cyanide and killed herself."

"That's a change in CK's MO, but Jane Doe? You haven't ID'ed her yet?"

"Jane Doe number...something. Oh, I should have written that down. Anyway, Truax said that there was some kind of foul up last week and Latent lost her prints. Had to take another set, but they can't seem to locate the body. The ME has sent it on, already."

"Fuckin' great!" Nichols mumbled. Then he realized what he had said.

"Oh...I'm so sorry. It just slipped out."

Vecchio smiled her most delicious smile. "Don't fuckin' worry about it, Detective."

Nichols's grin spread from ear to ear.

"I knew I'd like you," he said, "but do you know how many J. Does we get here a week?"

"No. Sorry, I don't."

"Dozens! It will take me days— maybe weeks—to go through them all to find the one from the Glen Burnie bar."

"Yes," Vecchio said, letting the sex appeal work, "but isn't that what *good* cops do?"

CHAPTER 44

Forensics was located in the same building as the pathology lab, their adjacent locations making the evidence chain easier to manage.

Vecchio parked her Celica on OCME's street-level parking lot at exactly 7:05pm, forty minutes after talking to Browning, and half-trotted around to the front the building. Producing her credentials at the front desk, the swing-shift guard stole an admiring glance and directed her back to the forensics lab.

"I'll let him know you're on your way, Agent Vecchio."

Three minutes later, Vecchio walked into the forensics division.

"You've got to be Agent Vecchio," Browning said, looking her up and down, and pushing his oily brown hair back across the top of his head. "Harry Browning," he continued, and extended his hand.

From the way he looked at her, Vecchio figured he was either unaware of his leering, or indifferent to it. The man was a pervert, no doubt, but it was no matter. She'd play on his perversions to get what she wanted. It was something she was especially good at.

Accepting his outstretched hand, she found his a clingy, limp-wristed handshake, clammy and wet, as if he'd been perpetually nervous his whole life, and while he seemed eager to prolong the ritual, she couldn't release quickly enough.

She resisted the urge to wipe her palm on her slacks as she followed the overweight Browning through a double door, into the well-lit 20 X 30 lab, wondering all the while how long it would take before he broke into an outward sweat, caused by overexertion.

The air was cooler in the lab than in the hallway, and the clicking of her heels against the brick-red floor ricocheted off the white ceramic walls as she trod along behind the heavy-breathing Browning.

The lab was pretty much as she expected. Several wood-finished laminate counters measuring ten feet or more, each with a plethora of drawers and cabinets, and each topped off with a black resin countertop bristling with stainless-steel sinks, gooseneck faucets, and overhead storage.

What caught her eye were the smaller worktables with their matching roll-about chairs. They sat clustered together in groups, boasting state-of-the-art spectrometers and microscopes, computer and gas chromatography systems, and other specialized equipment whose purpose at which, she could only guess.

Browning finally led her into his shoebox of an office, and she watched as he squeezed his rotund girth between a beige cinder-block wall, and a tiny gray desk, ultimately planting himself in the chair tucked behind it before offering her a seat. She declined.

"I don't have a lot of time, Harry. Whatcha got?"

"Yes, of course," he said, glimpsing the area below her shoulders. "The reports." He slid a manila envelope across the top of his desk. "These are the tox and autopsy reports on Eiffel. They don't even come close to the MO of the Cyanide Killer. The poison is half the potency, three times the dosage, and nothing more than rat poison. Nowhere as pure as the stuff used on the other victims."

"Yes, you said on the phone." Vecchio picked up the folder. "Did you get in touch with your friend?"

Browning smiled. "You must have the luck of the Irish, Agent Vecchio. Not only did I catch him, but his lab is running ahead of schedule. He had the results from the vials, but I think maybe they rushed this one."

Vecchio frowned and shifted her weight to the other leg. Browning's eyes fell to her hips. "What do you mean, 'rushed'?" she asked.

"I mean rushed. As in not careful. Screwed up. Do you remember about a year ago? That DNA lab out west. The one that mixed—"

"Screwed up how, Harry?"

"The biological evidence from the vials found on the side of the road matched a CODIS control sample belonging to one of CK's victims. The second one. But that can't be possible. It has to be a mistake."

It was a long time before Vecchio spoke. Her dark brown eyes stared straight through him causing him to shift in his seat. When she did finally speak, she left no doubt as to how he should answer. She would tolerate no verbal mischief.

"Name," she said evenly. "Give me the name."

"The name? Brennermann... The DNA fingerprints matched the fluids to sixty-seven year old Harriett Brennermann. CK victim #2."

With Browning's revelation, Vecchio decided to accept the chair he had offered and began thumbing through the autopsy and toxicology reports on Anya Eiffel. Just as Browning had said, the cyanide that killed her was of an inferior grade compared to that of the other victims. But that wasn't what concerned her.

Eiffel's murder lacked all the earmarks of CK, and since Truax believed there was a second killer, she decided to reverse her stand and support his two-killer theory. By encouraging his belief of a second killer, she could distract him from what she had to do; that being, identify the source of the discarded vials containing the Brennermann specimens.

She cautioned Browning not to mention the vials to anyone, saying she didn't want him to inadvertently tip their hand. Then, she asked if the discarded fluids matched any other samples in the CODIS database, besides Harriett Brennermann.

Browning's expression became one of mirthful surprise. She wasn't sure if she had caught him off guard, or if he thought it a stupid question.

"What would be the point?" he replied. "There would be no need to continue a comparative search. Nuclear DNA is quite unique. It can only belong to a single biological organism. They would have stopped searching on the first match, since it would have been the *only* match."

Vecchio closed the folder with the reports, and stuffed it into her valise. Browning continued to reiterate the point of a possible lab mistake. He pointed out that stumbling across fluids, preserved in vials and matching such an old case, was damn unusual if not near impossible, given the chain of evidence. He insisted that there had to be a foul up in the DNA lab. That, or someone had intentionally kept samples of Harriett Brennermann's bodily fluids, which was utterly ridiculous. There were rules against outside testing of evidence, unless specifically authorized.

Vecchio offered him a flirtatious smile and agreed there must be a foul up, then asked if he could run the samples against the other victims of the CK killings, just to see if there were any more mistakes.

"I just told you," Browning said. "I'd need authorization."

"But you ran the samples initially," Vecchio countered without conviction.

"Unknown biological human samples. Standard procedure. Remember? I told you that! For identification purposes." Browning's friendly, cooperative, tone had become suddenly condescending, signaling a loss of sexual interest in her.

If this had involved anything else, she'd tell him where to stick it, but she required his expertise and had to nip his belligerence in the bud. She needed information, so she had to keep any fantasy he might have of bedding her down, alive for him. But more importantly, she needed him to keep his mouth shut.

"Okay, Harry," she said, a seductive quality easing into her voice. "I don't mean to seem dense, and you've been wonderful, explaining these things to me. I'm not used to working with someone as well informed as you. Your department is lucky to have you." She finished off the sentence with a smile that would place a torrid fantasy in any man's mind.

"So you need authorization," Vecchio continued, confident that she had his mind on other things. "Authorization from whom?"

Browning rolled his head, cracking the cartilage in his neck as one might crack their knuckles. "The lead detective can authorize the search," he said. "Truax in this case. Or the captain. Or higher. Those tests are expensive. Running comparisons takes time. Lots of it, labor wise. Unless there's a case, or a burning reason, they won't waste the money."

"But I only want to compare this DNA against just a few people," Vecchio said, making her voice as weak and vulnerable as she could, without sounding whiny.

Browning smiled. "I wish I could, Frances. But I have to have authorization. Why don't you give me a couple of days? Let me see what I can do. Maybe we can discuss it over drinks. And I hope you don't mind me saying...I really like that blouse on you."

In the parking lot outside of the Chief Medical Examiner's Office, Vecchio sat in her Celica and took a moment.

Her head lay against the headrest as her body absorbed the dry heat. As the air conditioner struggled to compensate, she wondered how the inside of a car could heat up so fast when the sun was going down.

Maybe it wasn't the heat, she mused. *Maybe it really was the humidity.*

Dabbing her forehead with an unused napkin from some fast food chain, she pulled her cell from her purse, pressed a speed-dial button, and listened to the electronic ringing from the other end.

She knew Browning couldn't do anything for her. If he could, he would have blurted it out right then and there. When it came right down to it, he was just a little man in a little job, doing his best to impress the prom queen. He didn't have the chops, and even though Truax could give the authorization to run the DNA comparisons against the other cyanide victims, she didn't want to reveal this latest development to him just yet.

She would tell him when she wanted him to know. Besides, it's not as if he would help her for help's sake. Getting him to do anything for her was like pulling teeth. He wasn't one to listen to anything a "rookie" had to say, and he had made that abundantly clear, while proving himself immune to her feminine charms. Something to which she was not accustomed.

The ringing of the phone she had dialed stopped abruptly and a man's voice took its place. The voice sounded pleased.

"Hello, Frances," Atkins said, his words light, and dancing from his lips. "I was hoping I'd hear from you."

Vecchio reached over and turned the knob on the Celica's air conditioner down to quiet the rush of air. "I hate to bother you Don, but I was hoping you might be able to cut through some red tape for me."

There was a slight gap before he spoke. "Sure, Frances."

Vecchio detected disappointment in his voice, as if she had dashed his expectations when she started in talking business, and avoiding the familiarity he'd come to look forward to during their easy phone conversations.

"To what red tape are you referring?" he continued.

Vecchio realized she had to be careful now. Breaking from the behavior he had come to expect was a thoughtless move on her part. She had to get him back where she wanted him emotionally, and while keeping Truax in the dark about the Ritchie Highway fluid vials was critical, keeping it from Atkins was even more so.

"I need a DNA comparison against the known Cyanide Killer's victims," she said. "Seems there is some inconsistency between the latest specimens and at least one CODUS control sample belonging to a cyanide victim. When I asked the tech...Browning I think his name was...to run the latest samples against the other CK victims, he said he needed authorization. Do you know who can do that? Provide the authorization?"

"Yeah. Sure," Atkins replied flatly. "Truax can do that. Why the hell didn't he just tell Browning to run the comparisons? Send the paperwork in the rears."

Vecchio paused for dramatic effect, laying her head back against the headrest, allowing herself a bit of a smile. "Well, that's just it, Don. Detective Truax doesn't know I want the DNA tests."

"What?" Atkins blurted. "Why doesn't he?"

Vecchio expelled a resigned sigh into the cell's mouthpiece, drawing it out for Atkins's benefit. "He doesn't know, Don, because I didn't tell him. This is my idea."

"*Your* idea?"

His admonishment was exactly what she hoped for. She inserted a tiny catch before speaking, spacing it out just enough to be recognized for what it was: A woman whose feelings had just been crushed. "I...I'm sorry, Captain. Did...did I do something wrong? I'm only trying..."

"Frances," he said softly, "I'm so sorry. That wasn't supposed to sound judgmental." He took a moment and then continued. "I admire your initiative, but why haven't you run it by Truax?"

Vecchio took care to insert the appropriate amount of anguish into her voice, using his misperception to her full advantage. She closed her eyes, and pressed back hard into the seat, visualizing despondency.

"He can be such a *bastard*!" she wailed. Letting her voice crack, she added just a touch of hysteria, as if she had just caught her boyfriend fucking the girl next door. She took a second for effect, letting slip a sob here and there, and then blurted out, "I just want to test a theory! That's all! I *told* him! He didn't want to hear it! Just rejected it off-hand. He never listens to *anything* I have to say!" Vecchio let the words hang in the air for two breaths, letting the silence work for her, and then softly added, "He's obsessed with the idea of a copycat."

"Okay, Frances. Okay," Atkins said, mustering a comforting tone. "I was afraid this might happen. I've been concerned about Truax for weeks, and I think it's time I gave serious consideration to putting him behind a desk. Now, please settle down and tell me the name of the tech you spoke with again."

CHAPTER 45

The lighting in the Back Woods Restaurant's lounge was subdued, and the snobby Severna Park crowd, upscale and well dressed. Harvey found it far and apart from The Governor's Tavern, and completely unexpected, being tucked in the backend of a shopping center.

The Oriole's game played silently on the Hi-Def TV mounted over the small inline bar, and Closed-Captioning relayed the play-by-play, while a lone entertainer played an acoustic version of *Layla* from a portable stage near the front picture window.

The bartender looked to be about twenty-three, and to say she was pretty would do her a disservice. Standing eye to eye, Harvey thought her a shade over a hundred-and-twenty, and from the way her baby-blue top protruded in his direction, he could imagine a nice set of tits as well.

The waistband of her denim shorts surrounded her bare waist with inches to spare, and her slender legs were as equally tanned as the rest of her, suggesting that she used a salon. Harvey tried not to leer as she brushed sandy brown hair from chocolate-brown eyes.

"What'll it be?" she asked.

"Lite beer," he replied. "Any kind. Bottle." He wiped the corner of his mouth with the back of his hand.

"Well, we have Miller, Bud, Heineken—"

"Miller. Miller is fine."

"Amstel, Michelob... I'm still learning. You don't mind if I practice on you, do you?" She loosed a dazzling smile and he faltered.

"No...no, not...not at all. I'll take whatever's handy."

"Okay," she said, perkier than the law should allow. "Miller it is."

He watched her ass all the way to the cooler with the intensity of a man who would do anything for her, or anything *to* her. The events from earlier that week allowed him to entertain thoughts for either, only because of an encouraging phone call from the Vehicle Theft Division.

Officer Horn's call from two days ago came as a welcomed surprise, like rain to a drought stricken farm. The police had recovered his Corvette. Or what little remained of it.

"I'm sorry, Doctor Morral, but all we recovered of your automobile was the frame and the basic body. The doors, all the glass, hardware, wheels, interior...all of it was removed. They even took the steering column. I'm afraid you're the victim of an auto theft ring that steals cars for their parts, and a car like yours would be a major prize, to say the least."

It concerned Harvey that there was no mention of vials filled with human fluids, and Harvey was fairly sure something as unusual as that would have generated great curiosity on the part of the police, had they found them. But he couldn't assume they didn't. He had to ask a few questions of his own.

"Are you certain it's my car, Officer? I mean, sure, it's rare, but I belong to a Corvette club. There are many Corvettes that match my car's description."

"Yes Sir, we're certain. We matched the Vehicle Identification Number to your registration. In case you don't know, the VIN is stamped on the instrument panel support brace. Fortunately, they didn't take that, but they took just about everything else."

"I had personal effects in the glove box, and a bit of work I was bringing home for testing," Harvey said, choosing his words carefully. "Did you find it?" It was a pointed question, but he had to ask. If they were holding back, his asking would make it seem he had nothing to hide, and he was sure he could talk his way around it if they were trying to trip him up.

"No Sir. There was nothing in the glove box, or anywhere else in what remained of the car. If your effects were valuable, I suggest you file a claim with your insurance company."

Harvey allowed himself a smile. It seemed he was still in business.

"Wanna start a tab?" the lovely barkeep said, ripping him from his thoughts. "And what's your name anyways?"

"Uh...Harvey. My name is Harvey. No. No tab."

"Hi!" she said. "I'm Riki."

"Nice to meet you, Riki." *And you are a beauty,* he said to himself. He slid a five onto the bar, making her pull it from under his fingertips, and when she returned with the change, he held up his hand and said, "Keep it."

Smiling her thanks, she tossed the cash into the tip bucket and moved on to another customer. Harvey picked up the bottle, and as two young men who were nothing more than muscle and testosterone pushed their way into his space, he yielded his spot, giving them the hard look toward the backs of their heads before turning away.

"Hey! Bitch!" one bellowed at the young bartender. "Fuckin' get us some beers."

Harvey turned, astonished at what he had heard, his thoughts reflecting on their parents, and not in a positive way. *Their mommies should have taught them some respect,* he thought.

Images of confrontation flashed in his mind. Maybe he should admonish them. He wanted to, but then again, why should he? It wasn't his job to teach manners today.

But then Riki turned, squealed in delight, and scampered from behind the bar. She threw her arms around the boys, and as Harvey watched in disbelief, something turned sour inside him.

Her delight in their refusal to show her the smallest amount of respect now cast her in a very different light, and Harvey's short-lived appreciation for her sweet outward appearance dissolved like so much sugar in a hot cup of tea. His eyes narrowed and his jaw set. In spite of her looks, she was no better than the others, and after seeing her for who she truly was, the decision wasn't difficult to make. He checked his watch. 7:54. Still early. He decided to finish his beer and wait outside to see when her shift ended. Then, in a day's time, he would have her.

CHAPTER 46

Vecchio regarded the sun as it dipped below the city's skyline, its waning rays painting the clouds a reddish orange. Twisting the ignition key, an ancient proverb recited itself in her head.

Red sky at morning, sailor take warning.
Red sky at night, sailor's delight.
Red sky at night, she thought. *A good omen.*

Atkins had assured her he would send the authorization she requested to Browning, and that she'd have her DNA comparisons the next day—then, in the same breath, asked her out for drinks.

The damsel in distress. That bit always worked on men like Atkins: the frantic utterances, the catches she inserted in her voice, the hopelessness of her situation—the helpless female in need.

It's a basic drive that spurs men to action for a woman in trouble. Something about the way they're wired. It's all about being the White Knight, and doing the honorable thing. Either that, or they're trying to get laid.

A look of satisfaction fell across her face in the way of a smile. She set the date with Atkins for Sunday night, three nights from now. The worst that could happen? Another free dinner courtesy of Captain Donald Atkins. The best? She wouldn't have to keep the date at all.

That the inmate work detail stumbled across the vials containing human fluids matching Harriett Brennermann, so close to where Anya Eiffel was poisoned, was more than coincidental. It was a lead. Or as Browning put it, a *strong* lead. There had to be a connection.

Vecchio allowed her mind to float back to her interviews of The Governor's Tavern patrons, and their recollections of the night Anya dropped dead on a filthy bathroom floor.

Allowing her photographic memory to sort through the seemingly unimportant observations of the customers, she dismissed the obvious and focused on the events that were barely noteworthy that night.

One woman stuck out in her mind, an older bottle-blonde who had bleached her hair to a crisp, wore too much rouge, and was in dire need of a bra. Her particular recount of events floated to the surface.

"I didn't see nuttin'," she had said. "I was outside talkin' to dis guy...can't remember his name...smokin' one o' his cigarettes an' swappin' a little spit, an' all of a sudden dis red fuckin' Vette goes peelin' off the fuckin' lot. Tires screamin', smoke pourin' out the backend...had one 'o dem special vanity tags, not like regular plates, ya know? Started wid a "H" I think... Went right over the curb like he couldn't take time to back up an' use the fuckin' driveway. Fuckin' showoff! Its assholes like dat who bring the fuckin' cops down on us, ya know? No offense to youse guys. Anyways, I was outside when dat girl OD'ed, an' didn't see nuttin'."

Remembering what the blonde said was important, but remembering her gesture was even more so. It was the sweep of her hand as she indicated the direction the Vette took, the suggestion it headed north toward the city, the same direction in which the vials were found.

Gunning the engine once, Vecchio put the Celica in gear and rolled out of OCME's lot. Turning left on Pratt, another name floated to the forefront of her mind, presented to her by an infallible memory.

The name was Morral. Harvey Morral, the medical examiner who performed the autopsy on Harriett Brennermann, the ME who performed the autopsies on *all* the CK victims, original and copycat alike. She decided to look into Doctor Harvey Morral, but before she headed back to SIU, she needed to know where Truax was.

She grabbed her phone from the passenger seat and pressed the speed-dial key for Truax's cell, unconsciously tapping the floor-shift knob with a turquoise fingernail, and waiting for him to answer.

"Moby! Where have you been? Your phone just rolled over to voice mail. I was beginning to worry."

Truax drew a breath. "You ain't gotta worry about me, Frankie. I got a mommy for that. The battery in my phone died. Wouldn't hold a charge. Took me over an hour to find a damn cellular store with a battery that fit my phone. They kept trying to sell me a new one. Assholes! So where are you?"

"I just left the toxicology lab," she said. "Got a call from the tech saying the autopsy and tox reports on the Eiffel woman were ready, but the email system was down. So I drove over to pick up hardcopies. I needed something to do...since you weren't around."

"Yeah…well shit happens, don't it."

"Yes, it does. Listen...okay with you if we pick this up in the morning? I'm beat."

Truax checked his watch. 7:54pm. "What's tomorrow?"

"Friday, Moby. Tomorrow's Friday. Jesus! You need some sleep too if you don't know what day it—"

"You eyeball those reports?"

"Yeah...I looked them over briefly. Why?"

"Whadda ya think? Anything jump out at you? Something that screams CK?"

Vecchio glanced at the folder sitting on the front seat knowing it wasn't CK's work. The rat poison was a new wrinkle, but the discovery of the fluid vials was huge.

The reports didn't mention the vials, though. That information came by word of mouth. Straight from Browning. There would be a report on that tomorrow probably. Maybe the next day. But there was no mention of them in the documents she had.

Truax would find out about the vials soon enough. The rat poison too, but for now, she didn't want him to know. Withholding that information would buy her the extra time she'd need.

"No, Moby. Nothing out of the norm. The MO's pretty much the same. Cyanide poisoning, the only difference being that she snorted the stuff like cocaine, but you already knew that. She wasn't a regular there. At least, nobody fessed up to knowing her. Looks like we're gonna burn some shoe leather digging up her acquaintances."

"You're sure…"

"Absolutely."

"Okay. If that's the case…I'll see you in the morning."

The trailing edge of outbound rush-hour traffic was long gone, replaced by the inbound night-time crowd spilling onto the sidewalks from the parking lots or the Light Rail trains; most heading for the Orioles game, and still others destined for the local pubs to push down one last brewski before heading to Camden Yards, and its 3-times priced beer.

The congestion of foot traffic slowed Vecchio's progress and taxed her patience, stretching the five minute drive from OCME to I-83, to a maddening twenty minute crawl along eastbound Pratt.

Oriole Park, the Convention Center, and the Inner Harbor with its centerpiece Amphitheater crept by before she reached Harbor Walk, and the replica of the Civil War era frigate *USS Constellation*.

The snail's pace would have served her well, granting her a look into Baltimore's nautical past were she a tourist, and the National Aquarium might have provided her daylong entertainment, but as it was, she had a deadline.

With Little Italy just ahead, Vecchio cleared the slow-of-foot and hit the I-83 intersection with the accelerator mashed to the floor, breaking the front tires loose as she swung the car north for the I-695 Beltway, Reisterstown Road, and eventually, SIU.

Once she made it back to Squad, she'd drop the autopsy and tox reports on Truax's desk and get out. It didn't make sense that specimen vials similar to those used in the pathology lab would somehow just turn up on the side of the road, and that those specimens would be a match for Harriett Brennermann—unless Browning was right and the lab just fucked up. But that would be about the only viable explanation.

Atkins said she would get the results from the DNA comparisons against the CK victim database tomorrow. That would answer some questions one way or the other, but until she got those answers, she couldn't just wait for things to unfold. She had to move, get back to basics, so she decided she would trump technology with instinct.

She was going to play a hunch.

CHAPTER 47

Vecchio was fuming after spending over four hours making her way back to SIU because some idiot forgot how to drive a tractor-trailer, and jackknifed the damn thing across the northbound lanes of I-83.

She fairly jogged to her desk after acknowledging the lone detective still working with a wave. It was after 2am, and she was surprised anyone was there at all, since it was in the early morning hours when all the killing happened.

Tossing the Eiffel reports on Truax's desk, she slid into her chair, logged into the state employee database, and quickly began a search for Harvey Morral.

Finding vials containing the bodily fluids of Harriett Brennermann in such close proximity to the scene of the Eiffel murder was, in fact, an investigative lead, just as Browning had said.

Add to that Morral's role as medical examiner, not only to this latest Eiffel murder, but also to the Brennermann woman, and all the other cyanide cases. Of course, because the murders happened late evening and early morning, it stood to reason that the mid-shift examiner would do the autopsies, and that would be Morral. A coincidence? Probably not. Truax wouldn't think so. He didn't believe in coincidence. Said there was no such thing, and that cops who thought otherwise were morons.

Like Nichols.

Vecchio knew Truax was no idiot, even if his boss was. He picked up on the differences in the MOs almost immediately. The shift from older women to younger, the differences in the times and places of the murders, how the delivery systems had changed from ingested morsels of food to other mediums like beer, and water, and most recently, powder.

The only constants that didn't change from murder to murder were the concentration of the poisons, and the medical examiner. But Truax hadn't made the connection to the ME yet, simply because he wasn't aware of the vials, and their identical match to Harriett Brennermann's DNA fingerprint, if that was *actually* the case. But it wouldn't be long before he found out, and when he did, he'd zero in. She was running out of time. She would look into Morral's government file, and if she found what she thought she would, she wouldn't be meeting Truax in the morning. She would be far too busy.

CHAPTER 48

The opening rays of the Friday morning sun wiped out Squad's fluorescents ceiling fixtures by the time Vecchio found what she was looking for.

Digging up Morral's photo from his OCME personnel file was easy enough, but the file containing the make, model, and tag number of the car he had registered for his secured underground parking sticker, as innocuous a piece of information as it was, proved far more elusive.

Initially she had accessed MVA's files, but a quick scan of the surname *Morral* persuaded her to go another route. All she knew about the car that left the parking lot of The Governor's Tavern that Monday night was its make: a red Corvette. Not the registration number or the model or the year. Several dozen listings with the name Morral had Corvettes registered in the state of Maryland, making a search of the MVA records cumbersome at best, but the OCME file listing his secure parking sticker had him owning a red 1965 Corvette, a revelation that was something more than simple coincidence.

The address on his MVA registration record matched the address listed in his personnel file, neither of which Vecchio took on faith. Glancing up, the wall clock read 5am. The midnight shift was still on duty at OCEM, but she couldn't be sure if Morral was on. She picked up the desk phone and dialed the number listed in his file.

"Pathology," a voice answered after the third ring.

"Yes," Vecchio replied. "This is...Officer Mayes, Baltimore City PD. I'm wondering if Doctor Morral is on duty. I'd like to speak to him regarding a John Doe autopsy he performed early last week."

"Morral?" the voice said. "I'm sorry, Officer. Doctor Morral isn't scheduled in until midnight tonight."

"Midnight," Vecchio replied. "I'll be off duty. What time does Doctor Morral usually leave in the morning?"

"His shift ends at 0800, but sometimes he stays over to finish up if we're busy. I'd say you could probably catch him between seven and eight. He usually wraps up around then."

"Seven to eight? Okay," she said. "I'll call back then."

CHAPTER 49

The morning dawned cooler than normal for the middle of summer in Baltimore. Truax heard something about a cold front pushing its way through the area from the north on the WTOP-FM weather report, and smiled at the thought of cooler temperatures. Seemed the heat bothered him a little more every year.

Walking into Squad, he hovered behind his chair and removed his jacket, eyeing the blue Post-it note adhered to the first of two manila folders that were stacked, squared, and perfectly centered in the middle of his desk. He immediately recognized it to be Vecchio's handiwork.

Hanging his jacket on the back of the chair, he sat down, put on his glasses, and pealed the Post-it note from the folder. The script was written in the flowery cursive swirls of a woman. He was right. The note was from Vecchio and easily readable, unlike his own illegible scrawl.

"Moby, I'm sorry, but I can't come in today. Maybe not tomorrow either. It's that time of the month."

Boy, Truax thought. *That's more information than I ever wanted.*

"I'm not on the pill so I'm not regulated and never know when I'm going to get it."

Pa-leeeeze! Frankie!

D.B. Corey

"And I get terrible cramps in the beginning. Debilitating, really, so I just have to stay off my feet for a day or two and cuddle up to a heating pad. I hope you understand. I'll touch base with you on Monday. Inside the folders you'll find the autopsy and tox reports on the Eiffel murder. Good luck."

It was signed Frances and he half expected to see a series of X's and O's beneath her signature. Thankfully, there were none.

Crumbling the note into a ball, he tossed it into the trash as he made his way to the small break room. Pouring his second cup of coffee, he stirred in three real sugars as he made his way back to his desk, and the reports.

He already knew the Eiffel woman snorted the cyanide thinking it cocaine, and short of the change in the delivery system, the MO was the same as it had been for the last five murders. The victims were young women, poisoned with cyanide and killed in some version of bar or nightclub venue, not outdoors on a bench like the earlier, older victims.

Truax dropped into his chair and placed his cup on the far right side of his desk, a maneuver that assured he wouldn't spill his coffee all over his paperwork.

He saw that the cyanide that killed Eiffel was rat poison, a lower grade, less refined version of the toxin used in the previous murders—a complete departure from the other killings. It was a significant difference in the MO, and that Vecchio didn't feel the need to mention that particular fact when he asked her about the report last night, bothered him.

The cyanide used in the other poisonings was potassium-cyanide of an industrial grade—stuff used by professionals in metallurgical applications involving precious metals such as gold and silver.

Rat poison, he remembered, was used in the Tylenol murders of some twenty-odd years ago, not very original

245

and a bit cloak & dagger, but effective. Cyanide attacks the central nervous system and the heart, so it's clean and it's quick, and twenty years ago, easy to get.

Not so much anymore. Cyanide is no longer used in rat poison, anticoagulants being the preferred agent now due to their elongated killing process.

Dropping the report on the desk, Truax picked up his coffee mug and leaned back in his chair to contemplate the change in MO, just as his desk phone rang. The voice on the other end was unhappy, and unwelcomed, and Truax felt the urge for a cigarette.

"What the hell have you been DOING?" Atkins screamed. "Another killing and you're doing what? Sitting at your desk?"

"Captain," Truax managed, keeping his head. "There's a break in the cyanide killings. This last murder...its rat poison"

"That's just it! This LAST murder. How many more people have to die before you DO something to catch this sonofa bitch? What do I have to do to motivate you?"

"Captain...this is not the same killer. The MO...it keeps changing."

"Of COURSE it keeps changing! That's how he keeps you off his ASS! He has you chasing your tail, chasing more than one killer, while he keeps putting people in the ground! I can't cover for you anymore! This is it, Truax! There is one killer! ONE! And you have forty-eight hours to find him or I'll replace you, even if I have to take over the investigation myself! Forty-eight hours! Am I making myself clear?"

Truax didn't have the chance to answer before the line went dead. Still holding the now disconnected phone, he let it drop into his lap. Savoring the last deep cleansing breath he would allow himself, he depressed the off-hook button for a moment and created a new dial tone.

Glancing at the tox report, he noted the signature and dialed the number printed across the top.

"Toxicology," the voice answered.

"This is Detective Truax. I want to speak to Harry Browning."

CHAPTER 50

Browning paused his conversation when a tap on the door caught his attention, before his colleague stuck his head in.

"Can you hold just a sec?" Browning said into the phone. "I'm sorry. It's my associate." Without covering the mouthpiece, he said, "What is it, Russell?"

"Detective Truax is on the other line. Wants a word with you."

"Tell him I'm on another call, and that I'll call him back, please."

"Sure thing," Walters replied, and eased the door closed.

"That was your partner," Browning said, continuing his conversation.

"Yes," Vecchio replied. "I heard. We spoke just before I called you actually. I guess we got our wires crossed. Probably my fault, I'm still at home. Anyway, we want to know if the results from the DNA comparisons are back. Captain Atkins said we'd have them by this morning."

"I got 'em," Browning replied. "I was looking them over just as you called. Some weird shit going on over there, Agent Vecchio."

"What do you mean...weird?"

"I mean the comparison results...they don't make any sense. The samples must be contaminated. They re-ran the

DNA tests on the vials the cleanup crew found and confirmed the DNA match to Harriett Brennermann. Then they compared those same results to the rest of the CK victims' DNA charts as you requested. They found additional, 100% matches."

Vecchio took a long pause before uttering a single word. "Who?"

"Who?" Browning repeated. "According to the DNA comparisons, there are two additional matches to the Brennermann DNA: Emma Baumgartner and Stacy Culver."

"They're the only two?" Vecchio asked.

"The only two that match Brennermann," Browning replied nonchalantly. "That's why I think the samples were contaminated, and the chain of evidence compromised. Somebody must have—

"STOP PRATTLING!" Vecchio snapped, "And give me the rest of it! What do you mean, 'the only two that match Brennermann'?"

Browning became belligerent.

"I meant...that they were the only two that matched Brennermann. Two other victims, Kara Templeton and Georgia Parsons match Rosa Neunyo's DNA. Dorothy French is the only one without additional matches."

"Dorothy French..." Vecchio murmured, a tinge of reminiscence in her tone. "The first victim."

"Yeah... If you say so."

"Wait!' Vecchio blurted. "I only asked to run tests against Brennermann's DNA. How did they discover the matches to Neunyo?"

"When they discovered the discrepancies with Brennermann," he said, "they reviewed the other victims with a more discerning eye. They spotted similarities in a couple of the DNA charts and took a closer look. Overlays did the rest of the work. Didn't take long."

Vecchio's voice betrayed her shock and confusion. "Why wasn't this picked up initially? Back when the DNA samples were run the first time? How come we're just finding this out now?"

"Agent Vecchio," Browning began, using a tone that came off more as patronizing, than empathetic, speaking as an adult might speak to a child. "When pathology sends over evidence samples, in this case, blood or urine or bile, we test for toxins, and type, and disease. We only test for identification if the victim is unknown, comparing the results to known hair or skin or blood samples.

"In each case, the CK victims were identified by the documents the police found on their person, and then verified through follow-up investigations. There was no reason to doubt their identity, or verify their DNA fingerprints. We had an ID from the start, so when the VNTR fingerprint charts of the victims were created, we simply attached the charts to the victim's file.

"We didn't have to validate their identities. We already knew who they were, so we didn't *have* to compare them to any others."

"I see," Vecchio whispered.

"Good," Browning continued, "and to set your mind at ease, you'll be happy to know I've started an internal investigation. Somebody's head is gonna roll for this mix up. Just like last year when OCME's pathology and lab personnel didn't have their DNA on file. Screwed up many an investigation, boy. I tell you…"

Vecchio's demeanor changed. She ignored the chitchat Browning now seemed intent on engaging in. The informal air evident in her voice disappeared and was replaced by a sense of urgency.

"Email me the files," she ordered without regard to manners. "Copy Truax."

"He's expecting a return call from me," Browning reminded her.

"No need," Vecchio replied matter-of-factly. "Just email the files. I'll fill him in. What's your email address?"

CHAPTER 51

Vecchio scrambled to stuff her overnight bag with several bottles of water, half-a-loaf of whole grain bread, one jar each of peanut butter and strawberry jelly, a butter-knife, a pair of dark gray sweatpants and a tank top, also dark gray.

Pulling on a white tee-shirt and the loosest pair of jeans she owned, she slipped into her dingy white sneakers and dropped her cell phone into the bag. Placing the bag on the little kitchen dinette in her tiny extended-stay apartment, she pointed her personal laptop's browser to SIU's Webmail server. Since her laptop was not imaged for the department, it was the only way she had to access SIU's network from outside the firewalls.

Entering the specific URL, she accessed the SIU mail-server and typed in Truax.M@MSP.SIU.gov. When it asked for logon credentials, she entered the password she had covertly picked off when Truax logged in to his email account. A moment later she was scanning his Inbox.

There was no email from Browning yet, but she couldn't stay logged-in waiting for it to arrive. Accessing Truax's junk mail controls, she added Browning's email address to the SPAM filter, and toggled the Delete-On-Receipt feature to Enabled. Now Browning's email, with its attachments of the CK DNA comparisons, would go to Truax's Junk folder, and immediately from there, disappear into cyber nothingness.

Logging off, she stuffed the laptop into the bag with the 12V accessory power cord, snatched the overnight bag from the table, and locked the door before scampering down the two flights to her Celica. After stopping at a convenience store for adult diapers, she pulled back onto the highway and made a call.

"Vehicle Theft Division," the female voice said. "Officer Brzezinski speaking."

"Yes," Vecchio replied, identifying herself. "I'm checking on a stolen car from last Monday night. It would have been reported from Glen Burnie. A red Vette. 1965 Coupe."

Vecchio expected a wait while the officer looked through the reports and was surprised when that wait was less than two minutes long.

"Wellllll…" Brzezinski said. "Sorry Agent Vecchio. Nothing from Glen Burnie last Monday night."

"Shit! What about the surrounding areas? Severna Park? Annapolis? Ferndale? Baltimore City?"

"Wellllll…" the officer replied, starting a new search. "Let's see what we got here." A moment passed, then two. "Looks like a '65 Vette was reported stolen in the city Tuesday morning about 0830. That what you're lookin' for?"

"Could be. Model and year listed?"

"Of course. Red 1965 Corvette Coupe. Stolen from the OCME parking lot. Registered to a Harvey Morral."

"That might be it," Vecchio said. "It didn't happen to have vanity tags, did it?"

"Wellllll…let's see here. As a matter of fact. HARVEY. Same as the owners name. Go figure that one, huh?" Brzezinski snorted a laugh and then just stopped. "Looks like they found it already. Or parts of it. Not much left. Just the body and frame. Owner notified. That's all it says."

"One last thing," Vecchio said. "Can you verify Morral's home address? I have him listed—"

CHAPTER 52

Truax checked his watch like an expectant father. 11:50. Five minutes later than the last time he checked. That his captain chewed his ass and ordered him to treat the CK homicides as committed by a single killer—an order he knew he would have to disobey—was bad enough, but to have to sit around waiting for a phone call to get some answers was absolute bullshit.

He realized the lab techs were busy, and he hated pestering them with repeat phone calls, but he had waited long enough. He needed answers. He picked up the phone.

"Toxicology," the voice answered.

"This is Detective Truax. I want to speak with Harry Browning. Now!"

"I'm sorry, Detective," Walters said. "Harry is gone for the day. For two weeks, actually. Vacation."

There was empty space from Truax's end, before a measured reply came through. "Vacation..." Another long pause. "Who is this?"

"This is Walters...Russell Walters, Detective. I'm Harry's colleague. Is there something I can help you with?"

"That depends," Truax breathed, his tone advising against any forensic double-talk. "What do you know about the tox report on Anya Eiffel?"

CHAPTER 53

The Green Haven neighborhood was quaint, a quiet little community north of Annapolis, water all around—an older community. At twenty-seven minutes after one Friday afternoon, Vecchio pulled to the curb three houses down from the address Morral had listed as his home on the stolen vehicle report. It also matched the records on file with MVA and OCME.

On her first pass, Vecchio cruised by the house to get the lay of the land. On the next pass, she settled in at the curb on the small curved neighborhood street three houses down from Morral's.

Albatross Street was a long thoroughfare off Mountain Road that ended in a big circle, with both the entry and exit points being a fork off the main street. Across the three back yards belonging to the houses positioned around the curve, some with large oak trees, she had a relatively clear view of Morral's driveway, the side door, and the kitchen window of the white Cape Cod.

The entrance to the detached single-car garage behind the house was visible as well, and she knew that she had to get a look inside, not to verify the status of the stolen Vette, but just to see what she could see. In the middle of the day, with most people at work, she decided to chance it.

After a quick scan of the immediate area, and seeing no one other than children riding bikes and running here and there, she grabbed a clipboard from the back seat and piled out of the car. Acting as if she belonged, she stood stationary on the sidewalk for a moment, and gleaned the clipboard before strolling up the sidewalk toward Morral's house, pausing to compare each building against non-existent paperwork as she went.

Upon reaching the house just before Morral's, she stopped, glanced at the clipboard again, and then strolled up the driveway toward that home's garage, looking left and right, and making fictitious notations on the clipboard.

After peering into the neighbor's garage, she walked directly across the grass into Harvey's yard and up to his garage. Looking through the glass in the right-most door, she saw his mother's Ford Focus. Noting the dark blue color and the tag number, she proceeded back the way she came. That's when she spotted the elderly couple across the street, sitting on their front porch swing, intensely interested in her every move. She smiled and waved.

The couple waved back. Then the old man called, "Hello! Beautiful day to be working outside, eh?"

As always, she thought, offering them a broad smile as she continued down the sidewalk. *You catch more flies with sugar.*

Slipping back into the car, Vecchio sat for a few moments and considered several scenarios, the first of which seemed the most viable: Staying where she was until Morral showed himself.

Her best bet to acquire him was to monitor the house. Being early afternoon, with having to work that night, if he wasn't in the house sleeping, he would be before long. She had considered waiting for him at OCME, but with the dark of night, and the secure underground parking, she wouldn't be able to see his face. So the only sure way of knowing if he was in the house, short of knocking on the door, was to wait, and watch.

About dusk, she caught a break. Harvey trotted out from the house to fetch the evening paper. He left in his mother's car two hours after that.

Tailing him was child's play, even at night. When she followed him out of the neighborhood, she initially thought he was heading to work, until he passed the exit for Rt.10 North, and turned south on Ritchie Highway toward Annapolis instead.

She followed him to a small shopping center in Severna Park, nestled equidistant between Glen Burnie and Annapolis, where he pulled into a lot near the back of the retail stores at the south end of the mall.

Remaining at a safe distance, she circled around the far end of the lot, keeping an eye on where Morral parked. By the time she circled back, she saw the Ford parked in a space on a lot next to a copse of trees.

The trees separated the small lot from another larger lot closer to the building. The Ford was empty and Harvey was gone, and the only place still open at 11:30 at night was a small, unobtrusive lounge, sitting at the back of the building.

As she looked for an unobstructed parking space within eyeshot, Harvey materialized through the trees, walking from the lounge to his car at a fair clip. Vecchio found his short stint in the lounge puzzling, until she watched him enter his car, but not leave. He didn't even start the engine. He was waiting for someone.

Vecchio pulled onto the lot on the lounge side, keeping the tiny stand of trees squarely in the line-of-sight between her and Harvey's Ford. Then she hunkered down and waited.

When the bar closed, and a woman left the lounge she spotted Harvey homing in on her using the cover of the trees. It was over in less than a minute.

CHAPTER 54

Walters answered Truax's question with little enthusiasm.

"The Eiffel tox report? I...I know nothing about it. I didn't work it."

There was a pause before Truax asked in a voice devoid of emotion, "You're the same guy I spoke to a couple hours ago...ain't you..."

"Yes..."

"Didn't you tell me Browning would call me back?"

"Yes..."

"Then why the hell didn't he?"

"I r-r-reminded him. He s-s-s-said it was taken care of. I assumed it to mean that he c-c-called you."

"You assumed. You didn't ask?"

"No, I thought he—"

Walters stopped and heaved a labored sigh. His stammer eased. "Look Detective. It's Friday afternoon. It's summertime. People are running out of here as early as they can to s-start the weekend or their va-vacations or God knows what else. Maybe I can help you...if it doesn't take too long. Her report should be on file. What is it you need?"

"What I need is verification. Her tox report lists the killing agent as cyanide. Rat poison."

With the phone wedged between his shoulder and his ear, Walters sat down and dialed up the Eiffel file on his computer. Selecting the tox report, he opened the document and scrolled down until he found what he was looking for.

"Yes Sir. That's what it says. So what do you want to know?"

"I want to know if you guys came across any other cases where rat poison was used."

"Not that I'm aware of, but then again, I don't do the chemical testing."

"Then who does?"

"Browning."

"And he's on vacation…"

"Yes. I'm afraid so."

"Then that leaves you. You're a certified forensics specialist. You know how to run the tests, don't you?"

"Well, yes but what's that got to—"

"I hope you didn't have anything to do tonight, because you're going to run a couple of tests for me."

CHAPTER 55

In the wee hours of Saturday morning, the point of a syringe pierced a baby-blue top, a matching shear bra, and a left breast.

Passing between ribs #3 and #4, the hypo injected six CCs of a water-cyanide solution directly into Riki Harrison's heart. Riki recovered from the shock and hesitation of disbelief and managed a scream as Harvey withdrew the needle, but her cry for help proved no match for the blanket of sound that the crickets and tree frogs layered over the night. It became lost in the mayhem, unheard by two co-workers on the far side of the lot.

When he approached Riki, her initial reaction was one of recognition. She smiled when she saw him and that lovely upward curve of her mouth caused a stirring in his loins. As he drew closer, he looked ahead to her death. His pulse increased and he could hear his own breathing over the sweeping sounds of the woods.

When Riki's mind caught up, finally registering the terror that closed on her, her smile froze before her body stiffened and paled, and she more resembled a plastic mannequin in a department store window, than a living flesh and blood woman.

Harvey's hand shot toward her at near the speed of a cobra strike. Grabbing her hair, he released an audible moan as he yanked her to him and drove the needle into her chest. The power of the violence aroused him.

The *feel*... Plunging a needle into living flesh. The way her body froze. How the questions in her eyes became unspoken pleas for life. *How must she feel?* he thought, *to see death coming...*

Engaging in self-stimulation didn't compare to the endorphin-fueled mind-fuck of a beautiful woman begging for her life. To see them from afar one would think them lovers, lost in the embrace of a warm summer night, but as Riki fought to breathe, Harvey tightened his grip and pulled her to him. The sensation of her body against his, in its final throws of life, consumed him.

Feeling her die brought him to near orgasm, and because of this new excitement, the sex became almost secondary. He held her tight against him to feel her heart rate soar from the adrenalin flooding her system. With her blood circulating the poison through her body, she seized within seconds—about the same amount of time that it took Harvey to ejaculate in his pants.

As Riki drew her last breath, Harvey felt her body transition from rigid to limp. He let her go, dropping her in the dirt beside her Mini Cooper. Dirty was not an issue for him. Once at the lab she was easily cleaned up.

His thoughts turned to the hours yet to come. He'd be hard pressed to stay busy waiting for Riki to arrive if there was no autopsy scheduled, but once she was there, he'd be sure to do her proper. She would be his last for a while, considering he used the last of the old rat poison on her. Now he was forced to seek other, non-messy means of dispatch, but that was the least of his new problems.

He had just one last set of CK fluids remaining, the set he forgot to dispose of when he got rid of the rat poison. They belonged to CK's last victim—Rosa Neunyo, and later tonight, when he finished with Riki, he would send Neunyo's samples to the lab in place of her specimens.

In retrospect, he wished he'd had procured more fluid from the CK kills. Substituting them for specimens from his own activities was just too easy, and with the exception of that little faux pas when the Vette was stolen, his manipulation of the fluid samples went like clockwork.

Since the stolen vials didn't turn up with the Vette, and since Officer Horn said nothing of finding them even after Harvey asked him point-blank, he saw no reason to change his methods, except that CK had suddenly stopped his killing ways, and disappeared from the face of the earth. So until he showed himself again—began killing again—Harvey had no means of pointing the investigation in his direction.

Harvey turned and casually strolled into the billowy foliage at the edge of the parking lot. Ignoring the sounds of insects, he reminded himself to stop for cigarettes.

CHAPTER 56

Vecchio watched as Harvey let the woman drop onto the asphalt and disappear back into the trees. She waited until he reached his car, and after the headlights from the Ford Focus flashed to life, Vecchio rose from her stealthy position to watch him drive off. But she didn't follow. She knew where he was going.

Excited shouting ripped through the night, someone barking orders, and when she glanced back to the girl she saw someone, the doorman perhaps, hunched over her body. She considered rendering aid, but knowing what Morral used on the girl, Vecchio knew she was dead.

She couldn't stick around. Truax would catch this one and she didn't want to be anywhere nearby when he showed up. If he spotted her, how would she explain her presence? Besides, she had more important issues to deal with...like what to do about Morral.

CHAPTER 57

Truax steered left, then right, then left again, weaving slowly between the flashing red and blue chaos created by the county cars sprinkled about the lot. As the car veered, his mind veered with it, bouncing between Atkins's direct order to investigate the murders under the premise of a lone killer, and the anticipated results from the toxicology tests he had Walters running. He was playing the biggest hunch of his career, and if he got it wrong, Atkins would make him pay dearly.

Truax spotted Johnson kneeling next to the body when he exited the Crown Vic, wondering how it was that Johnson managed to beat him to the crime scenes. Didn't the guy ever sleep?

As Truax approached, Johnson paused his examination of the body and began peering around Truax in all directions.

"Where's that hot partner of yours?" Johnson asked with a grin. "I was looking forward to a little sunshine tonight."

"She ain't feeling well," Truax replied, a twinge of annoyance in his voice.

"Ah!" Johnson replied compassionately. "Nothing serious, I hope."

"Lady problems."

"Awwww," Johnson groaned. "There it goes… The perfect image of the perfect woman."

Truax grinned, happy to ruin his day. "You'll get over it. It only lasts a week, and then she'll be good as new. So what do we have here?"

Johnson gestured toward the body. "Riki Harrison, twenty-three. She tends bar here. Appears to be very much like the others. Same pink tint to the skin, same almond aroma, no external trauma. My initial read is that she was poisoned. Cyanide probably."

Truax stood over Riki's body, hands in his pockets, toeing the loose gravel into small mounds. He ran the other cyanide victims through his mind in the order of their deaths. His memory seemed good tonight.

The only common denominators were the weapon, the ME that performed the autopsies, and the lab. *Rat poison*, he thought, shifting gears. *Eiffel was killed with rat poison. Why the switch? Unless it wasn't a switch. Maybe, it was rat poison all along.* Kara Templeton jumped into his mind.

"Did you know," Truax said, staring at his gravel mounds, "the cyanide used in the last poisoning—Anya Eiffel, the girl in the bathroom—was rat poison?"

Since Truax now seemed to be thinking on another plane, Johnson squatted next to the body and continued his examination. "Heard through the grapevine," he replied. "Just 'cause I only do the field stuff, don't mean I don't hear things. It had to be some pretty old shit. They ain't used cyanide in rat poi—"

"Yeah," Truax said, "I know all that. But there's more to it. Each murder has had some minor difference in the MO, yet all the forensic results are identical for all the victims, both young and old...except for this last one. I gotta wonder why."

Johnson's eyes went wide. "You think there's some hanky-panky going on in the forensics lab?"

"Don't know. Maybe. Listen, can you do something for me?"

Johnson raised an eyebrow and waited, clutching his clipboard as if it were a winning poker hand.

"I want you to check something on our victim here before you release her to OCME. Can you do that?"

"Maybe. What?"

"I want you to pull specimens from her. The regular stuff...blood, urine. You know what to get. Then I want you, and *only* you, to do the tox screens on 'em. I want you to compare those samples to the lab reports when they come back. See if they're the same."

Johnson's skepticism took the forefront. "It'll never hold up in court," he counseled. "Breaks the chain of evidence."

"I don't give a shit about the evidence chain," Truax snapped. "I want to see if the results from the two sets of tests are the same or not. That's it. Nothing else."

"Okay...then yeah, I can do that for you. As long as the DA doesn't ask me to testify. My testimony will only hurt his case."

Truax's cell rang. "Just pull the samples and put 'em on ice," he said. "Get the tests done as soon as you can. ID the samples as Jane Doe number...whatever." Truax moved several steps away and pressed the green button on his cell, hoping he caught the call before it went to voice mail.

"Truax."

"Yes...Detective Truax? Russell Walters here. I know you said to call as soon as I had the results of the tox screens you wanted, but it's so late I worried you might be asleep. I didn't wake you, did I?"

"Hardly," Truax grumbled. "Whadda ya have?"

Walter's took a deep breath. "I tested the organ biopsies we keep in evidence cold storage for the cases you stipulated: Dorothy French, and Emma Baumgartner. Once I had the tox results from the organ biopsies for the two victims, I compared them against the tox reports that were in their case file.

The organ biopsy tox reports for Dorothy French match the tox report in her case file exactly: Died of acute cyanide poisoning. 250 parts per million, industrial grade, etc etc. Emma Baumgartner, however, was a different story."

Walters paused, waiting for a response from Truax, and he got it.

"Well don't fuckin' stop *now*!" Truax barked. "Keep going!"

"Baumgartner's *organ* tox results differ drastically with the case file results. The tox results in her *case* file are identical to those of *Dorothy French*. Probably a clerical mix-up of some kind. The tests—"

"WAIT! What do you mean...'identical'...to Dorothy French?"

"Exactly that. The original toxicology tests in Baumgartner's case file match the French woman exactly. They are identical. Almost as if the two separate tests were run from the same samples."

Truax said nothing for a moment, assembling the information, then told Walters to continue.

"As I was saying, the tests on Baumgartner's *organ* biopsies show the cyanide that killed her was half the potency, three times the dosage, and nothing more than rat poison. Nowhere near as pure as the stuff used on the French woman. Is that what you were looking to find out, Detective?"

Truax told him to hold on so he could sort through what Walter's told him. He wanted to attack this from the standpoint of identity, since it was beginning to look as if the samples had been compromised—swapped or mislabeled—or somehow mixed up with the others.

But if there was no accidental switch, if the sleight of hand was intentional, he had to be sure of what he had—of *who* he had—to pinpoint where in the evidence chain the swaps occurred. If he could prove the results had been tampered with, he might be able to prove the existence of a copycat killer and persuade Atkins to give him more time.

"Okay, Walters," he finally said. "Here's what I need you to do."

"Detective," Walters pleaded. "I had hoped you'd be finished with me after this. I am on my own time, here, and its Saturday morning. I worked all night on this and I have plans with my family this weekend."

"People are dying here, Walters," Truax said. "I need your help,"

A poignant sigh came through the phone from the far end. "Very well, Detective. What do you want me to do?"

"Atta-boy," Truax said. "Here's what I need. I want you to run those same tests again, but on all the other CK victims. I need to know if there are more of the same type of inconsistencies."

"Be thorough! Don't half-ass it! Then, I want you to run DNA comparisons on all the CK victims. I want to know who's who, here. I don't like that some of these test results are identical to others."

"We don't do the DNA," Walters interrupted. "The FBI lab in New Jersey does that."

"I know that, Walters," Truax said. "That's what I meant. I want you to get them to run the comparisons and send you the results. I'm lead on the investigation, so use my authorization to get it done. And I want the results as soon as they can get them to me. Think you can handle all that?"

"I'll do my best, Detective."

"There is one last thing."

The sound of exasperation from Walters' end was easily deciphered. "And what might that be, Detective?"

"Kara Templeton's case. The tox report had no mention of the baby's bottle, or if the contents were tested. Can you shed some light as to why?"

"The report contained the tox screens on the victim?"

"Yes."

"Did they list the killing agent?"

"Yes, of course."

"This is just a guess, you understand, but they probably didn't want to go to the time and expense to test the bottle's contents if they weren't relevant to the victim. I assume the victim didn't drink from a baby bottle, did she?"

"Of course not. It was the baby's water bottle."

"And the baby wasn't killed?"

"No."

"Then why test it? It wouldn't reveal anything we didn't already know."

"I see what you're getting at, Walter's, and under normal circumstances I'd agree with you, but the contents of that baby bottle may give us information we don't have. I need tox screens run on the water that was in the baby's bottle."

"Detective…"

"Just run it with the Templeton biopsy screens. Everything you need should be in evidence holding. I'll put a good word in for you." Truax knew that didn't mean shit when it came to Atkins, but Walters didn't know that.

"Fine," Walters griped. "I'll pull it with everything else. You'll hear from me when I have something."

"Good man," Truax said, then quickly added, "Day or night."

Truax ended the call, and turned back toward the field ME.

"JOHNSON!"

Johnson had finished up with Riki Harrison's body, and was overseeing its loading into the transport van when he heard Truax yelling his name. Turning, he spied Truax waving furiously. Johnson threw his hands out to his sides as if he were about to hug someone of substantial girth. "What?"

Truax ran the short distance toward Johnson, no easy task for a fifty-some-year-old man no matter how short the expanse. "HOLD THE BODY!" he gasped, flailing one hand in the air.

Johnson turned and halted the contractor, preventing Riki's body from entering the van. Then he turned to Truax. "What the fuck are you doing?"

"Wait," Truax managed between gasps. A few seconds later, after regaining his wind, he said, "Don't let her body out of your sight until you get fluid samples. In fact, I want you to do a preliminary autopsy on her."

"WHAT?" Johnson blurted. "Are you out of your fucking mind? I can't go cutting—"

"No cutting," Truax interrupted. "Just an epidermal exam. Take pictures. Note external marks, trauma, possible sexual assault."

"I've already made notations of external observations of exposed surfaces. I can't check for sexual assault. I'd have to remove her clothing. That's the medical examiner's job."

"*You're* a medical examiner. You can do it. I want you to record anything we can't see with her clothes on."

"They'll do a rape kit on her in the autopsy lab."

"That's exactly what I *don't* want. I want *you* to check her. Right here. Right now."

"Oh, Moby. That's highly irregular. There may even be regulations against field inspections of that sort. Besides, I don't have a rape kit."

"I just want you to check her out. Nothing fancy. Do it in the transport vehicle before they roll. Close the doors." Truax pointed to the cordoned off entrance to the parking lot. "I'll have that female officer over there stay with you as a witness in case somebody pitches a fit. Then, after her autopsy at OCME, I want you to transport the body to the university hospital to do a second autopsy. And keep it *quiet*! I want something to compare with OCME's findings."

Johnson's face turned ashen. "My *God*, Moby! What the hell has gotten *into* you?"

"Well, Doc," Truax said. "Not to put too fine a point on it...let's just say, I smell a rat."

CHAPTER 58

Sunday nights were the last of the nights out before the start of the workweek anywhere around town. Most places carried a fair crowd even with no band, and Harvey wanted—Harvey needed—a drink. He had to wind down after his pre-autopsy interlude with Riki.

She was as beautiful as the others he had taken, but she'd made it to the lab later than he had hoped, and he hadn't time enough for a thorough autopsy. He passed over several procedures, the simple ones such as epidermal inspection for lacerations, bruising, and the like, and he intentionally omitted the puncture wound in her left breast, same as he did with Georgia.

He wasn't concerned someone would notice. It was at the point now where no one from OCME scrutinized autopsy reports anymore, and they were never released to the families unless requested. Glossing over mundane sections of routine reports had become commonplace. It was like re-reading yesterday's newspaper.

Harvey found himself dealing with a new aspect of his extra-curricular liaisons, where the rush of being so close to them as they died, could easily replace having them on the table. It was all a very new and tasking experience, one he wanted to evaluate before repeating, unsure if the thrill was worth the risk.

He decided to ponder this new and exciting dilemma with a beer and a little music before going to work, but after Riki, it would be stupid to return to Severna Park, or any other place he had been.

He had heard of a place called Rascal's off Loch Raven Boulevard on the northeast side of Baltimore. It was nearly an hour from his mother's house, but roughly thirty minutes from OCME. He decided to check it out.

It was early when he walked in...not quite eight o'clock, and the amplified music pumping through a state-of-the-art sound-system was half of what it would be later. An undercurrent of voices lay just beneath the music flowing from the loudspeakers, interrupted occasionally by the snapping of ceiling-mounted smoke eaters, and Harvey noted that he could actually overhear other people talking.

Rascal's was longer than it was wide, the lighting was up a bit due to the early hour, and if one cared to look closely enough, they would see the grime and the burn marks on the carpets, stools, and chairs from countless spilled drinks, and untold forgotten cigarettes.

A waist-high, wood-paneled wall created a short hallway, separating the entrance from a rectangular front bar on the immediate right. Directly ahead, the main bar ran the length of the left wall, and a medium sized dance floor lay adjacent to them both. All the way in the back was a small one-man bar that serviced the surrounding tables that dotted the floor, providing a limited privacy, or at least a bit of refuge from the craziness of the main room.

Harvey headed for a stool at the sparsely populated front bar and, forgoing the beer, ordered bottled water. The memory of Kara seeped in. *Such a terrible waste,* he thought.

He decided he wouldn't stay long, thinking he'd hang around for twenty minutes or so and then head into work a little early. Maybe he'd even cut Rabbani loose. He did owe him a couple of favors.

When the bartender brought his water, movement from the entrance door caught the corner of his eye. Swiveling left he spotted a woman walking along the half-height front wall, and around the far side of the rectangular bar. She sat down directly across from him and ordered a drink, glanced up, and their eyes met.

Harvey could swear she was blushing when she quickly looked away, and it emboldened him to think the exchange afforded him an advantage of sorts. Something within told him to pay attention.

As the minutes passed, she grew on him a glance at a time. She was pretty, but not so pretty as to monopolize attention. Her dark hair cascaded down her back and her eyes fairly disappeared in the subdued lighting of the bar. Her complexion was rich Mediterranean, and her lips were thin, a minor flaw; as equally unimportant as the slight bend to her nose.

She wore a snug-fitting, adequately occupied, short-sleeved white V-neck, and from what he could see of her over the bar, he estimated she was lean with a medium frame.

He studied her and wondered what she was thinking, why she was there, who she was looking for. Her intrigue grew as the minutes passed, and had he been drinking, he would have credited the booze for the attraction she held. But he wasn't. She was wholesome. The kind of woman his mother would approve of. Not like the other women here, who carried themselves cheap in a gross and vulgar manner.

Her classy dress and soft appearance elevated her above common. And that was the problem. It was common that he sought. Like Riki. Like the Jane Doe cokehead from The Governor's Tavern. She wasn't what he was looking for, or what his Need sought.

He reluctantly looked away, and several moments passed before his eyes took on a will of their own and returned to her, and when they did, he found her watching him. Smiling a shy uncertain smile, her eyes fell to her drink and she stirred it intently. Just for a moment. Just before those near black eyes found him again, and her smile returned.

The back-and-forth, cat-and-mouse glimpses toward each other continued for what seemed to Harvey like an eternity. Shards of light reflecting from the depths of her eyes implied a smoldering yet controlled sexuality, and as he gazed upon her, he felt a longing to know her in a way different from the others. There was something compelling about this woman, and imagining himself with her allowed him a glimpse at the normalcy that had eluded him for all his years.

Time to shit or get off the pot, he thought. Calling the bartender over, he instructed her to buy the woman a drink. The woman rewarded his gesture with another smile and an unheard "thank you," mouthed across the bar. He rose to his feet and walked over. He decided that maybe he wouldn't go to work early tonight after all.

CHAPTER 59

It was late Monday morning and Truax still wandered around his kitchen in his old plaid robe, the frayed terrycloth keeping with the washed-out gray and purple that was once a vibrant black and burgundy.

Atkins's go-to-hell deadline had come and gone, and the only thing Truax had that he didn't have before was another dead girl. He thought for sure he'd have heard from Atkins by now, screaming at him to come in so he could fire him personally, face to face. But he supposed running SIU had him dealing with other things. He was sure Atkins would get around to him sooner or later. Truax preferred later.

His job, not to mention his livelihood, now appeared to hinge on two possibilities: The as yet unknown lab results he had Walters running, and Johnson turning up something on Riki Harrison's body. Something blatant. Something that differed from OCME's autopsy report—an omission, a variation, a modification of fact, a misrepresentation of evidence...hell, an out-n-out lie. Hunches and gut feelings were fine and they had their place, but they didn't carry the weight of cold hard fact.

He scratched his head, momentarily startled that he felt no hair. Even after shaving his dome for over a year, the barren area that was the top of his head, occasionally caught him off-guard. Atkins had him out of his routine, and worrying about his ass. He wanted to get his mind off Atkins and back on the case. The morning paper would go a long way toward that end. But he'd have to go get it first.

Gulping down the last of his third sugar-laden coffee, he snuck up to his living room window, reminiscent of a thief in the night. He pulled the blackout curtains back just enough to peer through the glass with a single eye, and searched the immediate area looking for the widow Ida. She was nowhere to be seen. Of course, that meant nothing.

The morning paper was there, on the front lawn, scant feet away. It was little more than bait, the kind of bait Ida would use to ask him in for a cup of tea, and if she saw him, he'd be like a hungry raccoon snared in a trap.

Giving the neighborhood a quick 180-degree glance, he scurried barefoot across the front lawn, picked up the paper, and then, swiveling his head like a praying mantis looking for something to eat, darted back into the house.

SAFE! he thought, slamming the door closed. The image of a home plate umpire gesturing wildly that the base runner beat the tag found its way into his conscious. Breathing a great sigh, he dropped the paper on the table, poured his fourth cup of coffee, and scooped in three spoonfuls of sugar. Setting himself gingerly into the chair, he turned to the grocery ads. They were easy to find, since they always popped out first.

Coffee was on sale for $6.99. Nearly half price. Coffee held the same importance to a cop as gasoline did to a police car. He'd stop on his way in and pick up several pounds.

The sports section came next and touted the Ravens at Cincinnati later that night, and wasn't it just their luck to draw a Monday night game for their season opener.

He continued working from the back forwards, finally making it to the front page of Saturdays' *Observer.* His eyes settled on an article he would have been surprised not to see.

CK Strikes Again.
Police Powerless.

Well you didn't really think a night in the pokey would scare Munroe away, did you? The kid must think he's Dan Rather.

Without reading the piece, Truax threw the paper on the couch and headed for the shower. He'd call Walters on the way to Squad and ask about the other toxicology tests, and the DNA comparisons. He needed the information if he were to solve this crime and keep his job.

Standing naked in the bathroom, he glanced at his reflection in the full-length mirror and grimaced. Seems he was losing the battle of the bulge, but more than that, sucking it in was becoming the only exercise he got anymore. Isometrics were good, but they couldn't work miracles.

The ringing of the phone in the kitchen snapped him out of his daydreams of the gym, his one-hundred-fifty-pound presses, and forty-pound curls. He wrapped a towel around his waist in case the widow Ida picked this particular moment to knock on the door, and hustled through the living room, past the side entrance, and into the kitchen.

"Truax," he answered, one hand holding the phone to his ear, the other holding the towel.

"I figured you'd still be home since you didn't answer your cell," Johnson said. "You sure you're not a banker?"

"I was going to call you in a little bit," Truax said, peeking through the blinds on the side door. "What'd you find out?"

"It looks like your instincts are spot on. There's something not kosher at OCME."

"Okay," Truax said. "Keep going."

"The field inspection of Riki Harrison's body proved uneventful, with the exception of a fresh puncture wound of the left breast by a small, needle-like object—probably a small-bore syringe. The wound was hidden by her bra. I'd have never seen it had I not removed her clothing."

"Is that what killed her?"

"Turns out, yes. It was. I had the tox lab run tests on the specimens I took from her at the scene, the samples you asked me to take. They turned up cyanide in her blood. Pair that with the puncture wound, and I'd say there's a pretty strong case that the poison was injected directly into her heart."

"I'm not so sure the tox lab's not the problem," Truax said. "You sure about the samples? About the results?"

"Hand carried them there myself. Watched the whole process. There is no mistake. And you'll be thrilled to know that the source of the cyanide was rat poison. I had them compare it to the Eiffel woman's tox results. They were identical. I don't think the lab is the source of the bogus findings. What you see is what you get. Whoever killed Anya Eiffel, killed Riki Harrison too."

Truax mulled that information over in his mind. If it wasn't the lab misrepresenting the test results—intentionally or otherwise—then the tests results were legit, meaning the source samples had to be the problem. But in order to prove it, he needed more than Booleian concepts and conspiracy theories. He needed evidence. Finding discrepancies in OCME autopsy results for the Harrison girl, based on Johnson's follow-up autopsy, would be something he could use...assuming there *were* discrepancies.

OCME's autopsy should be complete, and he would have access to the autopsy report when he got to work, but he had to give Johnson time to do his follow-up, and since

OCME still held the body, Johnson's autopsy was still hours away. He needed something now.

The tox screens on the organ biopsies of the remaining CK victims were the key. If Walters found matches that shouldn't be matches, he needed to know. But more than that, he needed the results of the DNA comparisons verifying the identities of the CK victims. He'd get Vecchio on those, first thing.

"Thanks Johnson," Truax said. "Let me know what your autopsy turns up."

"OCME should release the body by noon," Johnson told him. "I'll send a transport to pick it up and get back to you later. Of course, you do know I'll miss my daughter's soccer game tonight."

"Keep this under wraps," Truax said, not allowing Johnson to bait him. "I don't want it getting out."

Truax went to drop the wall phone into its cradle when something flashed in his mind.

"WAIT! JOHNSON!"

A second passed and Johnson came back on the line.

"You're cutting into my nap time." Johnson said. "What'd you forget?"

"Can you pull the autopsy report for Georgia Parsons?"

"Sure. What do you need?"

"See if there is mention of her virginity."

"A virgin… In today's culture? You kiddin'?"

"Just check for me, please."

"Gimme a sec...OK, there is no mention of an intact hymen."

"Thanks, Johnson."

Truax went back to finish dressing as his mind dwelled on Georgia Parsons. Her best friend said that she was a virgin, yet there was no mention of that on her autopsy report, and there should have been, just like there should have been mention of the wound on Riki Harrison. Now he wanted to get a look at the OCME autopsy report on Harrison. But more than that, he wanted to see who performed it...and he was pretty sure he already knew.

CHAPTER 60

Harvey half listened to the TV, occasionally guessing the price of the brand new car as he removed the plates from the coffee table after lunch. Today it was pre-cooked ham-steak and a package of macaroni-and-cheese that came from a blue and yellow box. He never learned to cook, so directions were paramount. When he cooked his own food, edible was important. It was that, or yet another pizza. Pepperoni, mushrooms, and anchovies. He was certain the pepperoni was eating away at his stomach lining.

He considered the dishwasher, but decided it just wasn't worth the water for a couple of dishes. So he washed the few pieces of flatware himself. Once that small chore was complete, he picked up around the kitchen so as not to give his mother yet another reason to bitch.

Plopping onto the sofa, he turned the TV down before rummaging through his wallet and retrieving a folded bar napkin with a name and a phone number. Lovely Riki was a woman he would remember fondly, but unlike his normal post-interlude memories, he found himself preoccupied with thoughts of a living woman. The woman he'd met at Rascal's.

Reading the number over several times, he was undecided as to whether he was trying to commit it to memory, or just stalling.

"Alexandra Borrelli," he said aloud. "443-746…"

According to dating etiquette columns, there was a protocol to asking a new woman for a date. Calling too soon made him seem desperate. Waiting too long made him seem disinterested, or even worse, might cause *her* to lose interest. According to everything he'd read, three days was the magic number. He moved to the kitchen table next to the enamel-white wall phone, discerningly punched in the number, and took a deep breath.

An unseen phone at the far end began to ring. He tried to picture it in his mind. Was it a wall phone like his? Or maybe one sitting on the nightstand next to her bed. It was probably a light color...a blue, or maybe a green. He thought her a green person. He imagined her place. It would be soft and demure. With color on the walls. There'd be paintings. Landscapes or still life. Or maybe black & white photographs. Reprints of famous photographers like Ansel Adams or Annie Leibovitz. Or maybe she shot them herself. Maybe she—

"Hello?" The interrupting voice was feminine. His imaginings evaporated.

Harvey stumbled on his tongue. "Um, Alexandra? Uh...hi? This...this is Harvey. We met at Rascal's. Thursday night. Remember?"

"Rascal's…oh! Yes! Harvey! *Hi*, Harvey. Of *course* I remember. I'm so glad you called."

All of Harvey's great uncertainty dissolved and her words encouraged him to continue. "Well, I'm glad I caught you. I thought maybe you weren't home."

"Oh...the number I gave you is my cell. Actually, I just left the gym."

Harvey looked at the folded napkin in his hand. Beside her name, clearly printed, was the word, cell. "Oh...yes. I see. Sorry."

"That's okay. I'm happy you called anyway, regardless of which phone."

"That makes me feel better. I was afraid to call too soon. I didn't want you to think me over anxious."

"I see. You must read those stupid dating advice articles." Alexandra laughed, and after her quip registered, Harvey began laughing with her.

"Actually, I do."

Alexandra chuckled. "That's all right. So do I. It's hard meeting new people. A little advice is a good thing as long as you don't let it dominate you."

She was a talker, directing the conversation, inviting him in and helping him along, and for Harvey, a person who always seemed to be searching for something to say, that was just fine with him.

"So …" she continued, shifting gears, "you work nights, right?"

"Yes. I work the mid-shift at the pathology lab downtown."

"Yes, I remember you saying. I have to tell you, my mother always wanted me to marry a doctor." She laughed again. "Nothing like a little pressure, eh?" She paused. "So, Harvey, I'm curious."

"Curious? About what?"

"Well...there must be a reason why you called."

Harvey felt his heart begin the short climb into his throat. Calling her was just the first in a long series of steps. He wasn't sure how to ask, but he was here now, so he may as well bite the bullet.

"I was wondering, Alexandra," he stammered, "if you might be available for dinner one night this week." He wiped the trickle of sweat from his temple as his heart stopped.

"Dinner? Oh, I'd love to. What do you have in mind?"

Harvey's grin returned with a vengeance. He shuffled his feet like a schoolboy and composed the best response he could, his voice betraying his absolute glee.

"Oh, I don't know. I hadn't thought that far ahead. I was working on the hello part most of the morning."

A laugh that sounded much like music came to him from inside the phone. "You're so funny," she said. "I really like your sense of humor."

"Well, that's a good thing, Alexandra. So, is there someplace in particular you'd like to go?"

There was a short pause, then, "I am rather fond of Italian," she said. "I've never been there, but I hear Salvatore's is excellent. And I've been dying for linguini and white clam sauce."

"Salvatore's...Salvatore's...I don't know where that is."

"Salvatore's Ristorante. It's in Little Italy, over on Fawn Street. It's easy to find. If you work downtown, it can't be far from you."

"My work is only ten minutes from Little Italy. All right. Salvatore's it is. Is there a night that's good for you?"

"Well, let's see...this is Monday. How about tonight?" she said with a giggle.

Harvey was caught off guard. He had to work tonight, unusual for a Monday, but what McGovern wants, McGovern gets. It would be nice if he didn't have to work the night of their first date, in case the opportunity to get into her pants presented itself. He wasn't going to plan on it, but the possibility existed. And if it did, he could always call in sick.

Then, there was the other option. The option he used when he didn't call in sick, the option that was more the norm for the way he usually operated.

"I'll make the reservations for seven. Is that okay?"

"That's perfect."

"Great! How about I pick you up at six?"

"Ahhh… You know, Harvey. You're nice and all, and I trust you, but I think maybe I'd rather meet you there."

The dating etiquette advice came flooding back. In this day and age of women's lib, and as a matter of safety, it was entirely proper for first-time daters to meet at the appointed place, at the appointed time, as opposed to the man picking the woman up at home.

"Yes," he said. "Of course," "So, about seven then?"

Another short pause, and Harvey had the distinct impression she had something more to say, until finally she just said, "I'll be there."

CHAPTER 61

Truax didn't *hear* his stomach rumble, as much as *feel* it. He glanced up from half-reading Riki Harrison's autopsy report to the big wall clock in the squad room. It was after six and he wondered where the time had gone.

He drifted back to grade school and Miss Copanas's third-grade class and the giant wall clock that looked like this one, the big-faced clock with enormous black numbers; the one with the minute hand that never moved.

Time, he thought. *Moves faster the older you get.*

His mind was elsewhere. He knew because he found himself re-reading the same paragraph over and over in an attempt to assimilate its contents.

It's funny how one's mind applies the conscious piece of itself to one task and gains no ground, while the sub-conscious piece works to deal with an issue that's more important.

That's what his mind was doing. Dealing with something more important.

Dropping the hardcopy report in his lap, he leaned back and rubbed his eyes, and stewed over the voice mail message that greeted him when he arrived.

The phone message indicator was flashing when he walked in. His first impression was of Atkins handing him his marching orders. But the message wasn't from Atkins. The message was from Vecchio.

"Moby," she began, "I hate to do this to you, and I hate delivering the news over the phone, but my office has recalled me to San Diego. My flight leaves at 4:30 this afternoon. I don't handle goodbyes very well, so let me just say I hope you understand, and thanks for everything. I learned a lot from you. Good luck with the cyanide case. Knowing you, it's just a matter of time."

Short and abrupt. That in itself should have appealed to him, but it didn't. He wasn't sure why her message hit him the way it did. Why the sudden feeling of loss overtook him upon hearing her words, or why he could feel the color drain from his face. Maybe because she was beginning to grow on him, or maybe because he was beginning to like bouncing ideas off her. Maybe he just enjoyed looking down her blouse. Who knows? He tried to shrug it off as no big deal, but it was harder to do than he wanted to admit— like taking in a stray, and then having to give it back to its rightful owners.

Too bad, he thought. *She* was *kinda pretty.*

Clearing his desk, he locked his computer and pushed himself back. He needed to eat, so he thought he may as well take the opportunity to grab a burger. His doctor's warning trickled into his mind. *Okay...maybe a salad. High cholesterol. Shit. I hate salad.*

He stood and rolled his chair under his desk, pulling his jacket from the back just as the phone rang. Like a jilted lover pining in seclusion, his heart became light with the possibility it was Vecchio changing her mind. Leaning in, he lifted the handset.

"Truax."

"Hi Moby," Johnson said. "Didn't know if you'd still be there. I kinda lost track of time, working all day and all night an' all."

That it was Johnson, and not Vecchio on the other end of the phone, deflated him.

"Okay Johnson. You made your point. Whadda ya got?"

"This may take a while. You might want to sit down if you're not sitting already."

"It's been a long day Johnson. Out with it for God's sake!"

"I see you're even grumpier in the afternoon. Well, to begin with, there are glaring discrepancies in OCME's autopsy report on the Harrison girl in comparison to mine."

"Define, 'glaring'."

"The puncture wound I told you about. For starters, there is no mention of it in the OCME report. The photos don't show it either. It's so small there should have been a close-up. There isn't."

As a second thought, Truax decided to take Johnson's suggestion. He returned his jacket to the chair back and sat down. He placed the phone on speaker and began an inspection of his cuticles. "Yeah, I noticed that too," he replied. "I'm reading the report now. What about the tox screens from the samples you pulled?"

"The results came back about an hour ago. I compared the initial tox findings for stomach contents and blood samples. I couldn't re-test stomach contents since pathology had them cremated after the autopsy, and drained all the fluids, so I took fresh organ slices and vitreous humor samples instead, and sent them to the microbiology lab. You're gonna fucking love this.

"According to *my* tests, the cyanide in Riki Harrison's body came in the form of rat poison, just like Anya Eiffel. But the cyanide in the Harrison samples sent over from OCME match all the CK victims exactly. And I mean fucking *exactly*! No variation. I double-checked the official reports myself."

"Wait a minute!" Truax said. "Tox tested the original concentrations of the stomach contents and blood samples of all the victims. Different techs tested different victims. They all reported that the type of cyanide, and the concentration, was identical in all of the Cyanide Killer's victims. Now you're telling me they're not?"

"At least as far as the Harrison girl," Johnson replied. "And I'd bet a week's salary that they don't match up with the other victims either."

"How the fuck does *that* happen?"

"Simple, Moby. Someone altered the reports. Not hard to do with online documents. Who would check? And even if they did, do you really think some overworked tech in the toxicology lab would remember what report said what about which samples? I don't. I barely remember what I did yesterday."

Truax said nothing, a sure signal for Johnson to continue.

"Because we intercepted the Harrison woman, we know for a fact the pathology report isn't accurate. Not even close. Hell, the blood types aren't even the same. And except for stupidity or incompetence, I just don't understand why someone would do that."

"To make it look like something it's not," Truax mumbled, then paused, saying nothing for a moment, and Johnson checked to see if his cell phone dropped again.

"Yes, I'm here," Truax said when asked.

"There's one last thing, Moby, and it's a big 'one thing.' I don't know how you knew, but somebody had sex with the body after I examined it. Now I see why you asked me to check her out. But how'd you know?"

"I didn't," Truax said, glancing at Morral's name on Riki Harrison's autopsy report. He rubbed his temples and wished he had an aspirin. Or a cigarette. Or both. "Where are her clothes? We'll need to line up the hole with the puncture wound. Check for semen."

"Lost in transit to Trace."

"That's evidence! How the hell— Shit! Never mind. Okay, Johnson. Anything else?"

"That's it. Unless you have another chore for me."

"You didn't happen to speak with Walters at the Tox lab, did you?"

"Nope. I never saw Walters. Worked with a new kid. Never met him before today."

"I gotta talk to Walters. Okay. I can't think of anything else right now. Thanks for the help. Sorry about the soccer game."

"The season's young," Johnson said. "There'll be more."

CHAPTER 62

A mandolin played somewhere in the background. Alexandra was late, but only because Harvey was early. Early by thirty minutes.

He came directly from a top-shelf men's clothing store in Marley Station, wearing the tan cargo pants and the crisp white short-sleeve button-down shirt he bought for the occasion.

Nursing a beer, he sat on a bar stool tapping the ashes of his cigarette on the tea-rose marble floor. He felt the rumblings of his stomach, set to churning by the aroma of Italian delicacies; entrees carried into the main dining room on large round trays by waiters in classic black-and-whites with razor-sharp pleats.

The oak bar ran the length of the 10 X 25 room, its distressed surface littered with beer bottles, glass ashtrays, and long-stemmed wine glasses that paired with the patrons sitting across from them. The brick wall behind the bar gave the space a rustic feel, and the mirrors backing the lit shelves created the illusion of twice the number of liquor bottles than were actually there.

Backlit by recessed lighting overhead were cocktail glasses of every shape and size, hanging upside-down from their stems, waiting for a bartender to slide one out for some delightful concoction.

Anxious with anticipation, the motion of the front door drew Harvey's eyes to the brick entrance foyer when anyone walked in, and when it wasn't Alexandra, he'd check his watch in disappointment. Two cigarettes later the door opened and there she was, her olive skin enriched by the summer sun, her thick black hair falling in easy waves, framing her face as she turned to look at the photos pinned against the brick: photos of Frank Sinatra and Tony Bennett and Dean Martin—all taken with the elated owner. Harvey smiled, condemning his nay-saying lack of confidence, and as the certainty of being stood-up evaporated, he drank her in.

Catching her eye with a wave, she smiled and waved back as she began her walk toward him. She was taller tonight, he thought, and then realized why upon spotting the three-inch, light brown heels that made her legs appear longer than he remembered.

She dressed to the summer in a beige, above-the-knee pencil skirt with a slit that ran the length of her thigh. The yellow print blouse that peeked from under her light-brown summer jacket, and the simple gold chain that raced around her elegant neck, simply couldn't compete.

Swallowing hard, Harvey pulled out the neighboring barstool and failed as he tried not to gawk. His longing grew as she approached. Her body, the way it moved, more pleasing with her every step. He inwardly congratulated himself on his earlier decision, and whether he decided to use it or not, bringing the syringe tonight was absolutely the right move.

CHAPTER 63

"Walters?" Truax repeated. "That you?"

"Yes...yes...this is Walters," he said, rubbing the sleep from his eyes and fumbling with the phone against his ear. "Who is this please?"

"This is Truax, Walters! Detective Truax! I've been waiting to hear from you. Where the hell you been?"

"Truax? Shit! Shit...I fell asleep. Truax..."

"WAKE UP! *Damn* it...WALTERS!"

"Okaaay already! Give me a fucking minute, will ya?"

Truax said nothing, listening to Walters grunt and moan and clear his throat, emitting all the sounds he usually made upon waking. Some, Truax noted, were part of his own waking ritual. Some were not.

"Okay, Detective," Walters finally mumbled. "I'm here."

"You want to throw some water on your face Walters? I can wait."

"No...no. I'm awake. Sorry. Your tests took much longer than I anticipated. I worked...I worked...what time is it, anyway?"

"It's 7:43pm."

"Sunday night…"

"Monday night, Walters," Truax corrected.

"*Monday* night? *Monday*? Oh God. Please tell me it's not Monday. Shit. I'm in *big* trouble."

"I'm sorry to hear that, Walters," Truax said, "but I got my own problems. Whadda ya got for me on those tox screens?"

Truax could hear guttural clicks and heavy breathing, signals alerting him to the anger on the other end, and he knew it was directed at him. He ruined Walters's weekend and put him in the dog house in one fell swoop—like he cared. He had bigger fish. But he waited, giving Walters the time he needed to vent. He allowed him one minute, and when that minute passed, he said, "You ready now, Walters?"

There was a gap, and Truax thought he was going to have to repeat himself, but Walters finally spoke up.

"Yes, Detective," Walters said, each syllable uttered with measured emphasis, "I have your information."

Truax decided not to aggravate Walters further and waited, saying nothing, allowing Walters his disapproval and self-pity. Several seconds elapsed before Walters continued, no doubt taking the time to visualize how he would hang the blame for disappearing all weekend on Truax, in the hope his wife would believe him.

"In a nutshell, Detective, I found the same inconsistencies across the board with the CK victims, that we saw with the Dorothy French and Emma Baumgartner killings. I'll email my official reports to you."

Truax had allowed Walters ample time to seethe, but now he was becoming belligerent and difficult, and Truax didn't have time to pamper or placate him. His voice became hard, and it became clear that any expectation of consolation was ill founded. The pity-party was over.

"I don't have time to check my *fucking* emails, Walters," Truax snapped. "Spell it out for me."

There came a pause, the kind of pause that could have gone either way; a direct challenge to the authority on the other end of the phone, or submission.

"Yes, Detective. Of course," Walters said. The edge in his voice disappeared. "The tox screens I performed on the organ specimen from evidence holding revealed that two different cyanide compositions were used in the CK murders. However, the tox reports from the case files state all the victims died of acute cyanide poisoning of the *same* compound—that being industrial grade potassium-cyanide.

"The fact of the matter," Walters continued, "is that only three victims were actually poisoned with that particular concentration. They were—"

"Dorothy French, Harriett Brennermann, and Rosa Neunyo," Truax interjected. "The older victims, right?"

"Yes, Detective. That *is* right. But if you already knew, why did you have me—"

"Evidence, Walters. You've heard of that, I assume? What about the others?" Truax continued, referring to the younger victims, asking a question, to which he again, already had the answer.

"Rat poison. Half the potency, three times the dosage. It was the same with all the younger victims: Emma Baumgartner, Stacy Culver, Kara Templeton, Georgia Parsons, Anya Eiffel...looks like you got two killers on your hands, Detective."

"Yeah," Truax mumbled. "I kinda suspected that. What about the baby's water bottle from the Templeton file?"

"Ah, yes...the baby bottle. The water was laced with rat poison as well."

"Yeah...makes sense. And the DNA? Did you get the FBI lab to run comparisons on the CK victims?"

"You know, when I asked them for that, they wanted to know why I wanted to run them again."

"Again?" Truax started. "What do you mean, 'again'?"

"That's what I asked. Apparently, mine was the second request for that very same information. The first request came in late last week. Apparently, some fluid vials were found by a highway work crew. Blood evidence. They turned it into the microbiology lab and they, in turn, forwarded it to the FBI DNA lab for an ID. Turned out to belong to Harriett Brennermann. CK's second victim. When they determined that, the lab asked for a full comparison run on all the CK victims."

Truax could hardly believe what he was hearing. How could he have not known about this? His heart became a hammer and his blood began to surge, pronouncing the vein in the center of his forehead.

"WHO?" Truax screamed, forcing Walters to yank the phone from his ear. "WHO requested the DNA work? And who fucking authorized it!"

"It...it was requested b-by the FBI. An agent working the c-c-c-case. Someone named Vecchio."

"...*Vecchio?*"

"Yes Sir," Walters replied, just before dropping the final bomb. "Authorized by Captain Atkins."

Truax's heart jumped into his throat. It felt as if someone sucker-punched him in the gut and his stomach turned over, just before he felt the urge to retch.

CHAPTER 64

Alexandra smiled. "Hi," she said as she slowed to a tentative stop beside the stool Harvey held for her. Securing a seat was the polite and proper thing to do, especially for a woman, especially if he wanted to get laid, especially if she were still alive later.

Placing her hand on his shoulder, she sat down as he flexed the shoulder muscles under her hand, hardening them for her benefit. She wiggled a bit to settle herself and then turned to him with a perky smile. "I'm sorry I'm late."

The imaginings of the lab and the stainless-steel gurney that had crept in on her approach, quickly retreated to the back of his mind, idling there in the event they were needed again.

"It's just a little after eight, so let's just say, fashionably so," Harvey said, assisting her to within arm's reach of the bar. "You look incredible," Harvey continued. "And what's that fragrance? It's very nice."

"Christian Dior. I only wear it on special occasions. So...I see you found the restaurant okay," she said, gazing admiringly around the room, taking in the Greco-Roman décor.

"Oh, yes. Came right to it. Wasn't hard to find."

She smiled with satisfaction. "Told you."

"Yes, you did. I'll have to trust your judgment from here out."

Two drinks later, their hostess seated them. A short time after that, the waiter took their dinner order. Alexandra looked around the dining room. Another smile. "Geez...will you look at this place?" she said, referring to the Italian inspired oils and watercolors hanging around the space, each individually lit with wall-mounted satin-nickel fixtures. "You've never been here before either?" she asked.

"I think I might have been here years ago," he replied, "but I can't be sure. Everything looks different inside, but the outside looks familiar."

"I wouldn't know. This is my first time. I've always wanted to try this place, but I never had a reason to drive this far before."

"Really...No one ever brought you here for dinner?"

"'Fraid not. I don't get out much and I wasn't going to come all by myself. Too far to go unescorted."

"How far is far?"

"I live north of Perry Hall. It's just under an hour for me. Too far by myself."

There was a short pause in the conversation as Harvey groped for something to say, an uncomfortable gap in the stream of intercourse. Suddenly brain dead, he chose the obvious.

"Perry Hall. That's about thirty minutes from here. Not too bad." The tact did what he hoped, that was, lead to something else. "So, do you have a nickname, Alexandra? Alex maybe?"

"No, Alex is a boy's name. I go by Alexandra."

"Oh...sorry."

"Don't be. It's a question I hear a lot."

"You know, Alexandra, I have a hard time believing you don't date. You're—Damn! I shouldn't say this."

"No...go on. Please. I think I'm going to like it."

Harvey managed a fleeting smile, took a breath and said, "You're very attractive. I would think you have 'em lining up at the door."

"HA!" She covered a whimsical grin with her hand. "I wish, but thanks for the compliment."

"So," Harvey continued, "you work in customer service?"

It was her turn to provide a little background. He'd given her the version of his life's story he wanted her to have, mentioning nothing about his failure with women, and that he still lived in his mother's house. He told her why he decided to become a doctor, his trials and tribulations in medical school, and eventually, why he chose pathology.

Alexandra smiled, thanking the waiter as he placed her linguini in front of her, and declined his offer of extra fresh-ground parmesan cheese, from the peppermill grater. "Yes," she replied. "Customer service. It's really just a transitional job until I can work my way into some sort of management program. Mmmm...this linguini smells so good."

"Yes, it does. Maybe I should have ordered that instead."

"Want to try it?"

He smiled. "Yeah. Okay."

"And I'll have a bite of your lasagna in return," she teased, twirling her fork in the pasta like a seasoned pro. "It's so cozy here. Did you see those paintings?" She sighed. "The canals of Venice, Rome's Colosseum. Maybe I'll get there some day." She leaned toward him and offered him a silver fork, wrapped with layer upon layer of linguini, wound tight like a ball of yarn and dripping with white clam sauce. "And just look at that fireplace! So romantic… I wish they had a fire going. Oooh, watch out! It's loaded with garlic. You like garlic?"

"Umm-humm…I wuv garwic," he said, curving his words around a mouthful of noodles. The slurping sound that escaped as he gathered up the stragglers put an exclamation point on his remark. Catching a trickle of sauce with his napkin, he continued.

"I take it you like to travel."

CHAPTER 65

The purple of dusk absorbed what little blue remained in the sky, and Truax rolled toward Harvey Morral's house code 10-40—no lights, no siren. Pressing the Send button on his cell, he redialed Vecchio's number yet again, and her ringtone played in his head like an annoying tune that wouldn't go away.

Bad boys bad boys, whatcha gonna do?

He hated the TV theme song, but couldn't banish it from his mind. It was just after 8pm, 5 on the west coast, and there was still no answer.

His memory was acute tonight. He crunched and rehashed the information—forensic findings, autopsy reports, tox screens, DNA comparisons...and the nine victims who were only three. All the information was there, circumstantial evidence that pointed directly to Morral, evidence that Agent Vecchio possessed days before he did.

All that brain-working occupied the forefront of his mind, but in the back, his subconscious dwelled on a mistake. His mistake. The mistake of not seeing Vecchio for who she really was. For *what* she really was. A loose cannon, a backstabber, a rogue element that intentionally withheld information critical to his case; information that, had she passed it on, might have prevented the death of Riki Harrison. That made her complicit as far as he was concerned, even if the law didn't see it that way. But one thing was sure, after her superiors got wind of her shenanigans, she was toast. It would cost her her badge, and he didn't understand why she would chance that.

But what if it wasn't Vecchio? What if she was an unwitting pawn? Considering Atkins's agenda to get him behind a desk, maybe Atkins saw Vecchio as an opportunity to get him off the front lines. Maybe he wants her in this job. Maybe, he just wants *her*.

Truax would be more than happy to retire if he could afford it. The job had changed. The old guard was gone, his peers, retired. Long live The New Order! The new way of doing things. The sweeping away of the old to make room for the young—the likes of Vecchio and Nichols.

But even at that, even if all that were true, why wasn't Morral in custody? Why hadn't Vecchio arrested him and taken the credit for apprehending the Cyanide Killer? She had the same information he had, and she had it at least two days before he did.

And why hadn't Atkins busted him for incompetence? Surely, he knew what Vecchio knew. He authorized the DNA work for her for God's sake! But more puzzling still, why didn't any of this make sense? There was something else going on here. What was he missing?

Barreling east down Mountain Road, Truax passed Shahverdi's Foreign Car at well over the legal speed limit. He continued across Waterford Ave. approaching Escalon Ave., his thoughts distracted him to the point of overshooting his turn. The cruiser was equipped with a GPS navigational system, one of the top-shelf units with a voice synthesizer, and it would have announced that his turn was coming up if he hadn't powered the unit off.

He continued on to George Williams Avenue and yanked the wheel to the left. The big Crown Vic lurched and her tires screamed in protest. As it fishtailed through the turn, it cut deep into the lane that oncoming traffic would use, had there been oncoming traffic. Swerving back into his lane, Truax continued into the middle-class neighborhood and he tried to focus on Morral. He had no extra cycles to theorize why Vecchio did what she did, or why she was suddenly recalled to Home Office.

Something was rotten about all this. Maybe it was an elaborate ploy to discredit him in an effort to get rid of him, or maybe he was just becoming paranoid in his old age. But being paranoid didn't mean he was wrong. Either way, he didn't have the time or the luxury to ponder it.

Truax figured, at worst, he had Morral for tampering with evidence, falsifying autopsy reports, and obstruction; all of which gave him cause to hold him for weeks, and if a search turned up what he was looking for at Morral's house, he'd amend the charges to include the murders of Riki Harrison and the others.

Truax accelerated as he passed the first right for Escaion Avenue, and proceeded to the dead end a block away before ripping through the right-hand turn there. It was the most direct route to the Morral house sitting halfway down the block.

He intentionally used the cruiser to block Morral's driveway. Even though no car was in sight, from his location there was no telling what the garage concealed. He'd have to wait for the warrant to find out.

Climbing from the Crown Vic, a breeze rustled the tree branches, and he thought again of the storm clouds off in the distance. Closing the door, he leaned against the car to wait for the forensics team. Looking about the neighborhood, he saw yellow-green flashes, dancing in no particular pattern in the approaching dusk.

Lightning bugs, he thought. *Used to catch 'em when I was eight. Kept 'em in a jar with holes in the lid. Took 'em to bed with me and watched 'em flash in the dark. I wish I'da known then what a great time that was. Simple. Easy.*

The ol' man worked eight to five, Monday through Friday, weekends off. And the biggest worry he had was havin' enough money for a six-pack after paying the bills at the end of the week. Stress wasn't a medical condition back then. Jobs weren't 24/7.

There were no cell phones. No computers. Dad was home by five-thirty, Mom called us in at five-forty-five and dinner was at six. Everybody had a pension and people retired back then. Their money didn't vanish over-fucking-night. What the hell happened?

Sounds from approaching engines snapped him out of his funk. He pushed off from the Crown Vic and took two steps toward the rear of the car. A pair of Maryland state cruisers—army-green on black— took point. The first had a single uniformed trooper, and two troopers were in the second. Behind them came a department van and a black Denali SUV with the forensics team. The four vehicles slowed to a stop, surrounding Truax's sedan. The forensics vehicles killed their headlights. The police cruisers did not.

"Moby…" Usher said, exiting the van and nodding in Truax's direction.

Steve Usher was the field forensics lead. Truax nodded back, regarding a man he always considered to be a younger version of himself. Thirty *years* younger.

Steve Usher stood over six feet tall with what a novelist might describe as "rugged" good looks: dark wavy hair, dark blue eyes set a bit too deep in his skull, a regal nose proportional to his face, high cheekbones, square jaw, powerful shoulders...just an overall good-looking guy. *Probably gets laid a lot,* Truax thought as he offered his hand.

"How are you, Steve? Are you up to speed?"

"I guess. Pretty straight forward stuff," Usher said, slipping into a dark blue windbreaker, the word FORENSICS emblazoned in yellow across the back. "Just a standard evidence search."

"You have the warrant?" Truax asked.

"I do." He slapped the paperwork into Truax's open palm, and then began pulling on a pair of blue nitrile gloves, his glove of choice due to a bad reaction to latex. "So where's Vecchio tonight?" Usher asked.

Truax began to stew before responding with, "Wait here." He pointed to one of the uniformed troopers. "You," he said. "Around back," and to the other, "Come with me." Without another word, he left a confused Usher and the others, waiting by their respective vehicles.

He and the uniformed trooper approached the front of the house, knocked on the door, and waited for a response. A moment later, Harvey's mother filled the doorjamb in her flower-print robe. The flashing emergency lights painted her white Cape Cod blue and red, causing her to peer around Truax. She became visibly shaken at the sight of Maryland State cruisers stationed in front of her house.

"What...what is happening? What's going on? Why are those police cars here?"

"Yes ma'am," Truax said, identifying himself as he glanced past Marie Morral into the house. It was more a precaution, than an attempt to find something damning. "We'd like a word with Harvey Morral."

"Harvey? Why are you looking for Harvey?"

"Is he here, ma'am?"

"No. What's this about?"

"Do you know where he is?"

"He's out. On a date. What do you want?"

"I'm sorry ma'am, but we have a warrant to search the premises. My people will do their best not to damage your possessions. Now, if you would please step aside—"

"Search my house? You can't search my house! It's *my* house! And you don't belong here! My son is a doctor! You can't come in! "

"We have a warrant, ma'am. Now, please—"

"NO!" she screamed and she pushed Truax in the chest, but succeeded only in rocking him back an inch or so. Rushing to contain her, the trooper wrapped Marie Morral up in his arms, taking care not to hurt her, as Truax called in the third trooper to help. He wasn't going to arrest her for assaulting a police officer or failing to comply or obstruction. He just wanted her the hell out of the way.

CHAPTER 66

The undercurrent of white noise about the restaurant diminished as patrons finished their dinners, and departed in groups of two, three, and four. The scurry of wait staff subsided proportionally as the manager cut them when their customers left. The busboy clearing a nearby table glanced at the door, no doubt hoping the dawdling couple would get the message. Alexandra waited for his retreat before continuing.

"It's not much of a job," she said, summing up the menial and mind-numbing aspects of her current employment. "Could you pour me another glass of wine, please? I man the Help Desk, answer the phone, ask about their problem, and look it up in the Primus Database. Then I ask them questions from a script and have them do things. I don't understand the...thank you Harvey. I don't understand the technology."

"That sounds really...boring, I'm sorry to say."

"Believe me, it is. And let me tell you, if I didn't— Oh!" she blurted, jabbing a turquoise fingernail into space. "Look! The dessert tray!"

Harvey noted that it was more of a cart, than a tray, but it did mercifully shift the conversation from her excessively mundane line of work.

The waiter, a tall dark fellow, smiled as he rolled the cart to a stop in front of their table, his eyes riveted on Alexandra, perhaps regarding *her* as dessert.

"Cheesecake, apple pie, cannolis...oh!" she said pointing to some unknown layered dessert. "*This* looks *really* good," she said. "What is it?"

"*Tiramisu, Signorina,*" the waiter answered in a heavy Italian accent. "Very light. Very *cioccolata*. Is...how you say? Awesome?"

"Should we have dessert?" Her smile sent Harvey's imagination back to his lab. He began to wonder how it would be, actually knowing the girl beforehand. Not just as an acquaintance like the others, but actually *knowing* her. Would that make it better?

"Anything you want, Alexandra."

"Let's get one and share," she suggested. "Okay?"

Harvey nodded automatically as he began running through killing scenarios, and gave the high sign to the waiter. The waiter nodded his understanding and then rolled the cart to the next tableful of diners.

"So, you're not working tonight?" Alexandra asked.

"What?"

"Working. You're not working tonight?"

"Oh! Yes. Unfortunately. I couldn't get the night off. McGovern, my boss, put me on tonight. I tried to get out of it. I mean, what kind of a date..."

Harvey stopped himself as his breathing increased slightly. His Need was with him. Not like with Georgia or Anya or Riki, this was more. *Much* more. He never ruled out having Alexandra in the lab. It was always a possibility. A fantasy, ever since meeting her at Rascal's, and considering the way his life's normal relationships had gone, maybe it was just better this way. No strings or feelings to get in the way. No feelings to get hurt. *His* feelings.

No, maybe he should stick to what works for him. Just leave her here on the parking lot and head to work. He had his tools, although the hypo didn't contain cyanide. After dumping all his stock and using the last of it on Riki, he made the switch to potassium-chloride, a compound that stops the heart almost instantly. It worked with lethal injection, so it should work for him.

Unfortunately, he had no more CK fluids to substitute for hers, but that was of no consequence now. His Need was with him. He couldn't resist it. He'd just have to find another means of skewing the test results.

"Oh," Alexandra said, handling the awkward pause in stride. "That's okay. I understand having to work. They call me in all the time. There's no avoiding it." She smiled. "So, what time do you have to be in?"

Harvey looked at his watch, the hands of his gold Rolex knockoff, easy to see in the restaurant lighting. It was 10:53. He had just enough time to finish dessert, walk her to her car, and get to work. After that, all he had to do was wait for her to arrive.

"Midnight," he replied. "I have to get going after dessert if I'm to be on time. McGovern hates when his people are late."

"Well, we still have a little time," Alexandra, said. "The evening went by so fast. But I guess there's always next time." She smiled warmly. "There's an old Vaudeville saying about ending a show. Ever heard it?"

"No, Alexandra. I don't think I have."

"Well, I'll tell you, then." She separated out several strands of long black hair and twirled them around her fingers. "There's an old saying they use: 'Leave 'em wanting more.' So that's what we're doing, and this way we can look forward to the next time we're together. Hopefully, it won't be too long."

Harvey smiled, now sure of his course. "It won't be," Harvey said. "Promise."

CHAPTER 67

Truax stood in the hallway of Marie Morral's house as Forensics went about their business. He would have smoked a cigarette if he had one, but there was no one he could pan-handle from, since no one present smoked. They never did. It was as if someone had mounted a conspiracy against him—probably his mother.

Keeping track of the forensics teams, he tried not to interfere, deciding the best way to do that was to check on Marie Morral. He had to question her anyway.

She sat in a chair beside the kitchen table with the trooper who had restrained her. She sat uncuffed as per Truax's instructions. Cuffing a woman her age, in her own home, when she's done nothing really wrong, was not Truax's idea of law enforcement.

He could hear the trooper talking to her, keeping her calm, explaining to her that she had nothing to worry about. That this was routine and that her cooperation would have them out of her house more quickly than not.

As he watched the trooper work, he decided not to interrupt him just yet, thinking he would make a good detective someday. He was heading back into the living room when the sound of descending footsteps on the stairway caught his attention. It was Steve Usher.

"There's nothing here, Moby," Usher said as he reached the last step. "It's clean. Looks like he—"

Truax pursed his lips and placed his index finger north-south across them. Then he gestured toward the kitchen.

"Oh, sorry," Usher said, lowering his voice. "If he's your boy, he keeps nothing incriminating in his room, unless you're busting him for porn." He grinned. "His mother probably doesn't know about that. We'll check out the garage and the basement next."

Truax looked back to Marie Morral. *No time like the present*, he thought. Acknowledging Usher, he started back toward the kitchen, leaving the forensics team to probe the basement and garage. Pulling out a kitchen chair, Truax gestured for the trooper to leave them and sat down across from Marie Morral.

"Mrs. Morral…"

"Like I said to that young man that just left," she interrupted, "it's Ms."

"Yes. Of course," Truax said. "*Ms*. Morral. I need to find your son. I have to ask him some questions concerning several cases he worked. Would you happen to know where he went on his date? It's very important."

"No. I'm afraid I don't. He don't tell me those things. All I know is he was going to dinner. Taking a woman he met just last week. Besides, it ain't none of my business where he goes. He's a grown man. He don't need his mother looking after him. At least that's what I tell him."

"Yes ma'am. Maybe you know what restaurant?"

"He ain't got no favorite place. He don't eat out much."

"Did he tell you what part of town? Maybe the kind of food? American, Mexican, Italian?"

After fifteen minutes of questioning, Marie Morral continued to insist she didn't know where Harvey was. Truax didn't believe her. Mothers tend to protect their sons, but while questioning her, she let slip that Harvey had borrowed her car. When pressed for the make, model, and year, she became conveniently absent minded once again, a condition Truax could relate to, but couldn't swallow in this particular case.

It was the same for her license number. She either didn't remember it or pretended she didn't, but either way, Truax would dig up the information from MVA, and dispatch a BOLO—Be On the Look Out.

He left Marie Morral in the house with her trooper escort, and walked outside to make the call while the forensics team continued to probe the basement and garage. Before he could call in the request for Marie Morral's MVA information, Usher called him over.

"Moby, I think you better come have a look at this. Found something in the crevices of the workbench in the garage."

Truax turned his task over to the first trooper he saw, told him what he wanted, and then followed Usher to the detached garage in the back of the yard. He was the only one not surprised at the discovery.

"Powder," Usher said. "Taste test says its rat poison, but we'll need the lab to confirm."

"No chance you found needles—"

"Nope. Sorry."

"Well, nothing about this case has been easy. Okay, when you're finished here, get everything you find to Tox and Latent," he said. "Have them call me with the results as soon as they're ready." Turning, he walked out to find the trooper that he tasked with getting his MVA information.

"What do you have?" Truax said.

"A dark-blue, 2007 Ford Focus is registered to a Marie Morral at this address, Detective."

Truax allowed his head to drop. Things just weren't going his way. There are thousands of Ford Focuses in the city. "Very well. Go ahead and dispatch the BOLO. Maybe we'll get lucky and someone will spot the tag."

"Yes Sir," the trooper replied. "But the car is equipped with LoJack. Why don't we just turn it on?"

As night settled on the neighborhood, a dog barked off in the distance, maybe at a rabbit or a fox. The locals, as Truax liked to refer to them, were inside getting ready for bed. Perhaps watching reruns of their crime shows, or the totally unbearable reality programs that had become all the rage.

The LoJack unit put Marie Morral's Ford, downtown. It was stationary, on a parking lot at the corners of Eastern Avenue and President Street. Little Italy. But Truax doubted it would remain there much longer. He instructed the two troopers in the single cruiser to follow him, and the two cars made a hasty departure for the city.

CHAPTER 68

Harvey fell in behind Alexandra as they started from the restaurant, and nearly knocked her over when she came to an abrupt stop beside the hostess station. Dipping her hand into a large glass bowl filled with green foil-wrapped dinner mints, she came away with five or six and dropped them into her purse, then turned to Harvey and smiled a meek apology.

"I love these things," she said. "I stock up when I go out. That's not stealing, is it?"

Harvey said nothing and managed a mechanical smile. His Need had his mind on the parking lot, and the How, Where, and When of what came next.

Harvey lit a cigarette once outside, and followed Alexandra down the narrow sidewalk along Fawn Street. Cars parked along the pavement likened themselves to sardines, packed tight against the curb and each other, a necessary compromise with single lane streets that posed the possibility of sideswipe.

Weaving in and out of unhurried people flowing in both directions, they made their way to the corner of Fawn and South High Streets.

"So," Harvey asked, his anticipation heightening. "Where did you park? I'm guessing it's okay if I walk you to your car."

Alexandra smiled broadly and elbowed him playfully in the ribs. "Smarty! Yes, it's o-kaaay! I'm parked way on the far side of the public lot around the next corner."

"Good," Harvey said. "I'm parked there too."

They continued at a dawdling after dinner pace, and after strolling a block down High Street, turned right on Trinity and crossed Albemarle to the parking lot. The crush of the dinner crowd had waned leaving few people on the street, and as they stepped onto the all but abandoned lot, Harvey's Need became acute. He reached into the thigh pocket of his cargo pants and touched the syringe to assure himself it was still there. He gestured with his free hand. "You're parked all the way over there?" he asked.

"Yes" she said. "About two rows from the road. I can go the rest of the way by myself if you want. I know you have to get to work."

"NO!" Harvey snapped. "I mean, no. I wouldn't have it. I'll walk you."

She smiled. "Okay. It *is* kinda dark over there."

She led Harvey across the lot, her route unencumbered now that few cars remained, and as she altered her course, she took a route that passed Harvey's Focus.

"Where's your car?" Harvey asked as they neared the fringe of the lot.

"It's right over there." She pointed to a white Toyota several rows over.

He took one last drag of his cigarette and flicked it into the night, not bothering to track it as he reached into his pocket. He removed the safety cover on the syringe when they cruised to a stop beside her car. Alexandra turned to him, her eyes dark and glistening, and she laid her hands on his chest.

"I had a wonderful time, Harvey."

Harvey said nothing as he began to withdraw the needle, but before it could clear his pocket, she slid her hands

319

upward, placing them on either side of his face. "Thank you so much for a lovely evening," she said, and she kissed him, her mouth open just enough to fire his lust. As her tongue found his, she quickly pushed away.

"YUCK...Cigarettes!"

With an impish smile, she stepped back and began digging through her purse. "Ah! Here it is," she said, removing a green foil-wrapped dinner mint. Peeling off the wrapper, she pressed the rectangular delight to his lips. "This will make a goodnight kiss, even better," she said.

He couldn't deny her what he knew would be a final request, and accepted the offering, allowing her to place the chocolate in his mouth, as a priest would a Communion wafer. She leaned back. "There!" she said, an expectant smile gracing her lips. "Isn't that better?"

"Yes...much," he said, swallowing before forcing a dull smile.

"Mustn't be a litterbug," she said whimsically, and she stuffed the empty wrapper into her purse. With Alexandra distracted, Harvey seized the moment and scanned the immediate area. There was no one close enough to concern him. He slid the syringe from his pocket and concealed it behind his back, anticipating the goodnight kiss that was destined to be her last.

D.B. Corey

CHAPTER 69

Little Italy sat on the edge of Baltimore's east side, a forty-minute drive from Green Haven. Truax and the trailing cruiser made the trip in less than twenty with lights. When they arrived, the flashing red and blue of emergency beacons that were all too common in his life, greeted them. The lights belonged to Baltimore City squad cars.

Truax turned the Crown Vic into the lot with the marked cruiser in tow and maneuvered to the far end of the lot. Before climbing from the car, he spotted the yellow crime scene tape that cordoned off the area. There was a body on the ground, covered with the familiar, ever-present, white sheet.

Truax summoned his troopers, and as they fell in behind him, he searched for a short-sleeved white shirt with the most chevrons on the sleeve. Spotting the biggest African-American cop he'd ever laid eyes on, an officer who could have easily played football for a living, Truax approached him.

"Sergeant," he said, displaying his shield. "You in charge here?"

Sergeant Blaylock eyed the cheap sports jacket and ten-dollar tie, open at the throat, and then focused on the man wearing them.

"I am," he said. "Nobody called the State in. What can I do for you?"

"Detective Truax. SIU." Truax said it like it should have some meaning to the big cop. When it didn't appear to impress him, he continued. "Whadda we got?"

"We? Detective? What do you mean, we?"

Being questioned by a subordinate was a sure way to get Truax's hackles up. "Well—Sergeant—I am in pursuit of a suspect. And that pursuit has led me here. This suspect may be involved in a series of murders, and now I see a body on the ground. So I'll ask again. What do we have here?"

Blaylock relented, but not easily. "We're not sure yet, *Sir*," he said, stressing the mocking tone in his voice. "We just arrived. But no matter what it is—for now, it's a City investigation."

Truax's gray eyes bore down on Blaylock without blinking. "It is what I say it is, Sergeant. And from where I'm standing, it looks like mine if I want it. Now…you said you just arrived. Who called it in?"

Blaylock turned straight on, face-to-face with Truax, and closed the distance between them with a single giant stride, leaving scant inches between them, and forcing Truax to tilt his head back to maintain eye contact. The man nearly blotted out the night sky.

"Listen, Detective," Blaylock said. "I know SIU is Homeland Security, and I also know Homeland trumps City. My pay grade don't give me the right-o-way to engage in a jurisdictional pissing match with you. I'm just a cop. Same as you. So if you wanna play big shot, that's fine with me."

Blaylock relinquished jurisdiction begrudgingly, but not the condescending slant in his voice. "So here it is. One of our regular patrols cruised through and observed the subject lying on the ground. They approached the subject and determined the subject was deceased. They placed the call not ten minutes ago." Blaylock paused for a moment, and then said, "I'm sorry, Sir...I forgot your name. Who are you again?" Blaylock didn't bother disguising the smirk spreading across his face.

Truax either didn't notice or didn't care. "Have you ID'd the body yet?" he asked.

"Yep, Blaylock said, producing the victim's ID. "Name's Morral. Harvey Morral."

CHAPTER 70

Truax leaned back in his chair and stared at the empty desk beside his. He was beginning to think that he liked it better when Vecchio was sitting there. At least the distraction of eyeing her up provided a temporary respite from his own thoughts.

Morral's murder brought everything to a head, culminating in the outcome Atkins's deadline had implied. Truax wasn't surprised Atkins was about to fire him. What surprised him was that Atkins let him hang around for as long as he did.

He didn't actually come right out and say it, and that in itself suggested that even Atkins considered it crass to fire someone over the phone. But Atkins's directive that Truax be in his office Friday morning told him all he needed to know. The writing, Truax noted, is on the wall.

Atkins was at the point where he had to deflect the cluster-fuck that was the Cyanide Killer fiasco away from him, caring not what Truax uncovered, and lending no credence to Truax's two-killer theory; even with forensic tests identifying rat poison as the second killing agent, and even with the new evidence discovered in Morral's garage.

When told of these new developments, Atkins replied with contempt. "If Morral was involved in some way, Detective Truax, then *why* is he *dead?*"

A good question. One Truax had no answer for. Seems that was happening to him a lot, lately. Morral's killing was the same as the others, more or less. He was dumped with little concern to dignity or worth, publicly, at the spot where he died. He had the pink coloring and the almond aroma of the other victims—a strong indication of cyanide. What didn't fit was the small-bore syringe found near Morral's body, perhaps of the same type that was used to murder Riki Harrison. Truax would have bet his paycheck that it was full of rat poison. But it wasn't. It contained potassium-chloride. The killer was still throwing curveballs.

It would take a bit of time to get the tox screens back to be sure of what killed Morral, but if it was indeed cyanide, the lab would make the determination as to what kind of cyanide killed him, and regardless of whether this was CK's work, or the copycat's, or the Easter Bunny's, Morral was the first male victim; a complete departure from either of the two previously established MOs for sure. And there was no way Truax would suggest a third killer to Atkins, even if he believed it himself.

There was no saving his job. Truax knew that much. But that was no reason to abandon the case that gobbled up half-a-year of his life. It was a matter of pride now, so for the next three days he would follow it through, until Atkins made his dismissal official. And until that happened, he was still a cop. He'd review the crime scene report, the lab reports, and the pathology findings—findings he could trust, since he had Johnson doing the autopsy on Morral.

CHAPTER 71

"That's about it, Moby," Johnson concluded. "Morral's autopsy went pretty much as I expected. The pink coloring of his skin suggested cyanide poisoning, and the lab confirmed that, and the composition. The delivery system was at least similar...a chocolate after dinner mint, found in Morral's stomach."

"How about the dosage?"

"Identical. 250 parts per million. This murder is consistent with CK's older victims, and in my professional opinion, CK is the one who committed it."

Reclining in a near prone position, a posture more suited to stargazing in an open field than a telephone conversation, Truax replied, "Yeah...I figured as much."

"If you want the rest of the minutia," Johnson added, "it's all there in my report. So, if you don't mind, I'd like to go home, play with the kids, and screw the wife."

Truax returned to a sitting position with a bounce. "Thanks Johnson," he said. "My regards to Maggie."

CK was invisible before, falling off the face of the earth, until now. What brought him back, Truax wondered. Why crawl out of the woodwork to kill Morral? It seemed the more answers he dug up, the more questions he had.

One of the witnesses on the parking lot that night, said she saw Morral walking with a woman near where he died.

The woman was as tall as Morral—long black hair, not unattractive—the witness wasn't sure if they were together, or if it was just coincidence they were in the same place at the same time.

Coincidence, Truax thought. *Unlikely. That description fits half the women in Baltimore. Hell, even Frankie fits that description.*

"Frankie…"

He glanced over to her desk. He ought to at least let her know the latest; that he was right about the copycat and that she should continue to pursue her original cyanide case out there. And while he was at it, he'd pick her brain for information. It was only fair. After all, she owed him.

He selected her cell number and pressed Send. A moment later, he heard her ringtone, the one he always hated.

Bad boys bad boys, whatcha ya gonna do? Whatcha ya gonna do when they come for you bad boys bad boys…

But this one wasn't coming from inside his head. This one, was in the room.

The ringtone was close, but muffled, as if coming from inside of something—a jacket, a purse, a drawer. He listened harder and found that it came from the bottom of Vecchio's desk. He pulled hard on the drawer handle, but it was locked. He forced it. Standard issue government desks weren't very hard to jimmy.

The fragrance of Christian Dior floated from the bottom of the drawer to meet him, lingering in his senses, and making him remember. The scent came from a black FBI t-shirt. Under the shirt were her bureau credentials and a pair of cell phones—one he remembered her using on a regular basis. The other, he never saw before. And, it was powered off.

The first phone displayed missed calls. His calls. As he began poking through the Incoming folder, he discovered that the only other calls to this phone came from Captain Atkins; something he found more than just curious, since most of the calls came in at night. And then, there was the 2nd phone. Why did she have it? A backup?

Truax thought that if he couldn't get through to her on her cell, he'd call her office. He fished out Vecchio's business card, dog-eared from its time in his wallet.

Special Agent Francis Vecchio
Federal Bureau of Investigation
San Diego Field Office

He dialed the number.

"FBI," the young female voice said. "San Diego Field Office."

"Yes…this is Detective Truax, Maryland State Police. I'm calling for Special Agent Frances Vecchio."

"Hold on, Sir. I'll connect you."

A moment passed and the line reconnected with a series of clicks. A man's voice came on the line.

"Special Agent Vecchio. How can I help you, Detective Truax?"

"Uhhhh…I'm sorry," Truax said, "I'm looking for Agent *Frances* Vecchio."

"This is Francis Vecchio," the voice stated without a trace of indignation. "How can I help you?"

"*You're* Vecchio? Ah…I'm looking for a *female* agent, the one working the Cyanide Killer case. Is there another agent there by that name? A woman? Frances Vecchio?"

"'Fraid not, Detective. I'm the only one in this office. Or any office for that matter, and I'm lead agent on the Cyanide Killer case. Is there something I can do for you?"

Managing to mutter a short explanation, Truax ended the call with an apology, and dropped the phone into its cradle. A familiar feeling overcame him, a gnawing in the pit of his stomach. It was the same gnawing that kick-started his curiosity when something wasn't right.

Vecchio was a man. The *real* Vecchio. And now, all his doubts about the Vecchio he knew as a cop, began to make sense; her un-FBI-like manner, the lack of discipline and focus, the apparent absence of general investigative knowledge, her lax procedures, and the suggestive way she dressed—a bit too provocative for the straight-laced FBI. She had lots of intuition, but when it came to investigative chops...well, she just didn't have any.

And apparently, neither did he. She pulled the wool where he was concerned, and as he began to feel like the fool she played him for, he could do nothing but push down the resulting anger—anger that would do him more harm than good.

Who was she really? What was her game? But most of all, he wanted to know why. But to answer that question, he had to find her.

He picked up her desk phone and dialed the lab, holding her cellphone carefully to preserve any prints, while at the same time, doubting she left any.

"How long will it take you to determine the origination point of a cell phone?" he asked Smitty, skirting all pleasantries when the digital forensics specialist picked up.

Harold Smith, thirty-one years-old, ran his fingers through wavy blonde hair, and leaned too close to the phone's external mic, almost as if the phone itself, was hard of hearing. "WHAT'S THE NUMBER, DETECTIVE?"

Truax jerked the handset away from his ear. Smitty was an annoyingly loud talker. "619-402…"

"HOLD ON."

Truax did as asked, and while he waited, he picked up the black leather case containing Vecchio's credentials. Right away, he knew something wasn't right.

It was light. Lighter than it should be. And when he flipped it open, he found a Post-it note stuck to the clear plastic lens that protected Vecchio's photo. The note was written in Vecchio's flowery cursive, and simply said, "Speed-dial #1."

Truax realized the only authentic aspect of her credentials was the imitation leather case. The badge proved to be a fake, made out of lightweight cast—a facsimile easily attained over the internet. The same held true with her photo ID. It looked authentic enough from arms length, but if inspected by a trained eye, up close, it couldn't hold up to the scrutiny.

He pressed the speed dial number, and when the number came up on the display, he noted it and ended the call before it could connect. About that time, Smitty returned.

"IT'S A SAN DIEGO AREA CODE AND EXCHANGE," he said, "BUT THE CELL'S—"

"SMITTY!" Truax blared. "STOP YELLING! I can hear you."

"Oh…sorry, Detective. It's always so loud in here. Anyway, as I was saying—the phone is a throw-away."

Truax allowed himself a grim smile, acknowledging his suspicions to himself.

"OK, Smitty. I want you to trace this number. Let me know when you're ready."

"Sure. What's the number?"

"619-402…"

"Doubt that's gonna help you, Detective. The area code and exchange are the same as the other one. Can't say for sure without checking, but it's probably a throw-away as well."

Truax sanded his fingers across his scalp. "And its San Diego," he mumbled. Truax hung up without another word. He stared at the note. She obviously wanted him to call, and after he did, she wouldn't be there long enough for the locals to pick her up, wherever that might be.

He pressed speed-dial #1 on Vecchio's cell, listening to the purr of several electronic rings before the circuit connected, and when the ringing stopped, Truax said nothing, electing to wait and see what developed. After a short pause, he heard soft rhythmic breathing, and then, a single probing word, spoken in a woman's voice.

"Moby?"

It didn't matter that he knew who he had called. It didn't matter that she had made a fool of him. Like a deceived lover, the soft tones of her voice did little to dispel the pain of betrayal, or keep his gut from knotting up like a piece of tangled rope. He remained silent before answering, not sure if he even should, but then he heard himself say, "Yes. I'm here."

"Moby...are you all right?"

His heart raced, his hands quivered, and he tried not to let on.

"I'm fine, Frankie," he lied, "If that's your real name."

"Frankie is a boy's name, Moby."

For the first time in his life he found himself having to work to remain professional. Commanding himself to breathe, he managed to find his purpose; the hunter seeking his prey.

"Where are you?"

"Detective! I'm surprised at you! You know I can't tell you."

"I know, but I had to ask. Thought I might get lucky."

"Moby, you *did* get lucky. You caught your killer."

"You're the killer, Frankie. You're CK."

"I really hate that the papers call me that. Do you think you can make them stop?"

"What would you prefer?"

"Oh, I don't know. I've always liked Angel. That's what they call me in San Diego."

"Angel of Death?"

"Angel of *Mercy*. They felt no pain, Moby. Not even Morral...and he deserved a bit of it."

"You made a fool of me, Frankie."

"Oh, I wouldn't feel too badly about that if I were you. Agent Vecchio's the one who will be pissed when he finds out I impersonated him, *and* represented the FBI, using only his business card and a couple of throw-away cell phones. You know, I really thought you'd have picked up on the way Francis was spelled. "*is*" for a guy, "*es*" for a gal. Shame on you!

"Besides, it was hardly your fault. It was that dweeby boss of yours who brought me in on the case. And it didn't take much doing either. A smile, a bit of cleavage...an implied roll in the hay. He really is a slime-ball, you know that?"

"Wait a minute, Frankie! The San Diego SAC *called* Atkins. Told him about similar homicides out there. Asked if she could send an agent to compare notes. Set the whole thing up before you ever set foot in the building. Are you saying—"

"Special Agent 'n Charge, Kaitlin Donahue," she said in a lovely Irish brogue. "'Tis a good strong Irish name, don't you tink?"

"That was *you*? *You're* Donahue?"

"There should be another phone there, Moby. Turn it on. You'll see only two numbers coming in or going out. One belongs to Atkins. The other is yours."

Truax glanced at the phone, but did not turn it on. "Atkins called the San Diego office," Truax added. "Verified the request. Talked to the SAC. Shit, I did too!"

"Yes, I know. Who do you think you guys spoke with? The real Donahue is on special assignment in the field. Her

332

admin wouldn't just hand out her cell number. All Atkins had to do was ask to have her return his call, but because he already had what he thought was her cell number, he never bothered. I expect after this, he'll be a bit more diligent. Probably, you too."

"You couldn't know Atkins would go for this."

"No, you're right about that. I was taking a big chance, but I was counting on my prowess as a woman to keep his mind on...other things, shall we say. And even if all that didn't work, I'd have found another way."

"So how'd you figure it was Morral?"

"Who else could it have been? It had to be the mid-shift ME. Besides, I had an advantage over you, Moby. I knew it wasn't *me* who killed them...not the young ones, anyway. It wasn't for me to take them. They were young. Vibrant. Full of life. Their lives needed living.

"The lives I took, I ended out of compassion. They lived empty lives. Wistful lives. Lives without hope or solace. Those blessed women were alone and in pain, isolated by their solitude, and in their own way, asked me to help them. I don't expect you or anyone else to understand.

"Chronic loneliness is a horrible way to live, waiting for the end to come. The never-ending sadness and depression. The hopelessness. Morral subverted my good work, made me look the monster, killing those young girls and leaving me the blame."

"The medical examiner," Truax mumbled. "He stacked the deck. But you broke your own rules, Frankie. You shouldn't have killed him because he didn't fit your criteria for euthanasia. It was murder, plain and simple. As clever as you are, you could have found a way to turn him in."

"I suppose," she replied, "and I did think about that, but your courts would have let him out in five years, so what would be the point? Besides, I remembered an old Texas saying...Some folks just need killin'...or something like that. He was giving me a bad name, killing those young women. Killing for his own sick purposes."

The comment jogged Truax's memory of the post-mortem sexual activity on Riki Harrison, but he didn't want to let on. He wanted to see what she knew. "What are you talking about? What sick purposes?"

"C'mon, Moby. Stop pretending to be clueless. He had to have some motive other than just murder. He targeted only young women. Gorgeous women. You pointed that out to me...on the map at Squad, remember? Young victims versus old victims. Different areas of town, different MOs, yet the poison was the same in all of them. You were spot on, but you didn't see what was right in front of you. You were too wrapped up in your own petty problems."

"I hardly call losing your life savings and facing dismissal, petty."

"Time's are tough for everybody, so get over it! You're not the only one who lost money. Man-up, for crap's sake and stop bellyaching! Self-pity doesn't become you!"

The impromptu ass-chewing actually had Truax grinning to himself. He perched on the edge of Vecchio's old desk.

"You let that little jerk Atkins dissuade you, Moby. You should have figured this out right away. I did!"

"You couldn't be sure it was him, Frankie. That's why we have laws to protect—"

"Oh don't lecture me on that innocent-until-proven-guilty bullshit!" she snapped. "Your prisons are full of innocent people. Don't you read the papers? DNA evidence has been overthrowing conviction after conviction. But Morral *manipulated* the DNA. Had you caught me, you'd have thought me guilty of his killings too. I watched that maniac kill that young bartender, and my only regret is that I didn't get to him before he did. Your laws would have put him in jail to continue his worthless life, and eventually put him back on the streets. *Your* way has too many laws that protect criminals. Too *many!*"

"Criminals...like you, Frankie?"

"Yes, Detective! Criminals! Like *me!*"

"You know I'll be coming after you."

"You wouldn't recognize me now if you fell over me. Besides, your jurisdiction stops at the Maryland State line, Luv. So no, you won't."

Truax didn't reply. Hard to argue with fact.

"I know you won't believe this," she continued, her voice softer now that she settled herself down, "but I really like you, even if you couldn't keep your eyes outta my shirt. And you thought I didn't notice. You big dope! *Every* woman notices. Half of us do it on purpose, just to see if you guys are paying attention. A plunging neckline. Very distracting. But even at that, it *was* kinda flattering, coming from you. I half thought that you'd ask me out. That little shit boss of yours sure did. What a dick."

Truax couldn't suppress his grin.

"You're a good cop, Moby," she continued. "Never forget that. So lookit...I enjoyed our time, but now I gotta run. You take care of you, you hear me?"

With that, there was a short hesitation, and then the line dropped. Truax found himself holding a dead cell to his ear for several seconds longer than he had to, and not sure why.

A moment passed before he shook it off and placed Vecchio's cell on her desk. Forensics would want to dissect it along with her forged credentials and the 2nd cell. Her desk would soon be combed over by Latent and Trace, looking for prints and the like.

He doubted they'd find anything. A woman with the stones and the smarts to pass herself off as FBI using only a business card, inject herself into the investigation, and work alongside of them—along side of *him*—certainly wouldn't make a stupid mistake like that.

It was ironic, now that he thought about it. She was an imposter hunting an imposter. Of course, that he didn't see through her little charade didn't bode well for him— something else to justify Atkins slapping him down, and pounding the final nail into his vocational coffin. Add to that, he never did figure out the common thread connecting the victims, but now, after talking with Frankie, it was right there the whole time.

All of her victims were alone in life. The French woman from the bowling alley, Harriett Brennermann from the library, and the third victim, Rosa Neunyo from the beauty salon. Everything was there, but he hadn't seen the *one* thing they all had in common.

Loneliness never occurred to him.

CHAPTER 72

The Friday morning sun brought with it the promise of a warm, late-summer's day, hampered only by the unavoidable face-off with Atkins; the outcome of which would have Truax serving the last two years of his career behind a desk—if he still had a job at all.

Procrastination wasn't one of his failings, but today it was necessary to maintain his sanity. Feeling as a criminal must before receiving his sentence from the judge, Truax put off embarking for his meeting for as long as possible. But once committed, the route to Atkins's office, an otherwise inviting path of carpeting, wallpaper, and sconce lighting, now seemed unfamiliar and hostile, and as he ambled down the hall, a scene from a Stephen King movie came to mind.

Walking the Mile. Walking the Green Mile.

The everyday dissonance of building sounds barely registered. The susurrus rush of the air conditioning, and clamor of jumbled conversations became whispers, and with each stride his anxiety grew, manifesting itself as shortness of breath, wet armpits, and the longing for a cigarette from the fresh pack he bought, still unopened in his shirt pocket.

Reaching the anteroom outside Atkins's office, Truax swallowed hard before entering. Carol was already there and greeted him with something other than what he had expected.

A smile.

Sympathy, he thought. *Comes between Shit and Syphilis in the dictionary.* She *had* to know what was going to happen. He reciprocated, forcing a weak, insincere, smile before speaking.

"Is he in yet?"

"You're early Moby," Carol said. There was an out-of-context lightness to her voice as she dodged the direct question, maintaining her attention on a silver serving tray containing a coffee pot, a pair of departmental mugs, and all the necessary accoutrements.

"You should go on in," she said, lifting the tray and starting for Atkins's office. "He's waiting for you."

Truax grimaced and questioned where Carol's uncharacteristic giddiness was coming from.

Didn't she know he was about to die?

Following her into Atkins's office, he answered his own question.

"Major *Taylor!*" he blurted, immediately recognizing the Commander of Investigation Command sitting at Atkins's desk. The spit & polish of the uniformed silver-haired trooper was well known and unmistakable. "Wha... What are...? I thought...I was ordered to..."

Truax paused, allowing himself to regain his composure. "Captain Atkins," he said with deliberate annunciation, "ordered me here this morning, Sir. He said nothing of your being here. I'm afraid I don't understand."

"Relax, Detective. I know all that. Please, have a seat."

Taylor thanked Carol and nodded. It was his way of asking her to leave them. A more considerate and respectful queue than those delivered by Atkins. She offered Truax a discrete smile and left, easing the door closed behind her.

Truax obeyed the informal order and sat opposite Atkins's desk, unable to shake the feeling he was in more trouble than he originally thought. His mind began to race and filled with more questions than he could possibly ask: Where was Atkins? Why was the agency commander here? What the *hell* was going on?

"Sir," Truax said, keeping his voice low. Speaking his thoughts, he failed to adjust for circumstances. "What the hell is going on?"

Taylor grinned at Truax's earthy frankness, a quality that his position seldom allowed. "Coffee, Detective?" Taylor asked.

Truax politely waved it off, thinking he was nervous enough.

"A situation has come to my attention that I felt I should address personally," Taylor said as he poured coffee into a single mug. "I understand the CK investigation has taken an unusual turn."

Truax nodded solemnly and felt his spine turn to ice. "Yes Sir. I'm afraid I couldn't solve this one. And that's my job, isn't it?"

"Yes, Detective, it is. And I dare say you'd have done your job, had you not been interfered with."

"Sir? I'm sorry. What?"

"When Agent Vecchio—the *real* Agent Vecchio— informed his SAC, Kaitlin Donahue, of the Cyanide Killer's impersonation, Agent Donahue's next call was to me, thanks to you."

"Me, Sir?"

"You did contact the real Agent Vecchio, did you not?"

"Well, yes Sir. But I thought—"

"That call set several things in motion. Patterns and details were disclosed, not the least of which was the discovery of Captain Atkins's lack of diligence, and insistence on a single killer; a concept planted, more than likely, by Vecchio's impostor.

"I'm sorry about Agent Vecchio, Truax responded. " I should have verified—"

"But you *did* verify," Taylor interrupted. "You checked into their case on the service. Placed calls and talked to who you believed to be the key players. I read all your reports. That's more than what Captain Atkins did.

"As you are well aware," Taylor continued, "we call in the FBI to assist, *if* we feel the need. In this case, the bogus agent just showed up on our doorstep, so to speak. You know, as do I, that CK played various roles, and played them exceedingly well. Impersonating real FBI agents, and possessing a bit of inside knowledge as to the activities of those agents. That allowed her to get away with her little charade.

"Captain Atkins brought her in based on a business card and a pretty face," Taylor said. "He didn't check her out thoroughly. He just spoke with her on the phone. You did the same, but you also checked her story on the service. Atkins did not.

"He did what she wanted him to do. He assigned her to you and the hottest case we had, making it that much easier for CK to insert herself into the investigation. Pretty ballsey of her, impersonating an FBI agent like she did, but it was Atkins's mistake, and I hold him responsible. Not you. He was too easily manipulated, too easily influenced, and from what we've been able to ascertain, made his decisions based on reasoning from below his belt. I had him reassigned."

Truax could relate. There was something about her.

"Reassigned, Sir?"

"Yes. Captain Atkins now commands the Traffic Division."

Truax pursed his lips and blew a silent whistle. Traffic was where careers went to die. Commander Taylor reached for the Winsor at his throat and re-centered his tie along the gig line.

"So, I know you were expecting a different scenario when you walked in this morning, Moby, and I'm here to tell you personally that you did an outstanding job."

"Outstanding, Sir? She played me like an old fiddle. Made a fool out of me and killed four people in the process. How can you say..."

"All of what you say is true," Taylor interrupted. Her strengths were distraction and misdirection. But I'm more disturbed by Atkins throwing obstacles in your way. CK herself, being one of those obstacles. Additionally, I believe you would have apprehended Doctor Morral, had CK not raided the game. She wasn't playing by the same rules as you, so it was easier for her to rid the city of a deranged killer. I wouldn't beat myself up too much if I were you."

"But, Sir. What about CK? She's still out there."

"She's the FBI's problem now. Impersonating a federal agent is a serious offense. That's not to say murder isn't, but the Feds take that sort of thing personally. They'll get her."

"Yes, Sir. So, have you decided who his replacement will be? I mean, with Captain Atkins reassigned, who do I report to?"

"You'll be reporting to me," Taylor said, leaning back into Atkins's oversized chair and filling it as if it were custom made for him. "I've been giving some thought to his replacement. You're the most senior detective I have. And the most qualified. I was hoping you might take the job."

"*Me, Sir?* I...I don't know if I can...I mean, I'm fifty-eight. Mandatory retirement is just two years away."

"I'm well aware of your age, Detective, and your feelings concerning desk duty are pretty much public knowledge. So how about we look at it as a temporary position? If you decide it isn't what you want to do for the next two years, I'll replace you as soon as I find a suitable candidate. Then I'll put you back on the streets."

Truax rolled it over in his mind. "Sir, I don't know if I can handle—"

"Well I do! It's not like I have time to scour the countryside to find someone for the job! So unless you want to get on my bad side, you'll help me out here. The position comes with a captain's salary and retirement package. So what's it going to be, Detective-Sergeant?"

Truax felt his stomach knotting up. Command was something he just wasn't interested in. Never was.

"Sir, you want me to take command of my peers. The very people with who I work side-by-side. People I've become friends with. Drank beer with. Caught bad guys with. To be truthful, Sir...it's uncomfortable to say the least. Except for maybe Detective Nichols."

Truax found himself suppressing a rancorous smile and became concerned it might give his thoughts away. After all, Taylor didn't get to where he was because he couldn't read people. And he was right.

"I see you're pondering something, Detective," Taylor said.

"Oh, it's nothing, Sir."

Taylor grinned. "I think you'll find him right where CK put him: At his desk, ploughing through J. Doe files from the last couple of weeks."

"Sir. With all due respect, how the hell do you do that?"

Taylor laughed. "I pay attention, Detective. Maybe if you take the job, you can turn that boy around. Make a detective of him. He has talent, you know. Just a bit too much piss & vinegar. Much like you, when you came to us."

Truax grinned. "Seems I don't have a choice, Sir, as long as I can get out if I want...without screwing up my retirement."

"Good man, Taylor said. "I'll cut the orders. Effective Monday, you're acting Captain, Special Investigations Unit. Don't be afraid to consult me if you feel the need, but something tells me you'll do just fine."

The two men stood, shook hands, and Taylor left without another word. Truax stood in place, his mind still reeling from the unexpected turn of events. Several seconds passed before Carol tapped at the door.

"You knew," Truax said, turning toward her. "Didn't you. You knew and you didn't warn me."

"*Warn you*?" she said, grinning. "Not a freaking chance!"

Her smile said what her words did not, and Truax felt like the brunt of a high school prank. But the fact remained, come Monday, he would command the SIU.

"Look, Moby," Carol said. "You've earned this. Enjoy it."

"Seems like I ended up behind a desk anyway," he said. "Exactly what I didn't want."

"Yeah, well take it from someone who's spent her life behind a desk." She twisted, scanned her bottom, and smiled. "If you can stay away from the bon-bons, it ain't so bad."

Truax laughed.

"So," Carol continued, "how about tonight I take you out for a drink? To celebrate?"

"A date?" Truax asked.

A seductive smile eased onto Carol's face.

"Thirty years is long enough to wait. I think it's about time, don't you?"

CHAPTER 73

Driving home Friday afternoon, Truax realized that few days in his life worked out the way this one had.

He woke that morning expecting a lambasting from Atkins, followed by a firing, or the inevitable demotion to desk duty, only to end up commanding the very unit from which he expected banishment. The unannounced appearance of Major Taylor set him on his heels, and virtually assured that he would accept just about any punishment handed down without a fight.

As he turned into his driveway, he spotted the widow Ida standing on her front stoop, an expectant look on her face as she watched him pull in. Seeing her took his mind back to CK and the women who died at the hands of the bogus Agent Vecchio.

CK regarded the slayings, not as murders, but as acts of mercy. Euthanasia. To her mind, they were a merciful release from painful and empty lives devoid of purpose, and wrought with loneliness; the kind that robbed each day of joy, leaving depression and emptiness in its wake.

Given the recent events of his own life, he could almost feel the burden they bore, but more than that, he could understand CK's motives. Ida reminded him of that.

"Officer Moby?" Ida called. "Officer Moby?"

Truax smiled. "Yes, Miss Ida?"

"Oh, Officer Moby," she called from her stoop, her voice wavering and faint, barely audible over the sounds of summer. "Would you please help me?"

"Yes ma'am," he called back.

Truax climbed from the cruiser and hopped the chain-link fence like he did when he was a boy. The unopened pack of cigarettes he carried in his shirt pocket popped out. He picked them up and crushed the pack, then dropped them into Ida's outside garbage can.

He held open the door, and followed her in.

"I need my blender down from my cupboard," she explained, shuffling toward her kitchen. "It's too high for me to reach and I can't climb up on a chair. My balance isn't so good anymore, and I might fall and break something. At my age, I'm afraid it wouldn't heal."

Truax nodded his understanding as he guided her gently to one side before retrieving the blender from the top shelf, reaching it without effort. Setting it on the counter, he turned to her.

"Here you go, Miss Ida."

"Oh, thank you, Officer Moby. I'd never have been able to reach it by myself."

"You're very welcome, Miss Ida. Now, is there anything else I can do while I'm here?"

Ida placed a frail hand to her cheek and thought for a moment.

"No," she said. "No, I can't think of anything else."

Truax smiled at her as a son would his own mother. "Then I was wondering, Miss Ida…"

Ida's green eyes lit up, faded with age, but sparkling with the anticipation of a child.

"Yes, Officer Moby?"

"I was wondering, Miss Ida, if I might trouble you for a cup of tea."

Biography

Author D.B. Corey

DB Corey lives in the Baltimore area with his lovely wife Maggie, an offish Chocolate Lab named Murphy, and a Catahoula-Leopard Hound they call Bond—James Bond.

After a rather uninspired stint in college, he spent twelve years with the U.S. Naval Reserves flying aircrew aboard a Navy P-3 Orion chasing down Russian subs. During his time with the USNR, he began a career in data processing, or as we know it today, Information Technology. He began writing in his mid-50s.

He is currently working on his next police procedural, and keeps a political thriller on the back burner. Corey has contributed opinion columns to online periodicals, and appeared on local talk radio, all under the *nom de plume*, Bernie Thomas.